D0583658

CHOICE   SEP. '72

Sociology & Anthropology

SNELLING, William Joseph. Tales of the Northwest. Ross & Haines, Inc., 11 E. Lake St., Minneapolis, Minn. 55408, 1971 (orig. pub. by Minnesota, 1936). 254p 70-180636. 10.00. ISBN 0-87018-058-4

First published in 1830, and reissued in 1936 with a biographical introduction by John T. Flanagan added, these are short stories by an early traveler among the Indians and fur trappers of the old Northwest territory. Drawing upon eight years residence at a military post in Minnesota, Snelling, in stilted prose, depicts the actions and personalities of the Indians and whites of this region. Although attempting realism, the villains, both Indian and white, are stereotyped evil and the heroes brave, forthright, and pure. Unfortunately, little understanding of Indian culture can be gleamed except that the Indians are bound to a way of life devoid of the refinements of civilization. The book's value, lies not as a literary or ethnographic effort but as an example of white beliefs about savage Indians, prevalent in the literature of the period. For a critical perspective between this book and other early fictional works dealing with the American Indian, see R. H. Pearce's *The savages of America* (CHOICE, May 1966).

Tales of the Northwest

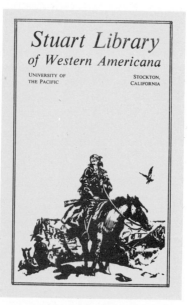

William Joseph Snelling's

TALES OF THE
NORTHWEST

WITH AN INTRODUCTION BY

JOHN T. FLANAGAN

ROSS & HAINES, INC.

Minneapolis, Minnesota

1971

L.C. #70-180636
ISBN #0-87018-058-4

Original reprint by
The University of Minnesota Press
in 1936

_____

Introduction and Notes
Copyright renewal by
John T. Flanagan, Urbana, Illinois
1964

_____

Reprinted by
Ross & Haines, Inc.
Minneapolis, Minnesota 55408
1971

Contents

INTRODUCTION
William Joseph Snelling

A LITTLE over a century ago, in 1830 to be exact, there was published anonymously in Boston a small volume entitled *Tales of the Northwest*, a thick duodecimo which chronicled with authenticity the life of the Indian, as the author had experienced it, in the Mississippi Valley. Unheralded and soon overlooked, the book never reached a second edition and has long since been known only to antiquarians and to special students of the frontier.[1] Nevertheless this volume is highly significant, not only as one of the first collections of short tales published in the United States but also as the first literary treatment of the territory lying at the headwaters of the Mississippi. For *Tales of the Northwest* marks the earliest appearance in American literature of the plains Indians who once claimed as their heritage eternal the right to roam over the land that now comprises the states of Minnesota, Iowa, Wisconsin, and the two Dakotas.

Collections of short stories and sketches were not numerous in America during the first decades of the nineteenth century. Certain writers, it is true, were known; and one,

[1] Even today the rarity of the book has caused it to be overlooked by scholars and historians of frontier literature. Thus Lucy Lockwood Hazard, in *The Frontier in American Literature* (New York, 1927), and Albert Keiser, in *The Indian in American Literature* (New York, 1933), ignore

Irving, had achieved fame; but the tale as a genus was a sporadic phenomenon until the annuals began to provide a permanent outlet for this relatively new literary form. Moreover, what stories existed were pallid and imitative, sentimental, and structurally weak. The influence of Addison and Steele was pronounced in Irving and through Irving in his successors. Moralistic and didactic elements bulked large in the American imitations of the eighteenth-century periodical essays; and even the author who was exacting enough to exclude the hortatory too often allowed it to be supplanted by the sentimental. Thus Pattee could well say that Irving's influence as a whole was rather a baneful one, since although he gave popularity to the short story as a literary form, he postponed its artistic development.[2] This unrealistic depiction of life extended even to Indian themes in the 1820's, for, although the Indian was a fairly common subject for literary treatment, few authors wrote of him with either understanding or sympathy. The red man was either brutalized and portrayed as the arch-fiend, or sentimentalized and described as a veritable lord of creation living nakedly but nobly beneath the boughs of the forest.

Obviously the readers of sentimental romances in which anemic heroes strove to win hysterical and weeping heroines would not have been interested in a volume that pictured conditions as they actually existed. Nor would a

it completely. R. L. Rusk, in *The Literature of the Middle Western Frontier* (New York, 1925), quotes from an early criticism of the book in the *North American Review*, fails to identify the author as Snelling, and admits that he has never seen a copy of *Tales of the Northwest* (1:286). Only Dorothy Dondore, in *The Prairie and the Making of Middle America* (Cedar Rapids, 1926), seems to be aware of Snelling's importance as an authentic portrayer of Indian life (p. 234).

[2] Fred Lewis Pattee, *Cambridge History of American Literature* (New York, 1931), 2:368.

conventional audience have responded enthusiastically to tales in which poetic justice was ignored, in which the uncouth was not glossed over and the brutal not disguised. Thus the reason for the apathy of the public toward *Tales of the Northwest* is not hard to discover. Readers were not ready for "one of the earliest calls for realism ever made in America" [3]; they preferred the quiet, inchoate tales with which they were familiar and which are embalmed today in countless magazines and annuals. Cooper had done much to develop an autochthonous literature, and the 1830's were to reveal talents as disparate as those of Hawthorne, Simms, and Poe; but it must be remembered that for several decades the most popular American novel had been *Charlotte Temple*. Thus, though this little volume of 1830 contained ten examples of an unusual literary genre and though it dealt with a locale far removed from the Atlantic seaboard and yet not entirely unknown to Americans, the book received little contemporary recognition. [4]

The author of *Tales of the Northwest*, William Joseph Snelling, was born in 1804. His father, Colonel Josiah Snelling, had entered military service early and had distinguished himself in the War of 1812. As a result of the father's frequent absences and the mother's early death, the son was entrusted largely to the care of relatives and was early sent to Dr. Luther Stearns's private boarding school, located about five miles out of Boston. But the lacunae are many in Joseph Snelling's life story. [5] Indeed if, as some contend,

[3] Fred Lewis Pattee, *The Development of the American Short Story* (New York and London, 1923), p. 64.

[4] The only contemporary review I have found is that in the *North American Review*, 68:200–13 (July, 1830).

[5] The only extant biography of Snelling is a manuscript doctoral dissertation by Allen E. Woodall presented at the University of Pittsburgh in 1932 and even this gives only an outline of Snelling's life. A short biographical sketch by the same author which emphasizes Snelling's

obscurity is necessary for literary fame, Snelling's immortality must be assured. For the only other definite facts about his youth are his enrollment at West Point on September 7, 1818, and his dismissal from that institution some two years later. Exactly why Snelling did not finish his course no one knows. A breach of discipline and a failure to achieve scholastic promotion have been alleged as reasons for his early departure,[6] but the whole episode is wrapped in shadow. It is just as conceivable that Snelling, an adventurous and restless lad, simply tired of the military routine and chose flight as the simplest escape.

His schooling definitely over at the age of sixteen, young Joseph eagerly embarked on a career of wandering. Indeed the keynote of his life seems to have been an independence which revealed itself first in a life of nomadic adventure and secondly in a fearless expression of the truth at all costs. In 1820 Colonel Snelling had been assigned command of a detachment of the Fifth Infantry stationed at the confluence of the Minnesota and Mississippi rivers and had begun to construct the military post first called Fort St. Anthony and later, on recommendation of General Scott,[7] Fort Snelling. Obviously, then, when young Snelling left West Point and began the life of adventure that was to occupy the next ten years, it was logical that he should eventually have gravitated toward his father's residence. A number of apparently apocryphal stories, however, have been told about his pere-

Minnesota sojourn appeared in *Minnesota History*, 10:367–85 (December, 1929). There is also a brief notice in the *Dictionary of American Biography*, 17:381–82 (New York, 1935).

[6] According to Mrs. Adams (née Barbara Ann Shadecker), who had come to Minnesota in the Selkirk colonizing group and who acted as a maid in the Snelling family, Joseph lived an ungoverned life and was dismissed from West Point for a breach of discipline. See *Collections of the Minnesota Historical Society*, 6:96 (St. Paul, 1894).

[7] Marcus L. Hansen, *Old Fort Snelling* (Iowa City, 1918), p. 30.

grinations before he reached Minnesota. Thus he is said to have been a trapper in the country about St. Louis and to have worked for a time in the Galena lead mines.[8] Although neither of these stories has ever been definitely refuted, they seem somewhat far-fetched, particularly when one considers Snelling's extreme youth and inexperience. At any rate he was independent enough to reach Minnesota safely late in 1820, for there is evidence that he met friendly Dakota Indians and spent the following winter in their wigwams, fraternizing with them, learning their language, sharing their food and their hardships. In May, 1821, he proudly brought the Yankton chief Wahnatah to visit Colonel Snelling at the garrison.[9]

Fort Snelling at this time was little more than a crude military outpost in the Indian territory, yet its significance cannot be adequately measured by its rough barracks and its irregular fortifications. When Joseph Snelling was reunited with his father in 1821 the fort had not yet assumed its permanent shape, but Colonel Snelling had already established a reputation as a shrewd and tactful commander who cooperated well with the honest and efficient Indian agent, Major Lawrence Taliaferro. To the fort came Sioux and Chippewa on trading ventures, and from the fort departed numerous exploring expeditions, such as that headed by Major Stephen H. Long in 1823. Thus the post was a kind of clearing house for trader and soldier, explorer and traveler, *bois brulé* and Indian.

Nevertheless, life on a military reservation in time of peace is rarely exciting, and upon Joseph Snelling particu-

[8] *Appletons' Cyclopaedia of American Biography*, ed. by James G. Wilson and John Fiske (New York, 1888), 5:601. This account, incidentally, contains several obvious inaccuracies.
[9] Woodall, "William Joseph Snelling," manuscript doctoral dissertation, p. 12.

larly it must often have palled. During the years that Colonel Snelling was in command (1820–27) there was little disturbance among the Indians. Indeed the troops were employed much more often as farmers, teamsters, quarriers, and millers than as soldiers. When Lewis Cass visited the spot in the summer of 1820 he found ninety acres planted in corn, potatoes, and wheat.[10] One observer, some years later, even went so far as to say that "the strong stone wall was rather erected to keep the garrison in, than the enemy out" and that the only weapon he saw outside the magazine was an old churn thrust through one of the embrasures.[11] In summer the life of the garrison was sufficiently varied, picnicking and hunting on the shores of Lake Calhoun being a pleasant variation of the routine of reveille, guard mount, fatigue duty, agricultural labor, dress parades, and five daily roll calls within the walls of the fort.[12] But in winter the residents of the post were almost completely isolated. Ice in the river blocked communication with St. Louis, the cold was severe, and heavy snow made any kind of travel wearisome and precarious. Colonel Snelling was a stern disciplinarian, but even he was not free from the vice of intemperance, and drinking, gambling, and quarrelsome behavior were far from uncommon among the soldiers.[13] Once the commandant himself was challenged to a duel and Joseph took upon himself the duty of defending his father's honor, receiving a slight wound for his temerity.[14]

To escape from the monotony of garrison life and to satisfy his craving for adventure, Joseph seized every avail-

[10] Hansen, *op. cit.*, p. 30.
[11] Charles Joseph Latrobe, *The Rambler in North America* (New York, 1835), 2:213.
[12] Hansen, *op. cit.*, p. 85.
[13] Hansen, *op. cit.*, p. 89. See also Mrs. Adams, *op. cit.*, p. 97.
[14] Edward D. Neill, *History of Minnesota* (Minneapolis, 1882), p. 920.

INTRODUCTION

able opportunity that promised excitement. Never an enlisted soldier,[15] he was exempt from the usual duties of the
fort, and in addition, as the son of the commandant, he was
probably allowed extra privileges. Furthermore, Colonel
Snelling had remarried, and between Joseph and his step-
mother relations were not invariably pleasant.[16] For some
time after his arrival at Fort Snelling Joseph contented himself with minor exploratory expeditions, most significant of
which was his trip with Joseph R. Brown in 1822 along
Minnehaha Creek and around Lake Minnetonka.[17] But in
1823 he was attached in the role of assistant interpreter to
the party, led by Major Long, which followed the Minnesota River to its headwaters and continued up the Red
River valley to Pembina and Lake Winnipeg.[18] The readiness of Major Long to accept this youth, despite the fact
that he had already engaged a competent interpreter and
guide in Joseph Renville, testifies to the general respect for
Snelling's proficiency as frontiersman and linguist. The expedition, consisting of thirty-three men (including a military escort commanded by Lieutenant St. Clair Denny),
left Fort Snelling on July 9, 1823, and by July 22 had
reached Big Stone Lake. Their next destination was the
Columbia Fur Company's trading post on Lake Traverse,
from which they took their departure four days later; by
August 5 they were at Pembina on the Red River, having
covered about six hundred miles in slightly less than a

[15] The assertion that Joseph Snelling was an under officer in the army
has never been substantiated.
[16] Mrs. Adams, op. cit., p. 96. Colonel Snelling had several children by
this second marriage, and one son, Henry Hunt Snelling (1817–97), later
became famous for his pioneer work in photographic journalism.
[17] Neill, op. cit., p. 331.
[18] William H. Keating, Narrative of an Expedition to the Source of
the St. Peter's River (London, 1825), 1:327. The St. Peter's River, of
course, is the old designation of the Minnesota River.

month. The chronicler of the journey, William H. Keating, states that several times Snelling was called on to interpret the conversation that ensued when the party met wandering bands of Sioux and that on one occasion his knowledge of the Indian tongue enabled him to warn the commander and avert a possible clash.[19] At Pembina Snelling left the expedition and, with a corporal and two privates, retraced his steps to Fort Snelling, which he reached safely.[20] This is the longest journey of which any record remains; Snelling's other excursions are cloaked in obscurity.

Back at the fort again, Snelling resumed his occupations of hunter, fur trader, and wanderer. He was one of six men licensed by Major Taliaferro in 1823 to trade with the Sioux.[21] Tradition has it that he married a French girl from Prairie du Chien in the same year but that she died after spending the ensuing winter in a hut outside the walls of the stockade; after her death he is said to have departed for Lake Traverse, there to pursue his trading ventures.[22] But Snelling did not confine his rambles to Minnesota for, according to Drake, he saw One-eyed Decorie, one of the more conspicuous of the Winnebago chiefs, at Portage, Wisconsin, in 1826.[23] Better authenticated are the reports of his presence on two occasions when Indian hostilities threatened. In May, 1827, a party of Chippewa from Sandy Lake had come to the fort for trading purposes and had encamped just beyond the walls. Here they were visited

[19] *Ibid.*, 2:12–13.   [20] *Ibid.*, 2:55.

[21] Neill, *op. cit.*, p. 896. See also "Auto-biography of Lawrence Taliaferro," in Collections of the Minnesota Historical Society, 6:249 (St. Paul, 1894).

[22] Mrs. Adams, *op. cit.*, p. 96. See also *Dictionary of American Biography*, 17:381-82.

[23] Samuel G. Drake, *Biography and History of Indians of North America* (Boston, 1851), p. 667.

by a delegation of Sioux, the two tribes feasting and fraternizing, apparently in perfect accord. But the Sioux, on leaving, murderously fired into the wigwams of their late hosts, with frightful effect. At this juncture Colonel Snelling intervened. Troops pursued the fugitives, took several prisoners, and handed them over to the bereaved Chippewa for vengeance. The result was a running of the gantlet on the open plain outside the fort,[24] of which occurrence Joseph Snelling has left a vivid account.[25] The second occasion on which Snelling was present was the Winnebago assault, in June of the same year, on the keelboats en route from Fort Snelling to Prairie du Chien with troops and supplies. The first craft, the *O. H. Perry*, was attacked on June 27 and two of its crew were killed; but the second, the *General Ashley*, on which Snelling was a passenger, went safely past the danger point at midnight of the same day.[26] When he arrived at Prairie du Chien, Snelling was immediately put in command of one of the hastily repaired blockhouses at Fort Crawford, where the terrified inhabitants had gathered to fight off the Indian attack which they were sure was coming. Later Colonel Snelling with four companies of infantry arrived to succor the community.[27] These episodes mark the end of Joseph Snelling's sojourn in the Northwest. The transfer of Colonel Snelling to St. Louis terminated the family's connection with Minnesota, and when his father died late in 1828 Joseph Snelling was already back in Boston.[28] He never returned to the scene of his early adventures.

[24] The best account of the incident is Neill's (*op. cit.*, 391–94).
[25] "Running the Gantlet," Collections of the Minnesota Historical Society, 1:439–56 (St. Paul, 1872).
[26] Neill, *op. cit.*, p. 901.
[27] *Minnesota in Three Centuries* (n. p., 1908), 2:189.
[28] Woodall, *op. cit.*, p. 22.

The rest of Snelling's life has little relevance to *Tales of the Northwest*. Plunging into journalism in Boston, he became editor of the *New England Galaxy* in 1833 and of the *Boston Herald* in 1847. As an editor Snelling was truculent, outspoken, militant in his attempts to reform the city and to expel the gamblers. The physical daring of his youth seems to have been transmuted by this time into the moral courage of the reformer. But he suffered from a fondness for drink and spent a period in prison for intemperance. (Conflicting reports state that political enmity and revenge may also have been responsible for his incarceration.[29]) Nevertheless his later years were marked by a fanatical devotion to his peculiar notion of truth. The restlessness of his adolescence had crystallized into a crusading zeal and a febrile desire to purify society. Never known for tact or patience, Snelling pounded away at this objective, and in his clumsy attempts to achieve his aim antagonized both friend and foe. He was an early member of the New England Anti-Slavery Society, founded in 1832,[30] and a relentless enemy of tyranny in all its forms. In the last decade of his life he married twice — Mary Leverett, who died in 1837, and Lucy Jordan, who with her two daughters (a third daughter was born posthumously) survived him.[31] At the summit of his journalistic success, when he had been editor of a really important metropolitan paper for little more than a year and when he had finally won the respect

[29] *Ibid.*, p. 102. According to Oliver Wendell Holmes, Snelling "found shelter at last under a roof which held numerous inmates, some of whom had seen better and many of whom had known worse days than those which they were passing within its friendly and not exclusive precincts." *The Writings of Oliver Wendell Holmes* (Boston and New York, 1894), 7:7.

[30] Oliver Johnson, *William Lloyd Garrison and His Times* (Boston, 1881), p. 84. Snelling later drew up the preamble and was one of the twelve signers (*op. cit.*, pp. 85–86).

[31] Woodall, *op. cit.*, pp. 101, 108, 116.

of his contemporaries, the improvidence with which he had spent his life exacted its toll; on December 24, 1848, he died at Chelsea, Massachusetts.

As a writer Snelling will not be remembered for a plenitude of work. Indeed the bulk of his literary production never rose above the level of journalistic hackwork and is hidden away in the dusty leaves of obscure annuals. Soon after his return to Boston he published a number of volumes, a scurrilous biography of Jackson, several juvenile travel books, in which he obviously relied either on published accounts or on his own fancy, an exposé of vice in Boston, and an account of his prison experiences. These can be quickly dismissed. Much more important is a rather long satire in verse, entitled *Truth: A New Year's Gift for Scribblers,* published in Boston in 1831, in which Snelling paid his respects to the poetasters of the time, riddling their pretensions and damning unmercifully their bombast and inanity. Willis especially bore the brunt of his anger; as Holmes said, Snelling "tomahawked him in heroics, ran him through in prose, and scalped him in barbarous epigrams." [32] On the other hand, for Halleck, Bryant, and Brainard, Snelling had only praise. *Truth,* which has been compared favorably with Lowell's *A Fable for Critics,* reveals Snelling's powers as a satirist and his mastery of the heroic couplet. Wanting neither wit nor terse and often vitriolic condemnation, it is acid in its attacks on the turgid and the artificial; indeed, its satire is so trenchant that the reader often wishes that Snelling had given greater rein to his critical powers.

Nevertheless, effective as *Truth* is, whatever fame the gods will mete to Snelling will depend, and deservedly, on the single volume *Tales of the Northwest.* With the excep-

[32] Holmes, *op. cit.,* p. 6.

tion of the poems "Birth of Thunder" and "The Snow Shoe" [33] and a few scattered sketches,[34] this work alone utilizes his frontier experiences and reveals how well Snelling had observed the raw life of the western prairies. As the author remarked in his preface, it was necessary for the true portrayer of Indian life to have lived among the characters he represented, to have seen their life, and to have experienced their hardships. Other men besides Snelling had of course penetrated the fastnesses of the wilderness and had seen the tepee from within. The early narratives of explorers and missionaries, of surveyors and amateur ethnologists, are filled with descriptions of the Indian, with accounts of his religion, his government, his method of life, his burial and marriage customs, even his probable origin. Charlevoix, for instance, wrote two huge tomes for the delectation of a nonexistent French countess; Beltrami filled a thick volume with his account of the true sources of the Mississippi; Schoolcraft and Carver and Lahontan added their contributions to the white man's knowledge of his red brother. But these adventurers contented themselves largely with external and often superficial estimates. Ceremonies and customs they reported accurately, very much in the manner of a naturalist recording a new bit of behavior by a captive ape. The clothes and weapons and food of the Indian received adequate treatment, but few of the observers took the pains to discover the essential man. It was the psychology of the savage as much as his choice of fish and tobacco that interested Snelling, and it is the emotional reactions of the Indian that are reflected so accurately, if admittedly sometimes

[33] Printed below, pages 248–54.
[34] See especially "Te Zahpahtah, A Sketch fom Indian History," in *The Token* (Boston, 1831); a review of the life of Black Hawk, in the *North American Review*, 40:68–87 (January, 1835); "A Night in the Woods," in *The Boston Book* (Boston, 1836).

crudely, in *Tales of the Northwest*. Snelling himself realized the superiority of his own attitude and with his customary bravado ridiculed the books of his predecessors, notably those of Carver and Schoolcraft.[35] And for the romanticists who from their distant havens depicted the red men as paragons of virtue, as orators and idealists, his contempt was unlimited. The doctrine of the noble savage and the Rousseauistic conception of the return to nature nauseated him. In all his years of experience he had never met a savage who remotely resembled the glorified and etherealized personages depicted in the pages of Chateaubriand. But neither did Snelling portray the Indian as the personification of villainy. The great lesson (if so didactic a term may be used) of his book is that the red men have just as many virtues and vices as the whites, and that virtues and vices are mixed together in that indiscriminate and inextricable fashion common to humanity. There are, indeed, certain characteristics peculiar to the Indian as Snelling saw him, notably inconsistency and an unfortunate addiction to the "firewater" of the trader. But the savage combined within himself, just as did the white man, curiosity and anger, jealousy and malice, egoism and unselfishness. The idealistic Payton Skah is just as unique in the wigwam as in the drawing room. It is no wonder that George Catlin declared that Snelling's portrayal of the Indian was the most faithful he had ever seen.[36]

The accuracy and truth of Snelling's picture may best be understood by comparing his tales with the later tales of James Hall. Hall also spent much of his early life on the

[35] "Early Days at Prairie du Chien, and the Winnebago Outbreak of 1827," Collections of the State Historical Society of Wisconsin, 5:123 (Madison, 1907).

[36] Quoted by Neill, *op. cit.*, p. 921. I have been unable to find the source of this statement.

frontier but in a rather different capacity. As attorney, editor, and circuit judge he traveled extensively in Indiana and Illinois, having an almost unparalleled opportunity to observe the encroachments of the white man on the wilderness. But his stories of the frontier, truthful as they are in depicting the pioneer husbandman, the squatter, the evangelist, and the border ruffian, do the red man scant justice. Hall saw the life of the Indian as an outsider, a spectator. The savages of his tales are wanderers or fugitives, portrayed without sympathy as the inveterate enemies of the frontiersmen, delineated as "varmints" that ought to be exterminated. There is seldom the slightest hint that Hall penetrated into the character of the Indian, understood his deficiencies and his wants, analyzed him as a human being rather than as an animal. Hall had not resided in the wigwams of his subjects, eaten their food, shared their troubles. As a result, whereas Snelling could draw with conviction a plains idealist, Hall's most unforgettable figure is that person so famous in frontier annals as the "Indian hater." Truly a comparison of Snelling's stories with those of any of his contemporaries only lends additional credence to Pattee's observation: "His Indian stories are undoubtedly the best written during the early period." [37]

Of the ten stories that comprise *Tales of the Northwest*, seven deal with the relations of white men and red, with heroes and villains appearing on both sides. The basis for these seven Snelling found largely in actuality, adding to them only the necessary embroidery of the narrator. Thus "Charles Hess" is little more than a series of incidents taken from life and telescoped to fit the framework of a story, the protagonist having been a well-known trapper and scout

[37] Pattee, *Development of the American Short Story*, p. 64.

in the 1820's.[38] "La Butte des Morts" records the practical
annihilation of the Sacs at a battle with the French near the
confluence of the Fox and Wisconsin rivers. This incident,
which occurred about 1725, put an end to the outrages inflicted on the *coureurs de bois* by the Indians living along
the trade route to Green Bay. The essential situation of
"The Bois Brulé" is enriched by a multifarious collection
of facts and observations derived from Snelling's personal
experiences in the country around Pembina. In particular,
the descriptions of the buffalo hunt, of the butchering and
curing of meat, and of life in a trading post could have
come only from the pen of one familiar with such scenes.
But the background, including the rivalry of the two great
fur companies and its culmination in the murder of one of
the factors, is historical.[39] Similarly, "Pinchon," which Dorothy Dondore calls "an extraordinary account of the au-
dacity, unscrupulousness, and strength of these early wood-
rovers," [40] is obviously a synthesis of many episodes taken
directly from life. Snelling must have seen many figures
similar to the unprincipled, Paul Bunyanesque exploiter of
the red men whose tale is here told so racily.

The genesis of the three remaining tales, two of which,
"The Hohays" and "Payton Skah," are among the best of
Snelling's work, is a little more uncertain, although it is
apparent that the author utilized legends that were fairly
common on the frontier and gave them literary form.[41] All

---

[38] To understand Snelling's technique better, compare this tale with
the accounts given in Keating (*op. cit.*, 1:425–30) and Neill (*op. cit.*, pp.
331–33).

[39] The slaying of Owen Keveny took place in 1816. See the account of
Henry R. Schoolcraft, *Narrative of an Expedition . . . to Itasca Lake*
(New York, 1834), pp. 37–39.

[40] Dondore, *op. cit.*, p. 234.

[41] Giacomo C. Beltrami alludes, for example, to the essential situation
which Snelling described in "The Hohays," in his *A Pilgrimage in*

three are set at a time anterior to the coming of whites, so that for his plots Snelling must obviously have relied on oral tradition; but for his adumbration of the characters, for his delineation of Indian emotions and reactions, his only source was his own experience. No one not endowed with sympathy toward and understanding of his subject could have portrayed so feelingly the self-sacrifice and grief of Payton Skah in his endeavor to end his life in the lodge of his enemies; or the intolerable misery that prompted the squaw of "Weenokhenchah Wandeeteekah" to commit suicide rather than live with a polygamous husband. In small points, too, Snelling was exact and convincing. Thus in the uncollected tale of "Te Zahpahtah" the French trader La Rocque, having arrived at the Sioux village, is feasted on wild rice, raccoon tallow, and "the carcass of a singed and boiled dog." In these stories Snelling brought details of life and costume to a framework of legend and breathed into the whole a vitality that is convincing even today.

Artistically his work is loose and very uneven. Indeed an early reviewer, Alexander Everett, censured him for not bestowing sufficient care and reflection on the arrangement of his material.[42] Certainly Snelling was not guiltless of such clumsy narrative methods as the tale within the tale, nor did he object to weighting down his plot with certain didactic elements. "The Captive" illustrates both these weaknesses, particularly the latter. Snelling, too, never overlooked a chance to criticize the United States government for its Indian policy or to ridicule the application to the red man of judicial processes which at their best were slow and cumbrous and at which the Indian invariably jeered. Some-

Europe and America (London, 1828), 2:210. The Sioux and Assiniboines were originally one tribe, Beltrami asserts, but separated because of the rape of a red Helen.

[42] *North American Review*, 68:200 (July, 1830).

times even the author's very amplitude of knowledge of frontier life proved disadvantageous, since it led him to clutter up his narrative with scenes and incidents which were essentially irrelevant. "Charles Hess," for example, is no more than a series of incidents loosely held together by the reappearance of the protagonist; it has no basic unity. "The Bois Brulé," perhaps richest in local color of all Snelling's stories, is the weakest artistically, for in it are jumbled together scraps of the romantic novels which the author bitterly detested, bits of conscientious character delineation, conventional moralizing out of the eighteenth century, and wild scenes of prairie life which only an eye witness could have reproduced. A better trained narrator and a more careful artist would have reduced this heterogeneous material to a unit, rigidly excising all that lacked pertinence; but Snelling included everything. His chief deficiency as a story-teller was a lack of firm structure. As Fullerton pointed out, this weakness alone prevented him from "standing with the greater authors of the early nineteenth century." [43]

In style Snelling was versatile and vivid, but often displayed little restraint or taste. Capable at his best of writing terse, vigorous narrative in the manner of Scott or Cooper (see, for example, "The Hohays" or "Te Zahpahtah"), narrative notable for economy and directness of language, he was also capable of tedious digressions, of moralizing in a tone reminiscent of Leatherstocking in his most grandiloquent vein, and of penning apostrophes to the "gentle reader." Combined indeed with his skill in marshalling facts was his inheritance from the eighteenth-century essayists. Even some of the archaisms of which Lamb was so

[43] Bradford M. Fullerton, *Selective Bibliography of American Literature 1775–1900* (New York, 1932), p. 252.

fond appear occasionally, and Snelling's style is free neither of redundancy nor of rhetoric. Probably the worst prose he ever wrote is the stilted dialogue between Flora Cameron and her half-breed lover, who, although the son of a Sioux squaw, talks frequently as though he had never been away from the influence of the drawing room. Nevertheless, his prose lacks the affectation that marked such writers about the West as Hall and Paulding; whatever else Snelling was, he was not a poseur. Nor is he often guilty of flippancy. He treated his material with dignity and as a result imparted to it the aura of genuineness. In general, his style is that of a man who lived midway between two literary generations and who anticipated the tastes of the one without being quite able to slough off the dogmatic formularies of the other.

But many of these criticisms are captious. Human nature may not change but literary taste does, and Snelling cannot fairly be judged by the standards of an age that looks with favor on the telescopic style of a Hemingway or the tortured ellipses of a Joyce. In 1830 no American save Cooper wrote better narrative than Snelling at his peak. His stories, whatever they may lack generally in coherence and continuity, are remarkable even today for their vigor and their freshness. Here is no pallid mimicry of English novels of manners. Snelling could sometimes tell a tale with objectivity and dispatch; he could sketch with unerring insight the emotional reactions of his savage figures; he could picture with vividness and accuracy a setting that even at present has not been fully utilized by romancers. The buffalo hunter, the squaw, the frontiersman, the *bois brulé*, the plains Indian, these characters live again in all their color and bizarreness in the pages of Joseph Snelling.

These narratives of the Northwest should be of interest

not only to those whose destiny has brought them to the valley of the Mississippi, not merely to those who today revere the watershed of the Great River as natal ground, but to everyone who is at all concerned with the development of American literature. For it must not be forgotten that Snelling was first to introduce into fictional art the life and the people of the early Northwest. Rich in local color and almost unique in their early ridicule of the noble savage of the sentimentalists, his tales treat with fidelity an existence and a scene which have not as yet found a worthy bard but which have stimulated the American fancy since the days of the Louisiana Purchase. Some day, perhaps, a genius will arise to do for the trans-Mississippi area what the ancient epics did for Greece and Rome; and he will have acquitted himself of his task nobly if he presents the red man and his white adversary with half the feeling and the knowledge evinced in the work of a man who does not deserve the oblivion that has been his portion.

JOHN T. FLANAGAN

University of Minnesota
July, 1936

Note on the First Edition

THE first edition of William Joseph Snelling's *Tales of the Northwest,* published anonymously in 1830, is now rare. Inquiries addressed to seventy-five libraries in the United States collecting Americana have revealed the existence of only eleven copies among them. Two copies in private hands have been located. Catalogues of book auctions held in this country during the last fifteen years record the sales of seven copies at prices ranging from $22.50 for one in old calf binding to $82.50 for an uncut copy in original cloth.

The first edition is a small duodecimo volume four by six and one-quarter inches, bound in light brown cloth. The backbone has a red leather label lettered in gilt as follows: (*double rule*) | Northwest | Tales | (*double rule*). The volume consists of viii + [292] pages, as follows:

TITLE PAGE, p. [i]. Tales of the Northwest; | or, | Sketches | of | Indian Life and Character. | By | A Resident beyond the Frontier. | (*short rule*) | Long have I roved afar in western clime, | In forests hoary with the frost of time; | Where the lone traveller, startled from his dream, | Lists to the wolf's dire howl, the panther's scream; | Where the red

Indian glides with silent pace | Upon the victims of his murd'rous chase. | (*short rule*) | (*ornamental rule*) | Boston. | Hilliard, Gray, Little, and Wilkins. | MDCCCXXX.

CERTIFICATE OF ISSUE, p. [ii]. District of Massachusetts, to Wit. | District Clerk's Office. | Be it remembered, that on the fifth day of April, A.D. 1830, | in the fiftyfourth year of the Independence of the United States of | America, Hilliard, Gray, Little, and Wilkins, of the said district have | deposited in this office the title of a book, ⸌ the right whereof they | claim as proprietors, in the words following, to wit:— | 'Tales of the Northwest; or, Sketches of Indian Life and Character. | By a Resident beyond the Frontier. | Long have I roved in western clime, | In forests hoary with the frosts of time; | Where the lone traveller, startled from his dream, | Lists to the wolf's dire howl, the panther's scream; | Where the red Indian glides with silent pace | Upon the victim of his murd'rous chase. | In conformity to the act of the Congress of the United States, entitled | 'An act for the encouragement of learning, by securing the copies of | maps, charts, and books, to the authors and proprietors of such copies | during the times therein mentioned;' and also to an act, entitled 'An | act supplementary to an act, entitled "An act for the encouragement | of learning, by securing the copies of maps, charts, and books, to the | authors and proprietors of such copies during the times therein men- | tioned;" and extending the benefits thereof to the arts of designing, | engraving, and etching historical and other prints.' | Jno. W Davis, | Clerk of the District of Massachusetts. | (*short rule*) | Printed by I. R. Butts....Boston. | (*short rule*)

DEDICATION, p. [iii], verso blank. To | John Pickering, Esquire, | The learned illustrator of Indian languages, | these pages | are respectfully inscribed | by | the author.

NOTE ON THE FIRST EDITION

PREFACE, pp. [v]–viii. Reprinted on pages 3–5 of the present edition.

CONTENTS. The Captive, pp. [1]–20; The Hohays, pp. [21]–38; The Devoted, pp. [39]–51; Payton Skah, pp. [52]–65; Charles Hess, pp. [66]–83; The Bois Brulé, pp. [84]–196; Weenokhenchah Wandeeteekah, pp. [197]–212; La Butte des Morts, pp. [213]–222; Pinchon, pp. [223]–262; The Lover's Leap, pp. [263]–278; Notes, pp. [279]–288.

There are numerous orthographic discrepancies, especially in proper names. No attempt has been made in the present edition to correct these, nor the occasional solecisms of which Snelling was guilty. Here and there an obvious typographical error has been corrected.

J.T.F.

Tales of the Northwest
or, Sketches of Indian Life
and Character by a Resident
beyond the Frontier

Preface to the First Edition

No MAN can learn much of the character of the aborigines of North America unless by personal observation. The Indian tales, novels, etc. which teem from the press and circulating libraries, in which the savages are dragged from their graves to be murdered and scalped anew, are proofs of the assertion. By personal observation, the author does not mean such as may be made while travelling through the Indian country, at the rate of an hundred miles per diem; and still less the knowledge that may be acquired by a residence near the degraded race that a constant intercourse with our frontier settlers has made miserable. No, a man must live, emphatically, *live*, with Indians; share with them their lodges, their food, and their blankets, for years, before he can comprehend their ideas, or enter into their feelings. Whether the Author has so lived or not, the reader must judge from the evidence of the following pages.

If the works above alluded to may be considered a criterion, it seems to be the commonly received opinion that the aborigines are all heroes; that they are all insensible of fear, and strangers to weakness. It would appear that their strongest passions are hourly called into exercise; that their lips never part but to give utterance to a sentiment, and that glory and honor are to them all as the breath of their nostrils. Is this their true character? No; the Author's experi-

3

ence teaches him that they are neither more nor less than barbarous, ignorant men. Their passions, when excited, are more furious than ours, because unrestrained by principle; and explode with more violence because they are instructed from early childhood to repress and conceal, till it may be safe to indulge them. There are wise and good men among Indians, but they are few and far apart, as in civilized nations, and about in the same proportion to their numbers.

They have as many of the vices and follies of human nature as other people, and it is believed no more. An Indian may be dishonest as well as a white, and is about as likely to forgive an injury; if it be not such, as according to the customs of his tribe, must be expiated with blood. The heart of man beats neither slower nor faster under a blanket than beneath a coat and waistcoat.

The key to much that appears strange in the character of the aborigines may be found in one word; inconsistency. No certain judgment can be formed of an Indian's future conduct, by the past. His behaviour in all probability will not be the same in the same circumstances. He is the child of nature, and her caprice will dictate his course. Thus he may steal from his neighbor one day, and return him fourfold the next. When suddenly attacked he may fly; yet when he has made up his mind to fight, no one shews more courage. He has no laws, but he has customs which have the force of laws; yet sometimes interest, or the instinct of self-preservation, prevails over pride and shame, and he evades their observance.

Another error is, that he is supposed to speak in the language of poetry on all occasions. It is thought he

'. . . . . .cannot ope
His mouth, but out there flies a trope.'

In consequence, those writers who introduce our savages

4

into their works make their discourse a farrago of metaphor and absurdity. This folly had its origin in speeches delivered in councils. Such effusions are not extemporary, but studied efforts, in which the speaker purposely obscures his meaning with parables and verbiage, often not understood by his brethren, and not always by himself. The author has frequently seen the half breed interpreters completely at a loss; unable to comprehend their mother tongue thus garbled. By a very natural mistake, these orations are taken for specimens of ordinary Indian discourse; a most lame and impotent conclusion. In truth, nothing is more flat and common place than their common conversation. They speak with as little circumlocution, and as directly to the point as any people. Some figurative idioms may indeed be found in their several tongues, as well as in those of civilized nations; but to cut the matter short; if any man were to address an Indian in such language as is put into his mouth by the novelists, he might as well speak Hebrew.

The object of this work is to give to the public a knowledge of the character and habits of the aborigines, gained during seven years' intimate acquaintance with the tribes in the northwest. To make it acceptable it has been thrown into short stories. Voltaire says, *l'histoire d'un prince n'est pas l'histoire de tout ce qu'il a fait; mais de tout ce qu'il a fait de digne d'etere rupporté.* With some modification the Author has conducted his undertaking upon this maxim. He has not written of *all* that Indians do and say; but of what they do and say, that may, in his opinion, instruct or amuse. It may be said of his book that it contains too much war and bloodshed; but he replies, in anticipation, that the defect is inherent in the subject and could not be avoided. And with this preamble he delivers himself up to the tender mercies of the critics and reviewers.

THE CAPTIVE

Die, would he, saidst thou? ay, indeed he would.
It is the letter of their own wild law,
The customs of his people, all exact,
That blood should be repaid with blood. And he
Would sooner die by inches; feel his limbs
Dissevered joint from joint, than see himself
In his own eyes degraded.
                        The Prisoner. A Tragedy.

WE READ with admiration how Curtius rode into the gulf
in the Forum, to save his country, amidst the shouts and ap-
plauses of surrounding thousands; but when a poor, ignorant savage, rather than do violence to his own rude notions
of honor, awaits a fate that he believes inevitable, in sadness
and silence, without the sympathy of an individual, or any
of the circumstances that spurred the Roman to a glorious
death, we think no more of it, and the story is soon forgotten.

Of all the traits of aboriginal character, none is more
striking than the tenacity with which an Indian adheres to
his word, given under circumstances when there is every
inducement to violate the pledge. Trust him in the way of
business and his conscience tallies with his convenience. Engage him to perform any service, but do not reckon upon
its performance. Make him a prisoner, and set him at large
on his parole, and no persuasion will induce him to violate
it. He will return to meet his fate on the appointed day, as
surely as the sun will rise and set. His education teaches him

that death is but a change for the better, and that it is more than anything unworthy and womanish to shun it. The feelings of nature do not often so far overcome the principles implanted in the breasts of Indians by such instruction, as to make them shrink from the penalty of their misdeeds. To proceed with our story.

It is not known to all our readers, that the little French village of Prairie du Chien was occupied by the British troops during the late war; but the fact is yet fresh in the memory of the Aborigines in that quarter. The liberality of the English government sunk deep into their minds, while the red coats of its officials elicited no small admiration. When the soldiery marched into the place, many a swarthy dame and damsel, in the extremity of wonder, displayed a set of teeth that might have made a wolf blush, and ejaculated, eenah! eenah! eenomaw! Before the forces evacuated the village, they had an opportunity to admire the promptitude of British justice also.

One evening, an Indian runner arrived at the house of M. Joseph Rolette, a gentleman from Montreal, who had settled at the Prairie, and acquired the supreme control of the Indian trade, which he still retains. He came to inform this magnate, that a party of Ioways, who were in his debt, had had a good hunt; and that they were encamped at the distance of two sleeps, west of the Mississippi. They wished M. Rolette to send for his furs, as it consisted neither with their plans nor their laziness, to bring them. The messenger might be about eighteen years of age; was tall, straight, and of a very mild and prepossessing physiognomy.

'I will guide your men myself, Sagandoshee,' (Englishman) said he, 'if you will give me a pair of red leggins, a looking-glass, and a paper of vermilion.'

To terms so reasonable, M. Rolette could have nothing to

object. So he took Washtay Wawkeeah (the Harmless Pigeon) into the kitchen, and offered him a glass of whiskey. The youth had not yet acquired that love of ardent spirits that grows into a mania in Indians, after a little indulgence; as, indeed, we believe it does in white men. He put the glass to his lips, tasted, and set it down with disgust, saying, 'I love my body too well to put a bad spirit into it.'

M. Rolette commanded that he should be hospitably entertained, and then went into the quarters of his engagès.[1] He ordered Jourdain and Champigny to prepare themselves forthwith to depart on a journey the next morning at daybreak. They cheerfully began to patch their moccasins, and to cut *nippes*[2] for their feet; for the weather was cold.

In the morning, at day light, they were awakened by Washtay Wawkeeah. He told them they must walk fast, to get to the Ioway camp in two days.

The morning was clear, cold, and bracing, and there was an inch or two of snow on the ground. They crossed the Mississippi on the ice, and began the route over a level prairie country, interspersed with clumps of wood. The Indian gaily led the way, humming a love song, with which, it is probable, he intended to delectate the ears of some red skinned damsel. Here it is.

> I see Hahparm in the edge of the prairie,
> She is handsomer than scarlet or wampum;
> I will put on a blue legging and run after her,[3]
> And she will flee as if afraid.
> But I see, as she turns her head over her shoulder,
> And mocks, and laughs, and rails at me,
> That her fears are nothing but pretence.
> She is handsomer than scarlet or wampum,
> I will put on a blue legging and run after her, &c. &c.

At sunrise all three were in high glee. Washtay Wawkeeah told them there were many pretty *witcheeannas* (girls) in the camp where they were going. 'Your wife is

9

old, and ugly,' said he to Champigny. 'You can throw her away and take another now, if you like; or you can have two instead.'

'That cannot be,' answered the voyageur. 'We never keep more than one wife at a time, and that is often too many.'

'Eoo-pee-do!' cried the young barbarian, laughing. 'That is a rule some of you forget, then. You are so eager to get our women, one would almost believe you had none of your own.'

A deer now bounded across the path, if path it could be called, that path was none. 'Meesoankeahpee,' (brothers) said Washtay Wawkeeah, 'keep for the blue hill you see yonder, and I will overtake you before you reach it, and bring some venison with me.' He snatched the gun from Jourdain, and plunged into the coppice where the deer had taken refuge.

The voyageurs continued their route, stopping every two or three miles to smoke, and beguiling the time with stories of the Indian country.

'When I was a *mangeur de lard*,' said Champigny, 'I wintered at Traverse de Sioux, with M. L'Hommedieu. One of our people was Nicolas Gorèe, a Quebec man. At that time he was about eighteen, six feet high, with blue eyes and yellow hair. He was not very good at lifting or carrying, but he could jump three feet further than the best of us, and few of the Sioux could keep up with him in a foot race. All the squaws said he was Weechashtah Washtay, (a handsome man) and he was in no wise backward to cultivate their good graces. When any of them wanted a maple knot to make a bowl of, he would volunteer to cut down the tree, and no one was so ready as he to catch an unruly horse for them. More than all, he had a bunch of splinters always ready, pour courir la lumette.[4] And though he never boasted, it was thought he was well received on such occasions.

But the time when he was in his turn to feel the pain he inflicted on the Dahcotah[5] maidens came at last. Sheenah Dootah Way, if her color be excepted, was one of the prettiest girls I ever saw; certainly, one of the most good natured and playful. If Gorèe was chopping wood, she would come and sit on a stump, and strain her eyes with looking at him. When the tree began to crackle, she would start, and cry to him to take care. If he laughed, she too disclosed two rows of teeth as white as ivory. She would mend his old moccasins, and make new ones for him; and once, when he had the fever and ague, she attended him with more than the affection of a mother. He had lighted his match in her father's lodge, and would fain have taken her to his bosom. He applied to her father, but he demanded such a price for her, as was quite beyond the lover's means. Gorèe was addicted to gambling, and being usually unsuccessful, he had spent all his wages, and run in debt besides. Still he might have obtained her, if she had been less attractive; but she was so handsome, that several traders and interpreters had offered her father a much higher price than could be expected from poor Gorèe.

Well; M'Donald, a Scotch trader from Hudson's Bay, cast the eyes, or rather the eye, for he had but one, of affection upon Sheenah Dootah Way. He offered, God knows how many guns, kettles, and blankets, and her father consented, notwithstanding her tears and remonstrances. The old man might have relented; but an eight gallon keg of high wines, promised by the suitor to be given after the consummation of the nuptials, silenced all scruples. The Scot endeavored to gain her heart with presents of scarlet cloth, silver brooches, and finery; but Sheenah Dootah Way preferred Gorèe in his red flannel toque and blanket capot to M'Donald with all his riches. But her repugnance to the match availed nothing. She was invested with a complete new suit by her parents, and carried neck and heels,[6] more dead than alive, to M'Donald's apartment, like a lamb to the sacrifice.

In the morning, Gorèe, sad and silent, went to his daily task of wood-chopping. The new made bride passed him again and again, hoping to attract his attention, and no doubt, willing to elope with him. But his feelings had received a deep wound, and in his own mind he accused her of too ready a compliance with the will of her parents. He fixed his eyes steadily on his work, striking his axe into the trees with convulsive energy, neither looking to the right nor the left. When Sheenah Dootah Way found herself totally disregarded, she withdrew into the depth of the wood, as the squaws will do, you know, when in affliction. There she wailed and sobbed the whole day, but after sunset was heard no more.

M'Donald was at first uneasy, and would have followed her into the wood, but her father, better acquainted with the disposition of the Indian girls, told him to let her alone. 'When she has done crying,' said he, 'she will return and get over her sorrow.'

Midnight came and she had not shown herself. M'Donald could be restrained no longer. He seized a torch of birch bark, and accompanied by her relations, and some of us, went in quest of her. After searching some time, we found her, but good God! in what condition. In her despair she had hanged herself, with a sash that was a present from Gorèe. I need not tell you that such instances of suicide are common with the Indian women.[7]

Gorèe was with us. When he first saw the corpse, his face became as pale as ashes, and he neither moved hand, foot, nor eye, till we took it on our shoulders to carry it away. Then he roused, rushed like a tiger on M'Donald, and dragged him to the ground. 'Villain,' he shrieked, 'This is your — your work;' and he grasped his throat with a force that all our efforts were barely able to overcome. When he found himself denied the boon of vengeance, he turned off into the darkness, and none dared to follow him.

In the night the ice formed across the river, and at sunrise Gorèe had not returned. We never saw him again alive; but in the spring, a body was found twenty miles below, on a sand bar. The wolves and ravens had so disfigured it, that had it not been for the moccasins on the feet, which we knew at once for the handy work of Sheenah Dootah Way, it could not have been identified. Whether he had fallen into the river, or wilfully destroyed himself, could never be ascertained. I hope the former; for Monsieur Le Curé says, a suicide has no chance to enter into paradise.'

This and other tales served to pass away the time till Washtay Wawkeeah overtook them. He had killed a buck, which he instantly transferred from his own shoulders to those of Champigny. The gun he restored to Jourdain. And shortly after, arriving at a pond bordered with trees, they kindled a fire, and regaled themselves with steaks cut from the yet warm carcass of the animal the Indian had killed.

At sunset, they halted for the night, and Washtay Wawkeeah informed them, that, by quick walking, they might reach the place of their destination on the morrow before nightfall. They cleared away the snow, and cut rushes to sleep on, and having dried their nippes and moccasins, laid down to sleep.

The long dismal howl of a wolf that had been attracted

to within twenty paces of them by the smell of the venison, was unheard by Jourdain and Champigny. Not so with the Indian. He woke from his slumber, and in an instant seized the gun that leaned against a tree within reach. A new and malignant expression stole over his features. He examined the priming of the piece, and tried the charge with the ramrod. Then, as he deliberately levelled it at the sleepers, as they lay under the same blanket, he perceived that while standing upright, he could shoot but one of them. He recovered the weapon, and laid himself flat on the earth, within five steps of his victims. Having them both in range, he fired, started to his feet, dropped the gun, and fled.

Jourdain did not wake from his sleep of death. Champigny, shot through the body, arose and looked for the author of his wound. He did not lose heart, but put on his moccasins, and tied his belt tight round his body, to stop the effusion of blood. The moon shone with unclouded brightness, and he slowly and feebly retraced his steps by its light. The remainder of that night and the next day passed and he was yet on the road.

The next evening, the party sitting over the wine at M. Rolette's table, was interrupted by a loud knocking at the door. The *bourgeois*[8] himself rose and opened it, and Champigny fell inward on his face. M. Rolette was startled to perceive that the man was bloody from head to foot, and asked what had happened. He received no answer; the voyageur was incapable of giving any, for he had fainted.

He was carried into the dining room, and brought to his senses with cold water and cordials. He was just able to tell his story before he swooned again. M. Rolette caused him to be put to bed, sent for the surgeon, and his wound was dressed. All was in vain: the wound, though not necessarily mortal, had become so from his exertions, and the delay of surgical aid; and he expired before morning.

When Champigny had told his tale, Captain Bulger, the British commanding officer, said, with true military non-chalance, that he would take the proper measures in the morning, and the party returned to the business of the evening.

The captain was not, however, destitute of humanity. Attached to his command were several Indian traders, who had received commissions from the British crown, and whose vocation it was to collect as many savages under the standard of St George as they might, and to direct their motions. Of these, Captain Bulger selected two, Duncan Graham and José De Reinville, and gave them the command of forty Indians, and half that number of soldiers. A guide was easily procured, and they were ordered to proceed to the Ioway camp and seize the murderer; or, if he could not be found, to take as many prisoners as they could, to be retained as security for his surrender. They set forward immediately, and after three days travel, reached the Indian camp. The Ioways were advised of their approach, and the measures they took to enter it by surprise were vain. They found it deserted by all who were able to walk. One old woman defended her lodge, axe in hand, but was easily subdued. Reader, imagine some hundreds of dogs, yelping in every note of the gamut, and the screams of a cracked female voice, and you have some idea of the sounds that greeted the party. In one of the lodges they found an old, gray haired man, who had either disdained to fly, or distrusted his own ability to escape. To him their object was easily explained.

'If one of my young men,' said the aged chief, (for a chief he was,) 'has proved himself a dog, let him die the death of one. Blood for blood is but just and right, and if he cannot be found, I am ready to pay the price in his stead. Do not, however, harm our women and children. Let me but see one of my people, and then if the fool is not given up to you before twenty sleeps, take my life for his. Or what will be better, kill me now, and put an end to it.'

De Reinville, himself a half breed Sioux,[9] told him they had no wish to harm him. But he must go with them to the English camp, there to abide the decision of the British chief. They understood each other well, for the Ioway tongue is a dialect of the Sioux.

'Let us set out immediately,' said the ancient. 'But walk slow, for I am very old, and unable to keep up with your young men.' The intentions of the officers were not in accordance with this request. After travelling all day, it will readily be believed they had no inclination to walk all night also. They posted a guard, and all, having appeased their hunger, resigned themselves to sleep. In the course of the night, the women and children dropped in, one after another, and great was the marvelling at the bright bayonets and splendid attire of the unwelcome visiters.

On its return, when the detachment arrived at the bluff of the Mississippi, the old man was exhausted with fatigue. Nevertheless, in order to cross the river, it was necessary to descend. In the descent, the octogenary slipped, rolled twenty feet downward, and was very nigh transfixing himself on the bayonet of a soldier at the bottom. As it was, he received a scratch. 'If you intend to kill me,' he cried, 'do it now. I can make no resistance. I am old and weary, and would rather die than walk another step. I have not long to live, at any rate.' And to receive the blow he expected with decency, he drew his blanket over his head, sat down, and refused to proceed.

With much difficulty he was induced to go on, but nothing could persuade him that the injury he had received, was
not inflicted intentionally. In a few minutes, the party arrived at the fort, and the old savage was quartered in the
guard house.

Indians, when incarcerated, commonly grow fat and
sleek, in spite of fretting and unhappiness. But this was not
the case with the Ioway. Confinement appeared to weigh
upon his spirits. In less than a week after his arrival, his appetite failed, his eyes lost their original lustre, and his flesh
began to shrink upon his bones. He seemed to suffer a complete prostration of body and mind, and was evidently fast
sinking into the grave.

'What does your cap-ee-tan intend to do with me?' said
he, one day to Graham, as the latter was passing before the
door of the guard house. 'Does he wait for me to grow fat,
before he kills and eats me? See,' he continued, holding up
his attenuated arm, 'I am not likely to be very good eating.
He had better kill me before it is any worse.'

'I should think,' replied Graham, 'that you were old
enough to speak with more wisdom. You are an Indian, but
not such a fool as to think that we eat men. You know
better.'

'Certainly: I do know better. I did but jest. Yet it is hard
for me, who for eighty winters have never slept under a
white man's roof, to be thus tied here. I tell you again,
I would rather die at once than remain here three days
longer. I ask you once more what the great Weechashchahtopee means to do to me.'

'I do not know. If the guilty person is not delivered into
his hands, it is likely that he will put you to death in his
stead.'

'I will tell you, Hohayteedah, (The Hoarse Voice, Graham's Indian name,) a thought has come into my head. If the Weechashchahtopee will let me out, I will go and kill the dog that has bitten the chain of friendship asunder. I will bring him Washtay Wawkeeah's scalp myself.'

'Do you think we are fools or women? If we should let you go, when should we see you again?'

The countenance of the Indian fell. His eyes, which the moment before had glistened with the eagerness of hope, grew dim again. He did not deign to reply to a suspicion he deemed so unworthy of him, but turned slowly away, and sitting down in a dark corner, began to sing his death song.

He was, however, affable in his demeanor towards the soldiers, and others whom fortune had brought into contact with him. For the men, who regarded such things as curiosities, he would carve pipe stems, and for the boys he made bows and arrows. These little services, and his gentle deportment, rendered him a favorite in the garrison. The women made soups for him and gave him clothes; and the men gave him tobacco, and sometimes a glass of spirits. 'The English are good people,' he said. 'They have pity on the old and miserable.'

Only once did he show any temper or ill humor. A soldier, who had shod himself according to the custom of the country, brought his moccasin to the Ioway, and desired him to repair it. 'Does he take me for a woman?' said the aged chief. 'I was once esteemed a man among my people.'

The day after his conversation with Graham, a messenger from his son arrived. He informed the prisoner that Washtay Wawkeeah had fled to the Missouri, but that the band was resolved to have him, and had sent several men for that purpose. 'Tell my son,' said the old man, 'to make haste, or I shall be dead before he arrives.'

Some days after, a private was sentenced to be flogged

on the parade. The chief looked out of the guard house door, and beheld the troops drawn up in hollow square, with no small admiration. But when the culprit stripped, and the adjutant began to count the stripes, he retired into the apartment, and held his hands before his eyes, as if to shut out the sight. For some hours he was unusually melancholy, and in the evening he desired to see Graham and the commanding officer.

'Tell my father,' said he to the former, 'that I wish to be taken out on the beach, and shot instantly.' The request was explained to Captain Bulger, who asked its reason.

'I have lived eighty winters,' said the ancient, 'and no man that wears a hat can say I ever injured him. On the contrary, I was always a friend to the whole race. I am so still. I do not blame my father for being angry at what Washtay Wawkeeah has done; but I am dying a lingering death here; and I cannot bear to see men whipped like dogs. It makes my heart sick, and my flesh creep. Take me out and shoot me, and so end my misery.'

Graham told Captain Bulger, that he verily believed the old man would die broken hearted, if kept thus closely confined. How to give him any more latitude, and yet be sure of his person, was the question. For this Graham offered to be responsible, body for body, and Captain Bulger accepted the pledge. 'Listen, old man,' said the Indian trader. 'Your father has concluded to set you at liberty. Now take notice. All day, and every day, you may go where you please; but when the sun sets, you must return to this apartment. Remember that you are a man and a chief, and ought not to be afraid to die. If you break the condition, put on a petticoat, and be called an old woman ever after.'

Tears streamed down the old man's cheeks. He put one hand on the head of the officer, and the other on Graham's, and poured forth a long prayer and blessing on them. In the morning, he drew his blanket round him, and left the fort.

In the daytime he would stroll about the village, then much larger and more important than it is now. Sometimes he would borrow a gun from the inhabitants, and shoot ducks about the islands. At others, he would spear fishes in the river, and a portion of the spoils of his chase and fishery always found its way to the tables of Graham and the captain. But as regularly as the sun went down, he presented himself at the gate of the fort, and demanded admission. Being under this restriction only, his eye brightened, and he recovered his health and spirits.

At last, the beating of drums, and the protracted death yell on the opposite side of the river, announced that the long expected Ioways were at hand, and that they brought with them the guilty person. A boat, for the ice was now gone, was despatched for them, and they came over, not without some doubts as to the treatment they were to receive. Their faces were painted black, and in addition Washtay Wawkeeah had his arms tied behind him, with sharp splinters of wood, thrust through the muscular parts, to prove his contempt of pain and death. His features were still mild and gentle. A stranger to the circumstances could not have believed him the perpetrator of a dreadful crime, nor that he was about to enact the principal part of a tragedy.

The other Ioways were hospitably received, and provisions were given them, while a court martial was instantly convened to try the criminal. When asked for his plea, he frankly confessed his guilt.

'What induced you to kill those men?' asked the Judge Advocate. 'Had either of them done you any wrong?'

'No,' replied Washtay Wawkeeah, 'neither they, nor any other white man, ever injured me.'

'Was it then for the sake of their gun and blankets, that you slew them?'

'Not so. I had a better gun than theirs in my father's lodge. I did not take anything that belonged to them.'

'Why then did you take away their lives?'

'I was asleep, and had it not been that a wolf awakened me, they would be alive now. But having the gun in my hand, the thought crossed my mind, that I had never killed a man, and that I could never have a better opportunity. That was my only reason for what I did.'

The court was cleared, and without much deliberation the prisoner was found guilty of the charge of murder, and of the specifications of time, place, and circumstance. Captain Bulger approved the proceedings, and ordered the sentence to be carried into immediate execution. The prisoner heard his doom with stoical indifference, and began to chaunt his death song.

The Ioways were invited to attend the execution, but they all declined. 'It is right,' they said. 'He ought to die. But do not ask us to behold it. He is one of us.' And they all departed forthwith.

On the beach a grave was dug, a little above the water's edge, and to it Washtay Wawkeeah was conducted by ten files, with fixed bayonets. But no precaution was needed to prevent his escaping. He would not have turned on his heel to save his life. He had painted a black spot on his skin, over his heart, and at this he requested the execution party to fire. On the way, he sung in a full, bold tone, and he took his stand at the head of the grave in which he knew he was to lie, with infinite composure. At the report of the muskets, he pitched headlong into it, and there he slept till the next freshet washed him away. In two hours from the instant he landed at Prairie du Chien, the sand was lying six feet deep over him. After his death, no white man was killed by an Ioway, till the summer of 1829.[10]

✦ ✦ ✦

Not long after, a Canadian, called Coursolles, was killed at the Prairie by a Saque. The case was thus. The man had retired to rest, but was aroused by a gentle knocking at the window. He went to see who was there, when the savage presented his piece and shot him dead. The Saque then concealed himself on the island in the river, opposite the village.

When Captain Bulger learned the place of his concealment, he sent a party over, which took him, not without an attempt at resistance. He was tried, condemned, and shot, in the same prompt manner that Washtay Wawkeeah had been before him.

This is the true way to live in peace with Indians. An eye for an eye, and a tooth for a tooth, is their own law, and with them, punishment follows crime closely. The civil law of the United States they cannot be made to understand. Under our government, when an Indian has been guilty of murder, he has been kept in prison months, nay, in some instances, years, and carried for trial a thousand miles from the place where the offence was committed, where no evidence could be procured. This would be of little consequence, if he were left to himself, for then he would certainly plead guilty; but the civil law assigns him a counsellor, who advises him to deny the crime, and as no evidence appears against him he is consequently discharged. It is believed, that in nine cases out of ten, where American citizens have been killed by Indians, the murderers have escaped in this manner.

THE CAPTIVE

A few years since, an Indian, guilty of a capital crime, committed on the upper lakes, could only be tried at Detroit. One who had done the like on the upper Mississippi, or its branches, must have been sent to St Louis for trial. Thus by removing him out of the reach of evidence, the ends of justice were inevitably frustrated. And the case is little better at the present day.

The evils attendant on this system were, principally, these. First, the Indians attribute an acquittal, under such circumstances, to fear on the part of the American people. They perfectly understand that a homicide ought to suffer death, but they cannot comprehend how his conviction is rendered so difficult, and they consequently despise us, and think they may take our lives with impunity. Secondly, confinement irritates the person who suffers and the tribe to which he belongs. That an Indian seldom remains long in prison before he asks to be put to death outright, like the Ioway chief in our story, proves this fact. His detention keeps his friends in constant suspense and anxiety too. They say that they prefer to have their relatives killed. To conclude, the French and English always tried them by law martial, and were in consequence much more esteemed by them than the Americans are.

THE HOHAYS

'I will have my revenge. I will have it if I die the moment
after. What shall stay me? It is the law, and who shall say
me nay? Wherefore, bring them forth; for I have bound it
on my soul that they shall both die.'

Spanish Curate

SOME years ago there lived in the plains between the Missouri and the Saskatchawayn a young Indian, who at the
termination of his nonage received from his tribe the appellation of Weeteeko, or the Fool. This name was conferred
on him, not that he was weak in intellect, but on account
of his notorious inability to command his passions; that
being in the opinion of the Dahcotahs the very worst kind
of folly. He was irritable, suspicious, and jealous, and unable to conceal it. His tongue gave vent to whatever came
uppermost in his mind, to his own great prejudice, for it
kept him in a constant broil.

Nevertheless one circumstance gave him a certain degree of consequence. Consanguinity, according to the Indians, extends much farther, and its obligations are of
greater force than in civilized nations. A cousin, with them,
is as near as a brother, and a man may not without incur-
ring great shame marry a woman in the most remote degree
allied to him by blood. Weeteeko belonged to a great family. Many noted braves and men of influence counted kin
with him.

He fixed his affection on Khotah Way (The Grey Woman) and obtained her in marriage. Never before nor since was a poor squaw fated to undergo such misery. If she spoke to a man, she sustained his reproaches, and not seldom his blows. If his moccasins were not ornamented, his lodge [1] not pitched, or his horse not tended to his liking, he raved and scolded, whereby his family as well as hers were terribly scandalized. His provoking jealousy at last drove her to what she would not otherwise have thought of. She engaged in an intrigue with Nahpay Tunkah (The Big Hand) a young man whose connections were as numerous as those of her husband. The affair became the common talk of the whole band long before the person most interested was aware of it, as no one liked him well enough to inform him.

But at length riding one day to the buffalo hunt, as he was vaunting the excellence of the animal he bestrode, and the carnage he intended to make by its help, another young man who cantered by his side smiled significantly and said, 'kill as many cows as you will Weeteeko, you had still much better have staid in your lodge.'

'And why so?'

'Why so! There is a cow there that Nahpay Tunkah loves to approach.[2] O, he has a good head. He was sick you know this morning.'

His suspicions now wide awake, Weeteeko asked question after question, which the other, enjoying his uneasiness, answered in a strain of banter admirably calculated to increase the confusion of the querist. He declared that on his return he would cut off his wife's nose [3] and slay her lover. Had he observed the usual Indian maxims of prudence he might have effected his intended revenge. But not curbing his tongue the brother of Nahpay Tunkah, who

rode close behind, overheard him. He separated from the
cavalcade the first opportunity and galloped back to the
camp. He found the pair in close confabulation. 'Fly,' he
said to Khotah Way, 'if you value your nose. And you,
fool, if you are not tired of your life, fly with her.' Few
words served to explain the danger. Nahpay Tunkah resolved to escape with the woman to the next camp of his
relatives, and there wait till the anger of Weeteeko should
blow over or be appeased with gifts. In a few minutes he
was on the way accompanied by his brother.

When Weeteeko returned he found the birds flown. His
passion was beyond all bounds and his speech was of blood
and cruelty. He declared that he would follow the dog that
had bitten him and take such vengeance as never was heard
of. In the mean while he ran to the lodge of the father of
Nahpay Tunkah and cut it in pieces with his knife, while
the family [4] of the absentee smoked their pipes within with
as little concern as if nothing had happened. The enraged
savage then let fly two arrows at as many dogs belonging
to the lodge and relieved his choler with harsh and abusive
speech, but nothing could disturb the serenity of the inmates. When he was gone one of the elders coolly remarked that Nahpay Tunkah was a fool for doing as he
had, but not so great a fool as Weeteeko either. It was then
resolved that the family of the absentee should follow him
to prevent further mischief.

Before daybreak the next morning, Weeteeko was off
in pursuit. A good horse, which he did not spare, soon
brought him in sight of the camp where Khotah Way and
her lover had taken refuge. Luckily for them, he was seen
afar off. At the cry of 'a man on horseback!' they guessed
who it must be. The guilty wife fled into the heart of the
wood, and concealed herself behind the trunk of a fallen

tree. At the solicitation of his friends, Nahpay Tunkah followed her with his bow and arrows.

In a few minutes Weeteeko was in the camp. He sprung from his horse which was almost spent with fatigue, and ranged furiously among the lodges, calling on his enemy, if he was a man, to show himself. As he found his summons disregarded, he rent the air with reproaches, calling Nahpay Tunkah dog, coward, old woman, and even *winktah*, the last of insults to a Dahcotah.[5] Enraged that he did not appear, Weeteeko entered all the lodges successively, overturning the piles of buffalo robes, and searching every corner that might have concealed a man. Finding his quest vain, he at last stood still, leaning on his bent bow, and casting fearfully ferocious glances around him.

'What ails you, Weeteeko?' asked an uncle of the person he sought. 'What mean these cries, and whom are you seeking?'

'As if you did not know,' replied the other. 'You have no need to be told that your dog of a nephew has carried away my woman; whose nose I will cut off before this snow melts away.'

'And if he has,' returned the senior, 'are you not ashamed to raise such a clamor about a poor silly woman? You cry after her as if you were an infant and she your mother. You have lost your wife, but what of that? Such things often happen. There are plenty more women left alive. I dare to say you may get another without leaving this camp. Come, enter my tent, and eat and smoke.'

'I care not for the woman,' rejoined Weeteeko, somewhat abashed at this rebuke. 'I care not for this, nor any other woman. But I am not a woman neither, and I will not be laughed at. Your nephew has done well to hide himself.'

'He has acted more wisely in running away than you

have in following him. Yet if he has done as you say, let him keep the woman, and I will give you six horses, and twenty painted robes, and ten strings of wampum.'

'No, I do not want your horses; I can steal enough myself. I have wampum and robes of my own. I came here to kill a dog, and I will kill one before I depart.'

'If you do seek a dog, you see it is not here you ought to look. You have taken the wrong track.'

At the last word a light seemed to break on the mind of the hot headed youth. His eyes sparkled, his nostrils expanded, and giving a shout of triumph he rushed out of the camp. Taking a wide circuit round the lodges, he examined every diverging foot print. At last he came to the tracks of the objects of his resentment, and recognised them at once. With a yell of delight he followed them up, at a pace that promised soon to overtake them. He had not, indeed, far to go, but in his blind fury he neglected the ordinary Indian precautions in approaching an enemy.

Nahpay Tunkah heard his cry, and saw him coming, and so did Khotah Way. She clung trembling to her lover, and besought him not to abandon her to the rage of her husband. Had he been disposed so to do he knew it would be in vain, for Weeteeko was wonderfully swift of foot. He told her to fear nothing, and bent his bow very calmly. Stepping behind a tree he fitted an arrow to the string, and awaited the approach of his inveterate pursuer. He remained motionless till Weeteeko was within ten yards of him. Then he drew the shaft to the head and discharged it with unerring aim. The point entered his adversary's eye and passed out over his ear, shattering the skull in a dreadful manner. The wood was splintered by the force of the blow. The homicide gave the usual crie de joie for the death of an enemy, and called on his companion to behold his work.

28

But in a revulsion of feeling she threw herself upon the bleeding corpse, and made the wood resound with her lamentations.

Roused at length by his reproaches and expostulations, she arose, and they wended their way, sad and fearful, to the camp. The youth called his kinsmen about him, and told them what he had done, at the same time declaring his resolution to give himself up quietly to the avengers of blood. They lamented for what had happened, but decided unanimously that Weeteeko had 'died as a fool dieth,' in the manner best befitting his name. He had refused all mediation and advice, and though he had certainly a right to do as he pleased with his delinquent wife, he ought to have been satisfied with the gifts offered to mollify his resentment. Nahpay Tunkah had killed him in self defence, and having paid the price of blood, was to be held guiltless. If the relations of the deceased should not acquiesce in these opinions, he ought not to be delivered into their hands, but on the contrary, defended to the last extremity. This decision was perhaps a little influenced by a strong jealousy that existed between the two families.

The body of Weeteeko was brought to the camp with much solemnity. A medicine dance took place,[6] after which it was consigned to the earth with all proper rites and marks of honor. The men afflicted their flesh as if it had been one of their relatives, and the women mourned as for a brother. Not the least vehement in these demonstrations of grief were the two persons by whose misconduct the misfortune had come to pass; and it is probable the fear of punishment did not mitigate their sorrow. All things fitting for the use of a hunter and warrior in the other world were buried with Weeteeko, and his own horse was sacrificed on the grave.

THE HOHAYS

To be in readiness for whatever might befall, runners were sent in every direction to summon the connections of the family. And as intelligence spreads nowhere faster than among Indians, ere three days the father of Weeteeko was apprised of what had taken place. The unfortunate youth had come honestly by his violent disposition, having inherited it from his parent, who now resolved to go straightway in quest of his son's murderer, and slay him with his own hand. Not dreaming that any opposition would be made to the observance of the unwritten law of the Dahcotahs, he set off, attended by his two brothers only. He reached the camp, and was invited into the soldier's lodge[7] to rest and refresh himself; but he declined the courtesy. In a loud speech he set forth his grievances. The wife of his only son had been clandestinely carried off; but it was not for a thing so trifling as the loss of a woman that he sought vengeance. Such an occurrence was beneath the notice of a man. His son, had he lived, could have found as many wives as he pleased. There were very many Dahcotahs who would have been glad to give their daughters to so good a hunter. But his son had been slain while seeking to recover what was his by just right, by the very man who had injured him. The rites of hospitality and the usages of the nation had been violated. Weeteeko had indeed behaved foolishly, and like a very young man as he was, but he was now dead. Therefore he demanded that the offender should be bound and delivered into his hands, to suffer the penalty of murder.

The old man spoke in a strain of angry eloquence, his eyes flashing, and every muscle quivering with emotion. We give the substance of his discourse, but the manner in which it was delivered we are unable to convey. He was heard with attention and respect. When he admitted that his son had acted like a fool, he was honored with the customary grunt of applause; but when he demanded the surrender of the homicide, that token of assent was withheld. The father of Nahpay Tunkah spoke in reply.

He, he said, who treated his wife like a dog, could not expect to be loved by her. So had Weeteeko done by Khotah Way; and in such circumstances it was but natural that she should turn to some other man for solace and consolation, and it was no matter of wonder if her regard had been reciprocated by Nahpay Tunkah, who was himself a very young man. He had, however, acted like a fool to take the life of another, when there were so many girls whom he might have obtained. Yet he had done what might be justified in killing Weeteeko. If that youth had been satisfied to use his right to recover and punish his wife, the case would have been different; though even then, he would have been in the wrong to have put her to death. Juvenile follies should not be visited with so much rigor. But he had insisted not only on killing her, but her paramour also, contrary to the custom of the Dahcotahs, from time immemorial. It never had been their practice to put an adulterer to death, unless in the first heat of passion. Weeteeko had had time to reflect, and had been offered a magnificent compensation for the injury he had sustained. He had refused to accept it, and would be content with nothing less than the blood of the offending party, and therefore Nahpay Tunkah was right to kill him in self defence. But to avoid dissension the speaker was willing to pay the price of blood, and he besought the bereaved parent to take all the family possessed, and suffer his anger to sleep. And to this harangue the women added their cries of 'spare my son! spare my brother!'

Instead of becoming pacified, the old man was violently

enraged. In the plenitude of his displeasure he bestowed on them all manner of abuse and opprobrious epithets, and asked if they thought he valued all the horses in existence as highly as his son. Weeteeko had been slain, and say what they might, he would have vengeance.

They now resorted to the last deprecatory measure. A child, the prettiest in the camp, and dressed in the finest attire they could procure came out of a lodge, leading Nahpay Tunkah by the hand. Coming before the senior, the culprit stood still, and the child lisped a prayer for mercy.[8] At the sight of the destroyer of his son the old man fixed an arrow to his bow, but refrained from discharging it for fear of hurting the infant. At the demand of forgiveness, coming as it did from the lips of childhood, he for a moment relented; but his anger suddenly reviving, he would have transfixed Nahpay Tunkah on the spot had not his arm been withheld by one who stood behind him. His brother, seeing his purpose thus prevented, levelled the person who had interfered with an arrow. This was the signal for the death of the three visiters. They fell covered with wounds, and a cry of exultation arose over them.

The bodies of the unfortunate father and uncles of Weeteeko were not treated with disrespect, nor were their scalps taken. They were laid in their kindred dust with tears and lamentations, and those by whose hands they fell looked sorrowfully at each other, and asked, 'what will be the end of this?'

Many of the friends of the party had now arrived, and after a long fast, it was resolved in council, that as they might expect a visit from the relatives of the slain, and as they had provisions enough to stand a siege, they would construct a fortification in the best manner they were able, and wait the result. About two arrow flights from the wood were two small hills, one a little in advance of the other. On the tops of these they made two enclosures with logs and brushwood. Within these they dug holes large enough to lie in, and at the same time use their weapons. A store of hay was cut for the horses by the women, and they all removed into these defences. A watch, too, was set on the highest ground in the vicinity.

The third day after, the sentinel discerned in the extreme verge of the horizon, a dark object, which he soon ascertained to be a large body of horsemen. The men repaired to their posts, and the women and children took shelter in the enclosures. Had the advancing party been aware that a hostile visit was expected, and that measures had been taken to repel it, they would have come under cover of the night; but, in fact, the friends of Weeteeko had intended to enter the camp with protestations of friendship, and to exterminate the obnoxious faction by surprise. When, however, they came near enough to see the preparations for their reception, they yelled with rage, and were promptly answered with shouts of defiance from the intrenched party. They then dismounted and consulted, when they scattered and each strung his bow.

The defendants were something over an hundred, and the assailants three times as many. Yet the difference in position more than compensated for the advantage in numbers. With the usual reluctance of Indians to attack fortified places, the besiegers advanced singly, skipping and dancing about, to avoid the aim of those within. Arrows were exchanged as occasion offered, but excepting that some of the horses in the forts, if forts they may be called, were wounded, no damage was done. So little danger was there in this way of fighting, that their grotesque gestures and barbarous cries might have been taken by a spectator for a game played for amusement.

At last a young man who had never before been in action, and who burned to gain a reputation, cried that his name was Wawkeean Woheteeka, (the Terrible Thunder) and that he would strike on the enemy, cost what it might. Dropping his bow and quiver, he flourished his war club, and running at the top of his speed to the nearest baricado, struck upon it, regardless of the shower of shafts that was aimed at him. A shrill, sharp cry announced that he had effected his purpose, and he turned and fled with the same speed at which he had advanced, bearing away three arrows sticking in him. If he had been killed it would have been an advantage to his party, for then they would probably have been discouraged by his death, and would have left the ground. But at short intervals several more, encouraged by his success, tried the same experiment, and not one of them came off with the like impunity. Seven of them laid stretched lifeless on the ground before the breastwork, and the besieged cried to the others to come on and share the same fate.[9]

Their ardor much abated by these losses, for Indians count every man killed, the assailants drew off to a safe distance, and it was resolved to blockade the fortifications and starve the inmates out. The idea of storming never entered their heads, and we leave it to our readers to reconcile this excess of caution with the desperate valor, sometimes displayed by Indians. These men, each of whom would, without the least hesitation, have thrown away his life on the slightest imputation of cowardice, or met a cruel death with unshaken constancy, could not conceive the idea of giving battle on fair and equal terms. If they had now been engaged with Chippeways, or any other tribe distinct from themselves, it is most likely they would have abandoned the enterprise as hopeless; but the strong excitement of the occasion urged them to leave nothing untried for vengeance.

They surrounded the position of the enemy, and excepting that now and then some one would advance, discharge an arrow, and receive one in return, nothing material occurred for three days. At length, weary of the length of the siege, they resolved that if the besieged were not obliged by hunger to abandon their cover by the morrow, they would break up the leaguer and return.

Hunger was no part of the evil to which the adherents of Nahpay Tunkah were subjected. They had enough dried buffaloes' flesh to have lasted a month. Enough hay, too, had been cut for the horses up to the present time; but now it gave out. But they were obliged to eat their meat raw, and were cut off from wood and water. Their thirst they might assuage with snow; but the cold they were obliged to endure; and it was no small hardship at that season. The old men voted to remain where they were till the patience of the enemy should be exhausted; but the younger, and by far the greater number, gave their voices for departure. The women seconded them unanimously; and their complaints and scolding prevailed over the better judgment of the elders. That very night then, was fixed on for their escape.

It was dark and favorable to their plans. Twenty of the most active sallied from the enclosures, and crawling on the bare spots of earth, that their dark forms might not be betrayed by contrast with the snow, succeeded in passing the enemies' line. Making a circuit round the wood they approached the scene of operations in the rear of the besiegers. It is well known what command Indians have of their voices, and our party exerted it to the utmost in the furious attack they now made on the enemy. They changed their tones at every cry, and called to each other by the names of their relations who were known to have been far away when the siege commenced. The adverse party was completely deceived; and believing the attack proceeded from a new band of the friends of Nahpay Tunkah, their whole force assembled in the edge of the wood. The darkness, and the cover of the trees prevented any great injury being done on either side; but while this was going on, those for whose benefit the stratagem was intended, stole out of their fortification, with their horses, wives and children. All were admonished to be silent, and the infants were hindered from crying by stuffing pieces of buffalo hide into their mouths. When fairly out of hearing, they exerted their speed till they reached the place appointed for a rendezvous with their detachment engaged.

These last, when sufficient time had elapsed for the fulfilment of their object, slackened their efforts, gradually withdrew from the scene of strife, and hastened to join their companions. When the two parties reunited, they made all speed toward a large encampment, which they reckoned upon reaching, by dint of hard travelling, before the next night; and one was sent forward on the fleetest horse they had, to require their friends to come and assist them, in case they should be overtaken.

The darkness for some time prevented the besiegers from discovering the trick that had been put upon them; and when they did find it out, they could not see which way the enemy was gone. Notwithstanding their anger, they were compelled to wait till dawn before they could discern the traces of the retreat. Yet they vented their wrath in some degree upon the goods and chattels the fugitives had left behind. When day at last broke, they mounted and made haste to pursue.

About noon they overtook the enemy, and attacked with greater advantage than before. Then were heard the cries of hate and wrath, of triumph and defiance; the screams of women and children, and the groans of the wounded; the wounded females we mean, for the men died like wolves, fighting to the last gasp without noise or complaint. The warriors placed their wives and infants in the centre, and kept the foe off by strenuous exertion and hard riding, such exertion as Indians only are capable of, when roused from their habitual apathy. Still they retreated.

Nahpay Tunkah was the first man who fell. It so chanced that the woman who had been the cause of all this evil received an arrow in her neck and fell from her horse. Though not mortally hurt, the cavalcade could not stop for her. She called on her paramour for aid, and in spite of the remonstrances of his friends, he was obedient to her voice. His brethren in arms saw him die; his life blood flowing from twenty wounds. Deeds of valor were done, worthy to be recorded in better language than our own. The weaker side had the worse. The arrow, the spear, and the war club, made fearful havoc among them. Twenty-seven of their best men had fallen; most of the survivors were wounded, and their horses were thoroughly jaded, when a band appeared coming at full speed to their relief. It was the party which their messenger had apprised of their peril, and it arrived just in time to prevent their total extermination. On its appearance, the avengers of the family of Weeteeko desisted from the work of death, and rode away to avoid coming to blows with fresh warriors. They were not pursued. The sufferers pursued their way and entered the camp in company with those who had come to their rescue.

This blow was felt by the whole tribe. Scarcely an individual in it but was in some degree connected with the slain, on one side or the other. Fasting, mourning, and medicine dances became the order of the day. When these observances ceased a war party of the friends and relations of Nahpay Tunkah and Khotah Way assembled to revenge the injury their families had sustained. And they amply retaliated on the adverse division of the nation. The feud was not to be staunched. Wrong succeeded to wrong, and battle to battle. Gradually the whole Dahcotah people took part in the strife, and finally, those who had espoused the cause of the Siou Helen were worsted. Then leaving their former hunting grounds, they roamed the prairies between the Missouri and the Saskatchawayn, and so they continue to do to this day. They are called by the legitimate Dahcotahs, Hohays, but are better known by the title of Assinneboins. They are the most primitive Indians we have seen in our travels and excursions. The war begun as above related continued till eighteen hundred twenty, when a peace was made between the belligerents.

The Hohays are seldom seen without arms in their hands, whether in peace or war. They are desperate robbers and expert horse thieves, and keep no measures with any people of whom they are not in fear. They have little intercourse with the whites, and they still retain their ancient manners; using the same saddles, earthen pots, dress, and implements of war, as of old. Heaven grant that none of our readers may ever come in contact with them.

THE DEVOTED

Life has no joys for me. For me the streams,
The clear, sweet waters of my native woods
Are streams of bitterness. The glorious sun
Shines on my path in vain, since he, my boy,
My brave, my best beloved, my first born,
Was torn from these old arms. I'll reckless rush
Upon the foemen's ranks; and with this blade
Will dig my own red grave.
                                    Unpublished Play.

IN THE year eighteen hundred and nineteen, or twenty, two
soldiers belonging to the sixth regiment of United States'
Infantry, then stationed at Council Bluffs, were shot by
two Dahcotahs of the Susseton band. No provocation was
given by the sufferers; at least none was alleged by the per-
petrators of the crime. They were induced to do the deed
by one of those unaccountable impulses that so often actu-
ate Indians.

The Sussetons, or 'People who end by Curing,' inhabit
the country on the St Peter's River. They dress in cloth
and blankets. Their original vesture and implements have
given place to articles manufactured by the whites, so that
they are in a great measure dependent on the traders for
the necessaries of life. An embargo on the Indian trade is
therefore the greatest evil that can be inflicted on them.

In order to compel the surrender of the offenders, the
Colonel commanding the post at the mouth of the St Peters

stopped the trading boats. Notice was duly given to the Sussetons that an absolute non-intercourse would be enforced till the persons demanded should be given up to justice. The good policy that dictated the measure was soon apparent. No Indian on the St Peters could shoot a duck, or catch a muskrat. The bow and arrow, weapons long out of use, were put in requisition, but to little purpose. The game taken by their means was insufficient for the support of life. As no knives could be had, if a deer was killed it was flayed with a flint or a clam shell. Tired of enduring such privations the Sussetons took measures to terminate them.

A large camp was convened at Munday Ean Tonkinkee, or The Big Stone Lake. A solemn council was held on the green sward, to devise means to avert the consequences of the folly of their 'young men.'

'I am willing,' said Mahzah Khotah, (The Grey Iron,) one of the criminals, 'to give my life to the Big Knives, as a reparation for that I have taken. They will put me to death. What then? I am a man. Better that one should suffer than many. I have been a fool, but now I will act with wisdom.'

The guttural ejaculation peculiar to an Indian council put the stamp of approbation to these generous sentiments. But one of the assembled elders did not join in the general applause. It was Ahkitcheetah Dootah, (The Red Soldier,) the father of the speaker. His head drooped, and he hid his face in his hands.

'I too,' said the other person implicated, 'will go to the chief of the Big Knives. I will throw away my body also.'

'Not so my son,' cried an old Susseton. 'You are my only boy, and how will your mother, and your sisters, and your wife, and your children eat, if you should die? I have long been unable to hunt. I am old and useless. Life for life is all the Big Knives can ask. They shall have mine. Come, young men, let us start immediately.'

This reasoning appeared conclusive to the assembly. Two men were to die and it seemed to the Sussetons immaterial which. The son himself made no opposition. The next day after leaving some worn out clothing and a quantity of tobacco on a rock, as a tribute to the Great Spirit, Mahzah Khotah and his intended fellow sufferer started for Fort Snelling, attended by a numerous retinue of friends and relatives.[1]

Arrived within a mile of the fort, the party halted, smoked, and sung a prayer, in a subdued and monotonous tone. If Handel could have heard, it is probable he would not have wished ever to hear a Dahcotah concert again. Then they smutted their faces anew, and wounded their arms with knives. The prisoners' elbows were secured with ropes of braided buffalo's hair, and great oaken skewers were thrust through their flesh. This unnecessary pain they bore without blenching in the least. The prisoners began to sing, and in this fashion the whole party advanced to the walls of the fort. A company was drawn up under arms, and the commanding officer came out to receive them.

The elders and warriors sat down in a circle on the ground, with the prisoners in the midst. The American officer was desired to take his place with them, and then the peace pipe was produced and smoked round the circle from left to right, or with the sun, as the Indians express it. This ceremony ended the elder of the prisoners rose and spoke.

'A cloud,' he said, 'has come between us and our father. We hope the beams of this day's sun will drive it away. Our hearts are sad that the chain of friendship has been broken. We wish to mend it. Two foolish young men have acted according to their folly, and the Master of Life [2] is angry about it. One of them was my son. I am here to suffer for him. We throw away the other also. Have pity on us father, for we are onsheekah. (pitiable.) Our women and children are starving. We have come a long distance to see you, and the path was overgrown with weeds. Father, take pity on us, and let the road between your people and ours be cleared.'

The pipe of peace was accepted. The prisoners were taken into custody, and the other Sussetons dismissed. Colonel Snelling wrote to Washington for instructions, but it was long before he received them. At that time, the facilities of communication were not so great as at present. It was not then known that the Mississippi was navigable for steamboats to the falls of St Anthony, and mail stages did not then run between Peoria and the Lead Mines. The breath of civilization has at length blown away all obstacles. Steam has conquered the Father of Waters, to the astonishment of the savages and the terror of the catfishes. Keelboats and their concomitant 'Salt River Roarers,' are seen no more. So much for the tide of emigration.

When the instructions did arrive, they directed that the old Susseton should be set at liberty, and that the young one should forthwith be sent to St Louis, there to be prosecuted by the United States' attorney, and dealt with as the law directs. So was the proverbial wisdom of our government in the management of Indian affairs exemplified!

Mahzah Khotah was put on board a boat and conveyed to the capital of Missouri as fast as three pairs of oars and a current of two miles an hour could carry him. When he was brought before the court on whose verdict his fate was to depend, his counsel advised him to retract his confession. There was no doubt of his guilt, for he had avowed it again and again at St Peters. Here, however, he pleaded not guilty, and as no witness appeared against him he was acquitted and discharged.

In a few days he left the city and began his journey across the prairies, directing his course to the Teton villages on the Missouri. Probably, these were his reflections: 'I have killed an American, and gained the name of a warrior. The Big Knives have not dared to revenge it, and I will therefore slay another the first opportunity.' Whether these were his thoughts or not, it is certain such were the common opinions of the more remote Indians before they were acquainted with the power of the whites; and this belief still prevails in many tribes.

But in an evil hour for Mahzah Khotah, he encountered with John Moredock, called from his inextinguishable hatred to the Aborigines, the Indian Hater. This man came into Illinois when the descendants of the French emigrants were its only inhabitants. The fourth husband of his mother had died like her three former spouses, being killed by the Indians. Yet this woman, who seemed a mark for the shafts of border warfare, left Vincennes in order to settle in Illinois with her children. As she was ascending the Mississippi she and the whole party with which she travelled were surprised and butchered by the savages. Of all her family John Moredock only escaped, he having voyaged in other company. From the day he heard of this calamity, revenge on those who had destroyed his kindred became his ruling passion. The Indians who had been active in their extermination did not escape him. By unremitting pursuit, he achieved the destruction of every individual of them. His vengeance did not sleep here. Though irreproachable in his dealings with his fellows, and though he afterwards obtained a seat in the legislature of Illinois, and the rank of colonel of militia, he never let slip an opportunity to dip his hands in Indian blood. He was famous as a hunter and a partizan warrior, and in the course of his life was said to have killed thirteen Indians with his own hand, and it is probable the truth rather exceeds than falls short of report.

He had been at Chariton on business, when he met Mahzah Khotah; both being on foot and alone. His rifle was in his hand. At the sight of the savage, his eyes flashed fire and his face grew black with passion. He '*sot* his triggers,' but the time required for this operation enabled Mahzah Khotah to get behind a tree. He too was armed with a gun, given him by the Indian agent at St Louis. Moredock gained a similar cover. There they stood, watching each other as the gladiator and the lion might do in the arena. Neither could raise his weapon, or take a more than momentary look, without exposing himself to certain death. But the fertile brain of Moredock suggested an expedient. He drew his ramrod, put his cap on the end of it, and protruded it from his cover at the height of his head. The Indian very naturally supposed that his head was in it. The lightning is not quicker than was the flash of his gun. The Indian Hater fell, and Mahzah Khotah, drawing his knife, rushed forward to take his scalp. But the white man was instantly on his feet again. 'Where are you going with your knife?' said he, with a fiendish laugh. He fired, and the Dahcotah dropped. 'That counts one more,' said Moredock, as he turned from the bleeding corpse to pursue his journey.

From the time his son was surrendered to the American officer at St Peters, Ahkitchetah Dootah pitched his tent in the vicinity of the garrison. He visited his offspring daily, wept over him, and asked many questions relative to his probable fate. When Mahzah Khotah was removed to St Louis, the old man lost hope. He became listless and inactive. He was no more seen spearing fishes in the river, nor did the echoes of his gun disturb the silence of the surrounding hills. To a white man, such a course would promise a speedy release from sorrow by starvation; but it was no great disadvantage to Ahkitchetah Dootah. Among Indians the indolent share the provision made by the industrious, and a refusal to give food or clothes, is a thing unheard of. This very generosity is the great bar to their improvement. Where the 'social system' prevails to its fullest extent, as with the Dahcotahs, it is not to be expected that any individual will exert himself more than is necessary to meet the wants of the hour. It is no benefit to a squaw to plant a cornfield, for the harvest must be reaped by hands that did not sow. It is useless for a hunter to kill more venison than is needed for the immediate consumption of his family, as the greater part will be eaten by those who have been smoking by the fireside, while he has been freezing his fingers and wearying his limbs in the chase. The obstacles to the civilization of the Aborigines are indeed many; but in the opinion of one who has had many opportunities for observation, this is the greatest. But, dear reader, we find we have been betrayed into a digression, and if it pleases thee we will return to our story.

Ahkitchetah Dootah continued his visits to the fort, and at last learned that his son had been tried. It was in vain to tell him that Mahzah Khotah had been acquitted and set at liberty, for no process of reasoning could make him believe it. 'He has been put to death,' he would answer to those who endeavored to convince him that his son might yet return. 'He has been killed, and you are afraid to acknowledge it. You think we might revenge him. But I will not long survive my boy.' Accordingly, he made a feast, at which he appeared as naked as he was born. No one spoke, for savages as the guests were, they respected the intensity of his grief. When the dog was devoured, and its bones burned in the fire,[3] he broke silence. He recapitulated the circumstances of his case and declared his belief as above stated. His auditors heartily concurred in it, for the way in which Mahzah Khotah had come to his end was unknown to the whites, and therefore could not be communicated to the Dahcotahs. In the same faith they remain to this day, and nothing can persuade them to the contrary.

'I have certainly,' said the old man, 'committed some heinous offence against the Master of Breath. I do not know in what it consists, but it is certain that his hand is laid heavily on me. He is angry, and it is useless to live any longer. I am alone of my race. I am *onsheekah*. I will throw away my body the first opportunity.'[4] And his discourse was applauded by all present.

He immediately removed, and pitched his lodge on the extreme verge of the Chippeway territory, where he was most likely to be visited by the enemy. But having thus devoted himself to destruction, he seemed to bear a charmed life. He could find no hand charitable enough to terminate his miserable existence. He twice joined the war parties of his people, but in neither instance did they find an enemy with whom to combat.

At last, in the year eighteen hundred and twenty-three, he joined a party of twenty of his tribe, which was going to the red pipe stone quarry. It has been said that this is holy ground, and that the savages forget their hostility there. But this is sheer fiction. No war parties have ever met at the quarry, and therefore no battle has ever taken place in its vicinity.

The companions of Ahkitchetah Dootah took as much

of the stone as they needed, and then left the place. We will not follow them till we have attempted a description of the spot.

The country on each side of the river is a bare prairie, in which the eye seeks in vain for a tree or a shrub. The only objects perceptible are the countless herds of buffaloes, and their constant attendants the wolves. These last accompany them, patiently waiting till one of them 'takes a hurt from the hunter's hand,' or falls exhausted by sickness or old age. Then they hurry to the feast. Through this vast plain the river runs, in a thousand crooks and windings, its banks thinly skirted with trees and shrubs. At the quarry the pipe stone is found imbedded between strata of limestone. It is red and friable, a kind of serpentine, easily cut with a knife when first taken from the earth, though it grows harder by exposure to the air. Asbestos is also found in the quarry. Here the bluff rises perpendicularly from the river, and directly in its front stands an isolated portion, rent from the parent cliff by some convulsion of nature. It is about twelve feet from the bluff, and the younger and more active Dahcotahs used to try their nerves by jumping upon it across the awful chasm below.

On the present occasion our friends wasted no time in such feats, or in contemplating the scenery. A trail had been found, which their sagacity discovered to have been made by the feet of Saques and Foxes, and it behoved them to make off with all convenient alacrity, for no people better understood that discretion is the better part of valor, than Indians. They travelled swiftly for two days, till they came to the north branch of the river Terre Bleue, where they halted and pitched their lodges. Ahkitcheetah Dootah indeed, remonstrated against such unseemly haste, but as the others were not so weary of life as he, his words were unheeded. Yet he followed a good distance in the rear, to give the Saques and Foxes an opportunity to take his scalp.

The Dahcotahs had gained their halting place unmolested, but not unobserved. The Saques and Foxes had seen them, but though trebly superior in number, they resolved to attack with as little risk as might be to themselves. They followed at a wary distance taking good care to keep out of sight. They were better armed too, than the Sioux, for their proximity to the whites enables them to procure weapons at pleasure. They had each a good rifle, whereas half their opponents had nothing but bows and arrows.

At daybreak the next morning, the usual time for Indian attacks, they approached the Siou camp, taking advantage of the trees and of the inequalities of the ground. When near enough they raised the war whoop, and poured a shower of balls into the lodges. Five men were killed by this first volley. The sleepers started, and boldly gave back the exulting shout of the enemy. They made so good a use of their knives, that in an incredibly short space of time each had dug a hole in the ground deep enough to protect his body, and with such effect did they project their missiles that in a few minutes the assailants were compelled to retire to a more respectful distance.

At the first fire Ahkitchetah Dootah sprang upon his feet, and exclaimed that his time was come at last, and that he should now rejoin his son. He snatched up his tomahawk and ran out of the lodge. A bullet through his thigh did not check his career in the least. He brained the Saque who had discharged it, and rushed upon the next with his tomahawk uplifted. The enemy waited till the old man was within five paces, and then fired his piece with a certain aim. The bullet struck the Siou between the eyes, and he was a dead man before his face touched the ground. Thus did Ahkitchetah Dootah fulfil his vow to 'throw away his body.'

The Saques and Foxes showed less than their wonted courage and the strife was soon over. They gave way before the Dahcotahs, and Keokok, their partizan, or war chief, was the first to throw off all encumbrances and fly. The Sioux were too few to urge the pursuit far. Seven of them had been killed, and twice that number of the enemies remained on the field of battle.

He whose avocations or pleasure may lead him to a wild and solitary glen on the north branch of the Terre Bleue, four or five miles from its junction with the other arm of the river, will there find the bones of the slain Saques and Foxes whitening on the earth. In the branches of the trees above, he will see the bodies of the fallen Dahcotahs, carefully wrapped up in buffalo robes.[5]

PAYTON SKAH

His hopes destroyed, his heart strings broke,
No words of wo the warrior spoke,
His bosom heav'd no sigh.
'Thine be the fair,' the hero said;
Then proudly rear'd his lofty head,
And turn'd away — to die.

WE HAVE before intimated that we cannot pretend to much
accuracy with regard to dates. So we are not certain that
the events we are about to relate did not happen five centuries ago, perhaps more; but it is probable that the time
was not so remote. Be that as it may, we shall give the facts
in the same order in which tradition hands them down.

The Dahcotahs were at war with the Mandans. Many
were the onslaughts they made on each other, and long were
they remembered. Among the Sioux warriors who struck
the post,[1] and took the war path, none was more conspicuous than Payton Skah, or The White Otter. He belonged
to the Yankton band. When he returned from the field with
his head crowned with laurels, or more properly with his
bridle rein adorned with Mandan scalps, the seniors of the
tribe pointed to him and exhorted their sons to ride, to draw
the bow, and to strike the enemy like Payton Skah.*

Payton Skah was a husband and a father. As soon as he
was reckoned a man, and able to support a family, he had
taken to his bosom the young and graceful Tahtokah, (The

* Vide 'The Hohays,' Note 8.

Antelope) thought to be the best hand at skinning the buffalo, making moccasins, whitening leather, and preparing marrow fat, in the tribe. She was not, as is common among the Dahcotahs, carried an unwilling or indifferent bride to her husband's lodge. No, he had lighted his match in her father's tent, and held it before her eyes, and she had blown it out, as instigated by love to do.[2] And when he had espoused her in form, her affection did not diminish. She never grumbled at pulling off his leggins and moccasins when he returned from the chase, nor at drying and rubbing them till they became soft and pliant.[3] A greater proof of her regard was, that she was strictly obedient to her mother in law. And Payton Skah's attachment, though his endearments were reserved for their private hours, was not less than hers. No woman in the camp could show more wampum and other ornaments, than the wife of the young warrior. He was even several times known, when she had been to bring home the meat procured by his arrows, to relieve her of a part of the burthen by taking it upon his own manly shoulders.[4] In due time, she gave him a son; a sure token that however many more wives he might see proper to take, he would never put her away. The boy was the idol of his old grandmother, who could never suffer him out of her sight a moment, and used constantly to prophecy, that he would become a brave warrior and an expert horse stealer; a prediction that his manhood abundantly verified.

In little more than a year the youngster was able to walk erect. About this time the band began to feel the approach of famine. Buffaloes were supposed to abound on the river Des Moines, and thither Payton Skah resolved to go. His mother had cut her foot while chopping wood and was unable to travel; but she would not part with her grandchild. Tahtokah unwillingly consented to leave her boy behind, at the request of her husband, which indeed she never thought of disputing. One other family accompanied them. They soon reached the Des Moines, and encamped on its banks. Many wild cattle were killed, and much of their flesh was cured. The young wife now reminded her spouse that his mother must by this time be able to walk, and that she longed to see her child. In compliance with her wishes he mounted his horse and departed, resolved to bring the rest of the band to the land of plenty.

At his arrival his compatriots, on his representations, packed up their baggage and threw down their lodges. A few days brought them to where he had left his wife and her companions. But the place was desolate. No voice hailed their approach; no welcome greeted their arrival. The lodges were cut to ribbons,* and a bloody trail marked where the bodies of their inmates had been dragged into the river. Following the course of the stream, the corpses of all but Tahtokah were found on the shores and sand-bars. Hers was missing, but this gave her husband no consolation. He knew that neither Sioux nor Mandans spared sex or age, and supposed it to be sunk in some eddy of the river. And Mandans the marks the spoilers had left behind them, proved them to be.

Now Payton Skah was, for an Indian, a kind and affectionate husband. The Sioux mothers wished their daughters might obtain partners like him; and it was proverbial to say of a fond couple, that they loved like Payton Skah and Tahtokah. Yet on this occasion, whatever his feelings might have been, he uttered no sigh, he shed no tear. But he gave what was, in the eyes of his co-mates, a more honorable proof of his grief. He vowed that he would not take another wife, nor cut his hair, till he had killed and scalped

* Vide 'The Hohays,' Note 4.

five Mandans. And he filled his quiver, saddled his horse, and raised the war song immediately. He found followers, and departed incontinently. At his return but three obstacles to his second marriage remained to be overcome.

In the course of the year he fulfilled the conditions of his vow. The five scalps were hanging in the smoke of his lodge, but he evinced no inclination towards matrimony. On the contrary, his countenance was sorrowful, he pined away, and every one thought he was in a consumption. His mother knew his disposition better. Thinking, not unwisely, that the best way to drive the old love out of his head was to provide him a new one, she with true female perseverance, compelled him by teazing and clamor to do as she wished.

So the old woman selected Chuntay Washtay (The Good Heart) for her son, and demanded her of her parents, who were not sorry to form such a connexion. The bride elect herself showed no alacrity in the matter; but this was too common a thing to excite any surprise or comment. She was formally made over to Payton Skah, and duly installed in his lodge.

He was not formed by nature to be alone. Notwithstanding the contempt an Indian education inculcates for the fair sex, he was as sensible to female blandishments as a man could be. Though his new wife was by no means so kind as the old one, yet as she fulfilled the duties of her station with all apparent decorum, he began to be attached to her. His health improved, he was again heard to laugh, and he hunted the buffalo with as much vigor as ever. Yet when Chuntay Washtay, as she sometimes would, raised her voice higher than was consistent with conjugal affection, he would think of his lost Tahtokah and struggle to keep down the rising sigh.

A young Yankton who had asked Chuntay Washtay of her parents previous to her marriage, and who had been rejected by them, now became a constant visiter in her husband's lodge. He came early, and staid and smoked late. But as Payton Skah saw no appearance of regard for the youth in his wife, he felt no uneasiness. If he had seen what was passing in her mind, he would have scorned to exhibit any jealousy. He would have proved by his demeanor 'that his heart was strong.' He was destined ere long to be more enlightened on this point.

His mother was gone with his child, on a visit to a neighboring camp, and he was left alone with his wife. It was reported that buffaloes were to be found at a little oasis in the prairie, at about the distance of a day's journey, and Chuntay Washtay desired him to go and kill one, and hang its flesh up in a tree out of the reach of the wolves. 'You cannot get back to night,' she said, 'but you can make a fire and sleep by it, and return tomorrow. If fat cows are to be found there we will take down our lodge and move.'

The White Otter did as he was desired. His wife brought his beautiful black horse, which he had selected and stolen from a drove near the Mandan village,[5] to the door of the lodge. He threw himself on its back, and having listened to her entreaties that he would be back soon, rode away.

His gallant steed carried him to the place of his destination with the speed of the wind. The buffaloes were plenty, and in the space of two hours he had killed and cut up two of them. Having hung the meat upon the branches, he concluded that as he had got some hours of daylight, he would return to his wife. He applied the lash, and arrived at the camp at midnight.

He picketed his horse carefully, and bent his way to his own lodge. All was silent within, and the dogs, scenting their master, gave no alarm. He took up a handful of dry twigs outside the door and entered. Raking open the coals in the centre of the lodge he laid on the fuel, which presently blazed and gave a bright light. By its aid he discovered a spectacle that drove the blood from his heart into his face. There lay Chantay Washtay, fast asleep by the side of her quondam lover. Payton Skah unsheathed his knife and stood for a moment irresolute; but his better feelings prevailing, he returned it to its place in his belt, and left the lodge without awakening them. Going to another place he laid himself down, but not to sleep.

But when the east began to be streaked with grey, he brought his horse, his favorite steed, to the door of the tent. Just as he reached it those within awoke, and the paramour of Chantay Washtay came forth and stood before him. He stood still. Fear of the famous hunter and renowned warrior kept him silent. Payton Skah, in a stern voice commanded him to re-enter; and when he had obeyed followed him in. The guilty wife spoke not, but covered her face with her hands, till her husband directed her to light a fire and prepare food. She then rose and hung the earthen utensil over the fire,[6] and the repast was soon ready. At the command of Payton Skah she placed a wooden platter or bowl before him, and another for his unwilling guest. This last had now arrived at the conclusion that he was to die, and had screwed up his courage to meet his fate with the unshrinking fortitude of an Indian warrior. He ate therefore, in silence, but without any sign of concern. When the repast was ended Payton Skah produced his pipe, filled the bowl with tobacco mixed with the inner bark of the red willow, and after smoking a few whiffs himself, gave it to the culprit. Having passed from one to the other till it was finished, the aggrieved husband ordered his wife to produce her clothing and effects, and pack them up in a bundle. This done he rose to speak.

'Another in my place,' he said to the young man, 'had he detected you as I did last night, would have driven an arrow through you before you awoke. But my heart is strong, and I have hold of the heart of Chantay Washtay. You sought her before I did, and I see she would rather be your companion than mine. She is yours; and that you may be able to support her, take my horse, and my bow and arrows also. Take her and depart, and let peace be between us.'

At this speech the wife, who had been trembling lest her nose should be cut off, and her lover, who had expected nothing less than death, recovered their assurance and left the lodge. Payton Skah remained; and while the whole band was singing his generosity, brooded over his misfortunes in sadness and silence.

Notwithstanding his boast of the firmness of his resolution, his mind was nearly unsettled by the shock. He had set his whole heart upon Tahtokah, and when the wound occasioned by her loss was healed, he had loved Chantay Washtay with all his might. He could vaunt of his indifference to any ill that woman could inflict to the warriors of his tribe, but the boast that they could have truly made, was not true coming from him.

Though one of the bravest of men his heart was as soft as a woman's, in spite of precept and example. At this second blight of his affections, he fell into a settled melancholy, and one or two unsuccessful hunts convinced him that he was a doomed man; an object of the displeasure of God; and that he need never more look for any good fortune. A post dance, at which the performers alternately sung their exploits, brought this morbid state of feeling to a crisis. Like the rest, he recounted the deeds he had done, and declared that to expiate the involuntary offence he had committed against the Great ·Spirit, he would go to the Mandan village and throw away his body. All expostulation was vain; and the next morning he started on foot and alone to put his purpose in execution.

He travelled onward with a heavy heart, and the eighth evening found him on the bank of the Missouri, opposite the Mandan village. He swam the river, and saw the lights shine through the crevices, and heard the dogs bark at his approach. Nothing dismayed, he entered the village, and promenaded through it two or three times. He saw no man abroad, and impatient of delay, entered the principal lodge. Within he found two women, who spoke to him, but he did not answer. He drew his robe over his face, and sat down in a dark corner, intending to await the entrance of some warrior, by whose hands he might honorably die. The women addressed him repeatedly, but could not draw from him any reply. Finding him impenetrable, they took no further notice, but continued their conversation as if no one had been present. Had they known to what tribe he belonged they would have fled in terror; but they supposed him to be a Mandan. He gathered from it that the men of the village were all gone to the buffalo hunt, and would not return till morning. Most of the females were with them. Here then, was an opportunity to wreak his vengeance on the tribe such as had never before occurred, and would probably never occur again. But he refrained in spite of his Indian nature. He had not come to kill any one as on former occasions, but to lay down his own life; and he remained constant in his resolution.

If it be asked why the Mandans left their village in this defenceless condition, we answer, that Indian camps are frequently left in the same manner. Perhaps they relied on the broad and rapid river, to keep off any roving band of Dahcotahs that might come thither. Payton Skah sat in the lodge of his enemies till the tramp of a horse on the frozen earth, and the jingling of the little bells round his neck, announced that a warrior had returned from the hunt. Then the White Otter prepared to go to whatever lodge the Mandan might enter, and die by his arrows or toma-hawk. But he had no occasion to stir. The horseman rode straight to the lodge in which he sat, dismounted, threw his bridle to a squaw, and entered. The women pointed to their silent guest, and related how unaccountably he had behaved. The new comer turned to Payton Skah and asked who and what he was. Then the Yankton, like Caius Marcius within the walls of Corioli, rose, threw off his robe, and drawing himself up with great dignity, bared his breast and spoke. 'I am a man. Of that, Mandan, be as-sured. Nay, more: I am a Dahcotah, and my name is Pay-ton Skah. You have heard it before. I have lost friends and kin by the arrows of your people, and well have I re-venged them. See, on my head I wear ten feathers of the war eagle.[7] Now it is the will of the Master of life that I should die, and to that purpose came I hither. Strike there-fore, and rid your tribe of the greatest enemy it ever had.'

Courage, among the aborigines as charity among Chris-tians, covereth a multitude of sins. The Mandan Warrior cast on his undaunted foe a look in which respect, delight, and admiration were blended. He raised his war club as if about to strike, but the Siou blenched not; not a nerve trembled — his eyelids did not quiver. The weapon dropped from the hand that held it. The Mandan tore open his own vestment, and said, 'No, I will not kill so brave a man. But

I will prove that my people are men also. I will not be out-done in generosity. Strike thou; then take my horse and fly.'

The Siou declined the offer, and insisted upon being him-self the victim. The Mandan was equally pertinacious; and this singular dispute lasted till the latter at last held out his hand in token of amity. He commanded the women to prepare a feast, and the two generous foes sat down and smoked together. The brave of the Missouri accounted for speaking the Dahcotah tongue by saying that he was him-self half a Siou. His mother had belonged to that tribe and so did his wife, having both been made prisoners. In the morning Payton Skah should see and converse with them. And the Yankton proffered, since it did not appear to be the will of the Great Spirit that he should die, to become the instrument to bring about a firm and lasting peace be-tween the two nations.

In the morning the rest of the band arrived, and were in-formed what visitor was in the village. The women screamed with rage and cried for revenge. The men grasped their weapons and rushed tumultuously to the lodge to obtain it. A great clamor ensued. The Mandan stood before the door, declaring that he would guarantee the rights of hospitality with his life. His resolute demeanor, as well as the bow and war club he held ready to make his words good made the impression he desired. The Mandans recoiled, consulted, and the elders decided that Payton Skah must be carried as a prisoner to the council lodge, there to abide the result of their deliberations.

Payton Skah, indifferent to whatever might befall him, walked proudly to the place appointed in the midst of a guard of Mandans, and accompanied by the taunts and exe-crations of the squaws. The preliminary of smoking over, the consultation did not last long. His new friend related

how the prisoner had entered the village, alone and unarmed save with his knife; how he had magnanimously
spared the women and children when at his mercy; and
how he had offered to negotiate a peace between the two
tribes. Admiration of his valor overcame the hostility of the
Mandans. Their hatred vanished like snow before the sun,
and it was carried by acclamation, that he should be treated
as became an Indian brave, and dismissed in safety and with
honor.

At this stage of proceedings a woman rushed into the
lodge, broke through the circle of stern and armed warriors, and threw herself into the arms of the Dahcotah hero.
It was Tahtokah, his first, his best beloved! He did not
return her caresses, that would have derogated from his
dignity; but he asked her how she had escaped from the
general slaughter at the Des Moines, and who was her present husband.

She pointed to the Mandan to whom he had offered his
breast. He it was she said, who had spared her, and subse-
quently taken her to wife. He now advanced and proposed
to Payton Skah to become his *kodah*, or comrade, and to receive his wife back again, two propositions to which the
latter gladly assented. For according to the customs of the
Dahcotahs, a wife may be lent to one's kodah without any
impropriety.[8]

The Mandans devoted five days to feasting the gallant
Yankton. At the end of that time he departed with his recovered wife, taking with him three horses laden with
robes and other gifts bestowed on him by his late enemies.
His kodah accompanied him half way on his return, with a
numerous retinue, and at parting received his promise that
he would soon return. We leave our readers to imagine the
joy of Tahtokah at seeing her child again on her arrival

among the Sioux, as well as the satisfaction of the tribe at hearing that its best man had returned from his perilous excursion alive and unhurt. In less than two months Payton Skah was again among the Mandans with six followers, who were hospitably received and entertained. An equal number of Mandans accompanied them on their return home, where they experienced the like treatment. As the intercourse between the tribes became more frequent hostilities were discontinued, and the feelings that prompted them were in time forgotten. The peace brought about as above related has continued without interruption to this day. As to Payton Skah, he recovered his health and spirits, was successful in war and the chase, and was finally convinced that the curse of the Almighty had departed from him.

CHARLES HESS

I oft have striven as becomes a man
With red and white. Ay stranger, and for sport
Have grappled with the grisly bear. But now
I am alone on earth; there runs no drop
Of blood akin to mine within the veins
Of any, save one only, who do live.
Destruction dogg'd the footsteps of my race,
And sank them sudden in one bloody grave.
                    Logan, an unpublished Tragedy.

THE Indians are not the only persons who excite interest in
the northwest. Among the many rude adventurers drawn
into that country by love of excitement and impatience of
restraint, there are some possessed of qualities that in other
situations would command respect, and perhaps admiration.
But these qualities are lost to the world. It has often been
observed, that men most exposed to hardships, danger, and
privation, by the nature of their employments, as for example soldiers and sailors, are more attached to their occupations than those of more tranquil habits. No where is this
more forcibly exemplified than by the persons actively engaged in the Indian trade. Once fairly drawn in, they are
seldom known to leave it. A very short residence among
the aborigines learns them to despise the refinement and
artificial wants of civilized society, and spurn the restraints
legally and conventionally established to bind men to each
other. The wild, independent habits of the wilderness are at

first pleasing from novelty, and soon become riveted by custom. An Indian wife, and a family of half breed children complete the change; and when they have thus encumbered themselves, they may be considered as chained to their occupation for life.

Charles Hess, the subject of this sketch, was an example of the truth of the foregoing remarks. With a strength of mind and body seldom equalled, and an energy and quickness of apprehension, that with the advantages of education would have insured him a high rank in any profession he might have chosen, the circumstances above detailed rendered him poor and miserable all his life.

Where he belonged cannot be ascertained. He had a faint recollection of having witnessed the burning of his paternal roof, and the slaughter of his family by a party of Indians, and as he retained his language and remembered his name, he believed himself an American. Having lived several years a savage, among savages, and after being many times transferred from one tribe to another, he found himself at last on the Red river of the north, and entered the service of the North American Fur Company, where his talents and activity soon obtained him a clerkship.[1] According to the custom of the country, he married a Chippeway squaw, by whom he had several children.

Hess was modest, and never boasted of his personal exploits. Yet sometimes when strongly urged, he would relate passages of his life of wild adventure; but on such occasions his own part of the story was always underrated. The author has heard him tell of what he had done and seen; and his account of himself fell far short of common report.

A grisly bear is an animal far more formidable than the common black bear of America: it is about the size of its polar namesake; much swifter, and more active; though its great weight hinders it from climbing trees. Of all beasts of prey it is perhaps the only one that neither fears fire nor the face of man. Such is its ferocity that when hungry it will follow the human track as a hound does that of a deer. When full grown its claws are six inches long. Those Indians who have killed one of these animals make a necklace of them and value it highly: the Dahcotahs think it as great a feat to destroy a grisly bear as to slay an enemy in battle, and never dare to hunt one but in large parties, nor without a previous religious ceremony.

'Once,' said Hess, as we were sitting before a blazing fire, 'I commanded a brigade of canoes that I was charged to conduct to the place of their destination on the Saskatchawayn.[2] At sunset we put ashore and encamped, for the boatmen were sorely fatigued with their day's work. It was a raw evening in October, and we built enormous fires. The men soon despatched their allowance of lyed corn and grease, for they were on short allowance, and there is no sauce like hunger.[3] They turned the canoes bottom upward to sleep under and laid down in safety, as they thought. I had spread my mat in my tent and was just beginning to doze, when I was roused by a yell as if all the fiends had broken loose. I seized my gun and ran out of the tent, when I was immediately aware of the cause of the tumult. Fifty tongues informed me that a grisly bear had paid our camp a visit. He had taken a man named Longtain out of his blanket, as he slept before a roaring fire, and was carrying him off with all possible expedition. The men had guns, but were afraid to fire, lest they should kill their comrade. Yet the poor fellow did not lose his presence of mind even in that moment of deadly peril. 'Fire, fire,' he cried; 'it is better to be shot than torn to pieces.' We could still see the willows bending under the bear by the starlight. I had raised my gun, but Louison Désmarets, a Kinisteneau half breed, was quicker. He fired, and a horrible growl told us that his bullet had taken effect. Directly after, Longtain joined us, sadly frightened, but not at all hurt. The thick blanket coat he wore had protected him from the bear's teeth, and the ball had gone through the animal's brain. It was a wonderful preservation, and all things considered, a lucky occurrence. Nobody was hurt; Longtain had a story to tell for the rest of his life, and Désmarets had the satisfaction to save his comrade. We fed on the intended feeder, and for the two next days our scanty pittance of corn and grease was exchanged for an abundance of good fat bear's meat.'

'Another time,' he continued, 'I was at my fort[4] on the river Qui Appelle, and an hundred Kinisteneaux lodges were pitched about me. One morning an Indian announced that he had seen a grisly bear in the adjacent prairie. I had disposed of all my trading guns, and the lock of my own was broken; yet I was not long in saddling and bridling my good horse, nor in equipping myself with a tough bow and a quiver of arrows. I found a party of forty Kinisteneaux assembled on the bear's tracks. They had peeled some willow sticks and laid them across the foot prints, and were smoking and praying lustily. I told them I would not be detained by such folly, but would ride on before the bear had time to escape. One old man said, "I have often been told that the men with hats are fools, and now I see it is true!" I did not wait to hear any more but gallopped away.

'There was a light snow on the ground, and the tracks were plainly to be seen. An hour of brisk riding brought me up to Bruin. My horse was afraid of him, trembled, snorted and made every effort to throw me; but I was not to be dismounted so easily. By a strong application of the bit I forced him to stand till the bear was within twenty steps of me, roaring terribly. I let fly an arrow at him, but it recoiled from his side as it would have recoiled from a stone wall. The reason of this was, as I afterwards discovered, that the point was not firmly fixed to the wood, and it turned when it struck him. I was now obliged to make all speed, for the beast was too close for safety, and if my horse had not been staunch I should hardly have escaped. However, Bruin soon tired of following, and I became the pursuer in my turn. After three hours hard riding I had stuck three arrows into him, and he laid down to die. While I sat on my horse, waiting for the death struggle, that I might approach him in safety, the Indians came up. The same old man who had before spoken to me cried, "Ah! I now see that the people with hats are not such fools as I thought!" We took off the bear's skin, which was all that was worth taking, for he was old and tough and rank, in short not fit to eat.'

In the winter of eighteen hundred and ———, Hess was stationed at the Lake of the Woods. An Indian called Opawgun Mokkeetay, or the Black Pipe, took offence at him for having refused to give him as much liquor as he desired. Shortly after Hess had occasion to go on a journey, and employed the Black Pipe as a guide. They travelled together half a day without any suspicion on the part of Hess. As they came to a ravine, the Indian proposed to stop and smoke before crossing it, and the white man cheerfully complied. 'Brother,' said Opawgun Mokkeetay, 'you have always been very kind to me. The other day you refused to let me make a fool of myself. You were right. I have a fast hold on your heart.' [5]

'I am glad,' replied Hess, 'that you are wise at last; but we have far to go; let us push on.'

'Directly,' rejoined the other, examining the lock and

priming of his gun. 'Go on brother. I will but tie my moccasin, and then follow.'

Hess took up his own piece and crossed the gap; just as
he attained the level ground on the other side, he heard the
report of the Indian's weapon, and felt his side grazed by a
bullet. He turned and saw that Opawgun Mokkeetay had
taken to his heels as soon as he fired. A ball from the white
man's gun overtook him, and he fell. The weapon levelled
for the destruction of Hess had been charged with two bullets, and this contrivance to make sure of him saved his life.
The balls had diverged; one grazed his right side, and the
other cut his belt in twain on his left. He returned in a few
days to his house.

Two or three evenings after his return, a cousin of the
deceased, by name Squibee, or the Drunkard, entered his
apartment with his gun in his hand and his face painted
black.[6] He seated himself before the fire without saying a
word. Hess saw that he was bent on mischief, and thought
it best to temporise. He offered the Drunkard a pipe, which
was refused. He then set before him a wooden platter of
boiled venison, but he would not taste it. He spoke several
times to the savage, but received no answer. Squibee sat
sullen and immoveable, his eyes steadfastly fixed on the
blazing logs before him. At intervals his eyes turned in their
sockets, though his head did not move, and he cast furtive
and scowling glances around. The engagés belonging to the
establishment, who were much attached to their principal,
looked in, but when they saw the expression of the Indian's
features, they shrunk back, and loaded their guns.

After a silence of half an hour Hess determined to bring
matters to an issue. 'Nitchee,' (i. e. friend) said he, 'what
makes your heart sorrowful, and what do you seek in my
house?'

CHARLES HESS

'My brother Opawgun Mokkeetay is dead,' replied the savage. 'My eyes are dry, and I want something to make the tears come in them.'

Hess went into his store house and drew a glass of spirits, which he gave to the Indian. The latter held it up between his eyes and the light, and then threw it into the fire. It blazed above the chimney.

'Why did you not drink it?' said Hess.

'It is not good, it is no better than water,' replied the other.

'It burned as if it was good,' said Hess, still desirous to conciliate him. 'I thought it was strong enough. I will get you some more.' And he went out to do so.

Squibee was evidently working himself to the pitch of resolution requisite for some desperate action. He began to examine his gun, and to look uneasily about him. At one moment he seemed to relent. He wiped the smut from one side of his face with the corner of his blanket; but one of the Canadians happening to look in, he turned away his head. The instant the man withdrew, he scraped some soot from the chimney back with his fingers, spat upon it, and renewed the color of his visage with the mixture. He had scarcely finished when Hess reappeared. 'Here,' said the trader, 'is liquor that is strong as fire. Drink.'

The Indian doggedly put the glass to his lips, took a mouthful, and spat it out again. He threw the remainder into the fire, saying, 'neither is that good. Bring more.'

Hess turned to obey, and as he stooped to pass through the door, heard the explosion of Squibee's gun, and saw the splinters fly from the timber over his head. Without testifying any concern he went out, and was asked by Ménard, one of his people, 'what is the matter? are you hurt, mon bourgeois?'

'I believe not,' he replied, 'but I have had a narrow escape. I felt the scoundrel's bullet stir my cap.' He took it off, and saw that he had indeed been near death: the ball had gone through it within an inch of his skull.

Without uttering another word he entered his store, drew a third glass of alcohol, and returned with it to the room where he had left the Indian sitting. He offered him the liquor, saying, 'You have been at the fort at the forks of the Assineboin river, and have seen the scales that are there used to weigh furs go up and down. Just so it is with your life. Shall I live? Shall I die? Dog!' he continued, his choler rising as he saw that the Indian's countenance did not relax its ferocious expression, 'your life is light in the balance. Look at that sun. It is the last time you shall ever look upon it. Drink that liquor. It is the last you shall ever drink.'

Squibee, as ready to suffer as he had been to inflict suffering, took the glass, coolly emptied its contents, and drew his blanket over his head.[7] Hess levelled a pistol and blew out his brains.

Ménard and the other engagés rushed into the room at the report, with their guns, and discharged them into the bleeding body of the Chippeway. 'If any harm is to come to you, mon bourgeois,' cried Ménard, 'we are resolved to share it. If the Indians revenge themselves on you, they shall kill us also.'

Some days after the Drunkard's brothers sent to invite Hess to a feast in their lodge.

This wigwam, like all Chippeway lodges, was made of mats of rushes, spread upon a frame of slight poles of an oval form; the fire was in the centre, and the smoke escaped through a hole in the top. Hess found the three brothers of the man he had slain, sitting, with their legs crossed under them; each had a wooden bowl full of dogs' flesh before him. A bear skin to sit upon, and a similar repast, were placed for Hess. The Indians had painted their faces black, and their arms were laid beside them. 'Sit,' said the elder of the brothers, and Hess sat down. The speaker then produced a red, stone pipe, with a stem three feet long, curiously ornamented with eagle feathers, porcupine quills, and human hair dyed red, which had been taken from the scalp of a Dahcotah. He filled it with a mixture of tobacco, and the dried and pulverized inner bark of the red willow; which compound is called *kinnikkinik* in the Chippeway tongue. He lighted the pipe, took a few whiffs, and passed it to the next, who imitated his example. When the brethren had smoked, it was handed to Hess, the elder saying, 'our brothers whom you have killed were foolish young men, and deserved their fate. We know they sought it, and that you are blameless in what has happened. If they had followed our advice they would now be alive: but they were fools, and a fool soon comes to his end. We offer you this pipe, and ask you to eat of the dish before you in token of amity, and assurance that no harm shall befall you for what you have been compelled to do.'

'Brothers,' replied Hess, 'I am a man: if you had intended me harm I should not have fallen alone.' And he showed the butts of two brace of pistols that he had brought under his garment. 'But,' he continued, 'I am not to blame for what has come to pass. If you wish me to believe your words, or to smoke your pipe, or to partake of your feast, you must first wash the black color of your faces away; and then I will comply with your invitation. I am not a woman, nor a child, to believe every bird that sings.'

The Indians rose, left the lodge, and soon returned with their faces washed. One of them said, 'If our faces *were* black, our hearts were clean. It was not in sign of malice towards you, but of grief for our relations that we were painted. Eat then, and smoke, without doubt or fear.'

Hess smoked and ate. When he had finished, the elder Indian said, 'we hope, brother, that you will give the widows and children of the dead something to cover their nakedness, and to relieve their hunger.' And Hess complied with the request, for he was a humane man when left quiet.

Whether, if they had not washed their faces, the family would have avenged their slain relatives or not, cannot now be ascertained; but it is certain he was never after molested for what he had done.

When the Hudson's Bay and North West Companies united, Hess, like many others, was thrown out of employment. He remained at Pembinaw (Lord Selkirk's settlement) and maintained his family by planting, trapping, and hunting the buffalo, till the autumn of 1822, when he received a proposal from the principal partners of the Columbian Fur Company, then just formed, to engage in their service. He accepted the offer, bought two carts and horses, and started with his family and little effects, to go across the plains to Lac au Travers, the principal post of his future employers. He was mounted on a good horse, and expected to subsist on the buffaloes he might find in his route. To the inhabitants of the Atlantic coast it may appear strange, that a family of eight, women and children, should undertake a journey of nearly three hundred miles under the protection of one elderly man only, with the sky for a covering, and relying on his success in the chase for support. But we can assure them that nothing is more common in the north-west than such excursions; and the hardships they must have reckoned on enduring are there accounted as trifles.

They had accomplished about half the distance they had

to go, without seeing any of the roving bands of Sioux that infest the prairies on the Red River, and expected to complete the journey in the like security. One day at noon they halted at the river Aux Outardes to refresh themselves, and give their horses time to graze. While they were eating, a drove of buffaloes came in sight, and Hess mounted his steed to pursue them. From a cause then unknown to him, the animals took fright, and he followed them far and long before he brought one down.

For two days the family had been observed by an erratic band of Dahcotahs, whose name cannot conveniently be expressed by the letters of the English alphabet; but translated, it signifies People of the Pole. They are the Ishmaelites of the north-west. None ever escaped from their hands without being plundered, unless too strong for them to meddle with: few whom they have ever plundered have survived to tell the tale. They knew Hess by report, and one or two of them had seen him; and from his character they inferred that they could not attack him openly, without the loss of one man at least. They had therefore hitherto kept out of sight; but when they saw him ride away after the buffaloes, they sent a runner to frighten the animals, in order that he might go too far to see or hear what was to take place. In this they succeeded too well. Does the reader ask their motive for aggression? The wife of Hess was a Chippeway, and the blood of that hated race ran in the veins of his children. And had this not been the case, the thirst of blood, the little property in the carts, the supply of ammunition and tobacco they expected to find, and the scanty clothing and pitiful ornaments of the victims, would have been to them sufficient inducements to butcher a thousand human beings. When Hess returned at sunset faint and weary, from his successful hunt, a sad sight for a husband and a parent met his view. The bodies of his wife and children were naked and had been thrown into the fire; their heads were divested of their natural covering, and the trunks bristled with arrows. His carts were broken in pieces, and the horses were led away. 'I have seen,' said Hess, 'many a sight of blood and horror, but never before anythng like this. For a moment my brain turned, and the world seemed to me to be annihilated. Had the enemy then come back, they might have taken me like a child. But other feelings soon arose in my breast. My blood boiled; I felt it flowing in my veins like molten lead; my voice became husky and my palate parched; I was almost suffocated with rage, which was not at all allayed by the reflection that I could do nothing for vengeance. I was alone; a poor, weak, friendless old man: the murderers had at least four hours the start of me; their trail I could see; but if I followed it what could one, even if he were younger and stronger than I, have done. But this would not have weighed with me for an instant, if my wearied horse could have carried me. Those only who have suffered such a loss, in such a manner, can have any idea of my feelings.

'When I came a little to myself, I found that my children were not all present. There lay my wife, her infant nailed to her bosom with an arrow. There was my brave boy, his face upward, still grasping the knife he had drawn to defend his mother and sisters, his teeth set, looking defiance, though cold and dead. Five of my children were there in one bloody pile; but my eldest daughter was gone. This did not console me, for I knew that some brutal savage had saved her, that she might become his wife.

'I dug their graves with the knife I wore in my belt. I had no fear that the wolves would disturb them, for the carcasses of the buffaloes cumbered the prairie. The work oc-

73

cupied me all night. I took one last embrace of her, who, although her hue was dark, had been my faithful partner through twenty years of joy and sorrow. With a weak and a trembling hand I laid my family in the earth, and I swore over them by God the Father Almighty, the omnipotent maker of heaven and earth, that if any of those who had thus bereaved me should ever fall within my power, I would not spare them; no, not the babe unborn.'

But when this first storm of passion was over, his better feelings prompted him to attempt the recovery of his daughter, rather than obey the dictates of revenge. Four days travel carried him to Lac au Travers. On his arrival he was kindly welcomed by Messrs M'Kenzie, Laidlaw, and other partners of the Columbian Fur Company. Another cup of bitterness was in store for the unfortunate old man; the next day he was taken ill, and was confined to his bed for several days. While he lay upon his fevered couch, he was informed that the Indian who had made his daughter a prisoner had taken her to wife. The gentlemen above mentioned offered him any amount of merchandise that might be needed for her ransom, and it was settled that he should go and demand her at the Indian camp as soon as his health would permit. A messenger was sent to ask on what terms she might be redeemed, and the answer was soon obtained.

As force could avail him nothing, Hess determined to go alone, and unarmed, in quest of his offspring. When he arrived at the camp another dreadful spectacle was prepared for him. The scalps of his family were hung upon a pole, and the savages were dancing around them in triumph. He was greeted, not with hostility, for the hospitality of the Sioux nation forbade that, but with evident exultation and insolence. Some sung the wrong they had done him. He presented himself before his daughter's husband, or master, and uncovering his breast said, 'I am worthy of pity. This is my only child; restore her, or strike me as you struck her mother. I am alone on earth; lo! here is a ransom.'

The features of the son of the Pole showed some feeling. 'I am the only child of *my* father,' he replied. 'The ransom is little, but you are old and need some one to make your clothes and moccasins, and to take care of you. Tarry and partake of our cheer before you depart. Then take your child, Tahtunkah Nahzhee,* and begone, and none shall molest you.'

If it were permitted to compare a poor Indian trader with a mighty monarch, we should say that this scene reminds us of Priam kneeling to Achilles for the body of his son.

Fearful to irritate the Indian, by any sign of impatience, the heart stricken old man entered the lodge, and sat down with his daughter to a dish of boiled buffalo meat. While at this repast, a young savage who had assisted at the massacre of his family entered, and holding out his bow and arrows to Hess, said, 'here, Tahtunkah Nahzhee, I used this once to your sorrow. Do you understand the use of it?'

His anger for the moment boiled over. He sprang to his feet, seized the weapons, and drawing the arrow to the head, replied, 'stand off a little and I shall show you.' For an instant the life of the Indian was in great danger. But the elder interfered. 'You are a fool,' said he. 'Go away, and let Tahtunkah Nahzhee depart in peace.'

Hess found his way back to Lac au Travers in safety, and the daughter thus redeemed was afterwards married to an Indian trader. In the year eighteen hundred and twenty ———, he went to Washington with Major Taliaferro, in the capacity of interpreter to a deputation of Indians. He had not dwelt in anything like a town before. He was tall and

* The Rising Buffalo, a name the Sioux had given to Hess.

thin to emaciation, but a life of constant exercise had indurated his muscles almost to the hardness of iron. He was strait and strong, and for his age, active. His eye had lost none of its quickness or brilliancy, and as he stole along the streets with the noiseless Indian step he had acquired, if a carriage rattled behind him, he would start and feel for his knife, as he used to do in the wilderness. He would cast sudden, furtive glances around him, as if he expected an attack, and was clearly out of his element. On his return to the north-west he died of a complication of disorders, and his bones lie on the bank of the St Peters river. Peace to his manes.

THE BOIS BRULE

Chapter 1

Yes, truly: for look you, the sins of the father are to be laid upon the children; therefore, I promise you I fear for you. I was always plain with you, and so now I speak my agitation of the matter: Therefore be of good cheer: for, truly, I think you are damned.

Merchant of Venice.

AT THE time of which we are about to treat, that is, between the years eighteen hundred and fourteen and eighteen hundred and twenty, the country west of the Mississippi, from the fortyninth degree of latitude to the Frozen Ocean, was the scene of bitter contention and fierce strife, between two rival trading companies; the Hudson's Bay and the Northwest. The former, existing as a body corporate under a charter granted by the second Charles to Prince Rupert and others, found its ancient privileges and possessions invaded by a new association, which at first supplied the want of experience by superior energy, and a double share of activity. It soon acquired an influence over the Indians, that gave it a considerable advantage in the trade. Fraud and deception became matters of boast on both sides, and fortunate would it have been had the opposition extended to no greater excess. But being beyond the reach of law, the traders came ere long to open hostility, and bloodshed was the order of

77

the day. The Earl of Selkirk was at the head of the Hudson's Bay Company, and whoever is desirous to learn the history of these dissensions, may read it in a book which that nobleman gave to the world; though it must be allowed that the work is partial.

The halfbreeds of the North-west are physically a fine race of men. The mixture of blood seems an improvement on the Indian and white. By it, the muscular strength of the one, and the easy grace, and power of endurance of the other, are blended. They are the offspring of intermarriages of the white traders, and their subordinates, with Indian women. Good boatmen, expert hunters, and inimitable horsemen, as they all are, they are sometimes engaged in the service of the actual Indian traders; but more frequently subsist by fishing, trapping, and hunting the buffalo. It is impossible to ascertain their number, so widely are they scattered; but probably it amounts to four or five thousands. Each speaks French, and the language of his mother; or to define more accurately, of his mother's tribe. They receive just enough religious instruction from their fathers, to despise the belief and superstitions of their savage kindred, but are as ignorant of Christianity as Hottentots. In manners and morals, they are on a par with the Indians.

The contending parties found in these people apt instruments of evil. For small pay they were ready to act as spies, boatmen, hunters, or banditti; as they were ordered. If a trader was to be killed or plundered, or a trading fort attacked, they were willing and unscrupulous. If a courier was to be intercepted, they would ease him of his despatches, and even of his life, when commanded. If a post was to be established, they could build log houses, and feed the inmates with buffalo meat, from one end of the year to the other. The Scotsmen and Canadians who controlled the trade, could not have found fitter tools wherewith to make mischief.

Besides the Indians and half breeds, there are other inhabitants of the prairies. Canadians, reluctant to labor, and unwilling to return to places where the restraints of law and religion are in force; or perhaps retained in the country by Indian connexions, mix with the half breeds, and live the same life. When hired by the traders, they are termed engagés: when out of employment they call themselves 'les gens libres,' or free men. It would seem, from the number of these last, that ten civilized men degenerate into barbarism, where one savage is reclaimed from it. Metaphysicians may speculate upon such a propensity as much and as long as they please, and devise means to counteract it; but the fact is thus, and it is believed, always will be.

This is a long preamble, but in order to a right understanding of the following story, it will be necessary to extend it still farther. By some strange infatuation, the Earl of Selkirk conceived the plan of establishing a colony at the junction of the Pembinaw and Red Rivers, at the fortyninth degree of latitude. For this purpose he sent an agent to Scotland, and another to Neufchatel in Switzerland, to procure colonists. A prospectus was printed, and circulated among the mountaineers of either country; describing the promised land in terms that might with more propriety have been applied to the garden of Eden. The trees, it said, broke down under the weight of their fruit. The buffaloes presented themselves at the doors, every morning, to be killed; and the climate was like that of the north of Spain, or of the Langue d'Oc. Not a word of this statement is true. There are trees on the water courses, indeed; but they are elms, or such other products of the soil as have never borne fruit since the days of Adam. There are buffaloes; but to be eaten, they must be hunted and killed. The climate is hot enough in summer; but the summer is brief, and in winter, Siberia is not colder. That the Scotch and Swiss ladies might not want an inducement to emigrate, the prospectus furthermore held forth that 'l'on avoit besoin de cinquante ou cent jeunes femmes, saines et robustes; pour unir en mariage avec autant de colons déjà établis.' Deceived by the missionaries of colonization, and their promises of assistance, some hundreds came to Hudson's Bay, and thence to Ossinneboia, as the settlement was called. There they found their error. The river rose every spring, and destroyed their plantations; and such as had ploughed above high water mark, saw their corn devoured in the milk before their eyes, by swarms of grasshoppers, more voracious than the locusts of Egypt. To cap the climax of their distress, the North-west Company began to look upon the colony as a part of a deep laid scheme of Lord Selkirk to ruin their trade, and threatened the harmless emigrants with fire and sword.

At this period our story commences. One clear afternoon in October, a boat might be seen making its way up the Red River, propelled by six oars, lustily plied by as many stout Canadians. It was laden with settlers for Pembinaw. There were a few men, and about twenty women and children. Their speech was truly a confusion of tongues: no two of the families spoke the same language: one addressed his neighbor in French, and was answered in German; and a third supported his share of the conversation in one of the patois dialects of the Canton of Berne. Add to this, the voices of some half dozen infants, crying with cold and hunger, (for the Swiss were beginning to discover the futility of the promises of his lordship's agent,) and the description is complete.

Two men stood on the bow of the boat. One of them,

who was clad in a blanket coat, and wore an otter skin cap, was Governor Semple; on his way to assume the reins of government over a population of five hundred souls, the inhabitants of the flourishing colony of Ossinneboia; in virtue of the powers vested in him by the Earl of Selkirk. His age might be forty, or upwards, and his features were indicative of his character; too gentle and humane to live in such a country, at such a time. The other was a tall, good looking youth, with sparkling dark eyes, and coarse, straight hair, as black as the raven's wing. His somewhat high cheek bones, and olive complexion, bespoke him of aboriginal descent, yet he would have been thought eminently handsome in any part of the civilized world. He was dressed in the costume of the *bois brulés*.[1] His nether man was invested with a pair of elk skin trowsers, the seams of which were ornamented with fringes. Over these he wore a capot, or surtout, of coarse blue cloth, reaching to the mid leg, and bound round the waist with a scarlet woollen sash, in which was stuck a dague, or broad two edged knife, used in that country to divide the carcass of the buffalo. Buck skin moccasins, and a *capuchon* of one piece with the surtout, completed his attire. He leaned on a short gun, such as the Indians in that quarter carry, and waited for Governor Semple to speak.

Roused from his meditations by a shrill cry from one of the children, that gentleman broke silence. 'William,' said he to the young man, 'I trust these good folk will find accommodations at Pembinaw, that will make them forget their present hardships.'

'No, sir;' replied the youth, 'unless some of those who are already housed take them in, they will not find a roof to shelter them. As to food, their chance is a poor one. When I was at Pembinaw, three weeks since, the settlers had nothing to eat but the fish they caught daily from the river. The ice will soon make, and then they will be deprived even of that resource.'

'That proves great neglect or mismanagement in them: there are plenty of cattle in the plains, and they have had the whole summer to make pemican [2] and raise corn.'

'With due respect for your better judgment, I should say it proves no such thing. It proves the folly, or wickedness of those who have persuaded them to leave their homes for such a country as this. They have planted; and the blackbirds [3] and grasshoppers have reaped the harvest. There are buffaloes for all the world, but the poor creatures are not hunters; nor do they know how to cure the meat when it is killed. If they could all ride and shoot as well as myself, they have no horses; and how could they, without the guns and ammunition that were promised? More than that, the Indians will not suffer them to hunt: it is not a month since the Yanktons drove a party of them in. In these circumstances, I should find some difficulty to live myself; bois brulé as I am.'

To these reasons, Governor Semple had nothing to reply. He drew his cap lower over his brows, and covered his face with his hands. A moment after, he opened his liquor case, and distributed brandy to the men, and wine and cordials to the women.

The young man now left his station in the bow of the boat, and took his place at the side of a girl who was busied in tending a sick child. 'Flora,' said he, 'for heaven's sake, take more care of yourself. Give the child to its mother, and let me throw this cloak over you: it is growing colder fast.'

'No, William,' replied the lady, in a slightly Scottish accent; 'let me take care of the poor baby: its mother is unwell, and not able to do it herself. It would do me more harm, believe me, to hear their complaints, and witness their sufferings, than any hardship or privation that I am likely to undergo.'

'This is but the beginning of their misery. I am afraid all will suffer bitterly when winter comes. If your father had had but a little common sense, you would have been exempt from it.'

'Alas! I know his prejudices too well. Though you are a Gordon by the father's side, he cannot overcome his dislike to your Indian blood. For your own sake, then, seek a fairer and richer bride than poor Flora Cameron.'

She spoke with evident effort, and turned away her head to conceal her emotion. We are inclined to believe that she was not very earnest in her request, nor displeased at the answer that followed. Gordon replied, in a whisper, 'Forsake you! may God forsake me if I do! Would you drive me mad, Flora? When you accepted the offer of my hand, you were ignorant of my family, but I know that the discovery has not lowered me in your opinion. I never sought to deceive you: I thought my descent was as plainly stamped on my features, as the mark on the brow of the first homicide. It seems I was mistaken. If your heart is still unchanged, why should the folly of an old dotard sunder us? True, he gave you life; but did I not save it, and his too? I have therefore as strong a claim on you, as he. My blood is tainted, forsooth! ay, that was the rub always. At the Catholic College, the boys, who were glad of my assistance at their tasks, called me "cursed Indian" when we quarrelled. I could hardly refrain from proving my right to the appellation with my dirk. And when I became a man, those who extended their courtesies to me, did it as though they thought it condescension. I had even thought to abjure the society of civilized man, and seek a refuge from his scorn in the tents of my Assinneboin kindred. But I saw Flora Cameron, and my purpose was changed. And having your plighted faith, do you think I will relinquish it? No, never! I will not give over the hope of obtaining your hand, till I hear the command so to do from your own lips. Seek a fairer bride, indeed! And where can such be found?'

'Do you think I believe such gross flattery? Beauty and I are strangers. You must either be mad, or exercising your wit at my expense. But why, if you apprehend so much hardship at Pembinaw, do you make it your place of residence? You have yet time to return to Montreal before the cold weather sets in, and I assure you it will be a consolation to me to know that you are well. Do not fear for me: if you wish it, I will again swear to you, never to marry another. Let that content you; and if you value my good opinion, do not again speak of my father as you have done. He is a good man, and it may be that his family pride will yield to affection; for what love is like the love of a parent for an only child? Why have you, contrary to my desire, attached yourself to my footsteps, to make him doubt me? Why will you remain in this unhappy land, where cold and hunger are the least evils? Return to Montreal, I entreat you.'

'If I have acted contrary to your desire, it was for your own sake. You are not safe in any part of this country. You have heard of the outrages already committed: more, and worse, are to happen. This winter, some will die of starvation, and some by violence. Your father cannot follow the elk and buffalo; but I need not tell you that I am the best hunter here; even among the half breeds. My skill shall be exerted for you and your father, and he shall be indebted to me for life again, whether he will or not. Do you think I could enjoy a moment's rest at Montreal, knowing as I do, that you need support and protection? Flora, speak to me no more of leaving you.'

'What you say is but too true. We have good reason to tremble. I have not eaten a morsel today, and there are women in the boat who need food more than I.'

'What then have you done with your portion of the provisions, and with what I added to it?'

'I have given it to these poor famishing women; but if I had known that what I gave was yours, I would not have taken it.'

'And have you indeed acted thus? Thank heaven; there is the track of a buffalo that has been to the river to drink within the hour! I will go ashore and try to bring a load of his flesh to the boat.'

'But William, dear William; do not go far. Those cruel People of the Pole are abroad; and if you meet them you will never return. Stay, stay, I beseech you: I am not at all hungry: I can fast very well till the next allowance is distributed.'

He did not hear her. He had already commanded the steersman to set him on shore, and the latter had cried *allume!* [4] The half breed mounted the bank, waved his hand to Flora, and disappeared.

When the boat had again put off, Mr Semple called to Flora to take her seat beside him. He was informed of the attachment between her and Gordon, and had endeavored to persuade old Duncan Cameron to consent to their union. The clansman was deaf to all reasoning on the subject. 'I am a gentleman born,' he said. 'The blood of Lochiel and Sir Evan Dhu runs in my veins, and it shall not be contaminated with my consent. The boy is a good boy, and the Gordons are an ancient and a noble race, but his mother is an insuperable objection. So, sir, it is of no use to argue. I cannot consent to it.'

Flora, notwithstanding her disavowal of all pretensions to beauty, was an uncommonly beautiful girl, and was as well aware of it as her lover. At the time when our tale begins, she had seen seventeen summers. She was such a maiden, in appearance at least, as the novelists of the last century usually took for a heroine. Her figure, though slight, was active, and perfectly symmetrical. Imagine a neck like a swan's, down which light hair fell in natural ringlets; a brilliant complexion; a forehead like Juno's; eyes rather mild than piercing; a straight and well formed nose; such a mouth as limners delight to delineate; and a faultless chin. Then add cheeks indented with such dimples as Love loves to lurk in: form a combination of these particulars, and you have a good picture of Flora Cameron.

Before we proceed farther in this history, we will give some account of its principal characters. Duncan Cameron was one of that class denominated originals. His father, who according to Highland ideas, was a gentleman, because collaterally descended from Sir Evan Dhu, had amassed money enough in his vocation of travelling packman, or pedlar, to enable him to send young Duncan to school, and afterwards to the University of Aberdeen. There the youthful Cameron made a reasonable progress in the humanities. But he most delighted to listen to Highland genealogies and traditions, and the tales of seneachies. He would go to Luckie M'Laughlin's change house, in the North Wynd, and having ensconced himself beyond the reach of interruption, in her cosey back parlor, he would call for a Scots pint of Glenlivat, and send for Donald Ben Lean Cameron. Inspired by the beverage, the piper would relate to him the traditional glories of the Camerons. The pedlar's son was by nature enthusiastic, and his early recollections co-operated with this intellectual study, to convince him that

Scotland was the first and greatest nation in the world; the clan Cameron the noblest clan in Scotland; and himself intimately connected with the honor of the clan Cameron. His father dying shortly after he graduated, he found himself in possession of a thousand pounds sterling. Much and long did he deliberate how to sustain the dignity of his name. While he hesitated between physic and divinity, the blind god stept in and counselled him to espouse the daughter of a farmer, a tenant of the Duke of Buccleugh. His father in law was embarrassed, and Duncan's thousand pounds were very useful. They managed the farm in tacit partnership, and the Cameron soon imagined himself the first agriculturalist in the three kingdoms; but notwithstanding, nothing that he undertook succeeded. He would sow wheat on the wettest soil on the farm, justifying his doings with a quotation from the Bucolics.

Twentyfive years after, his father in law died. His wife followed, leaving him a daughter, the sole fruit of their wedlock. Five years from this event, poor Duncan was obliged to sell his stock, and throw up his lease of the farm, to pay his debts. He found himself with a beautiful girl of fifteen hanging upon his arm, forty pounds in his pocket, and

> 'The world all before him,
> Where to choose.'

His pride had increased with his poverty. Yet he had considerable powers of conversation, and still remembered something of his classical education. When reduced to his last guinea, he had the good fortune to be introduced to the Earl of Selkirk, who after some confabulation, judged him to be a very proper person to superintend his infant colony, and to instruct the new comers in the mysteries of husbandry. He was much of the same opinion himself. The terms were agreed upon, and he embarked at Glasgow for Quebec, where he arrived in due time, without accident.

At Montreal, his situation as homme d'affaires to his Lordship, and his daughter's beauty, procured him many attentions from the M'Gillivrays, M'Leods, and other worthies concerned in the Indian trade. Many were the swains who sighed for Miss Cameron. Among these was William Gordon, with whom our readers are already a little acquainted. He was introduced to Cameron as the only son of a half brother of the Marquis of Huntly, then disputing the inheritance of a considerable estate, at law, with another member of the family in Scotland. The young man had been educated at the Catholic Seminary in Quebec. His gentlemanly demeanor, and implicit deference to the opinions of Duncan Cameron, made him a favorite with the old man; while his polite address, elegant person, and constant attention, awakened a stronger feeling in the bosom of his daughter. With all his good qualities, Flora remarked that his temperament was melancholy, and that he was subject to sudden starts of passion. The least appearance of neglect appeared to cut him to the soul. Once, in a large company, an outrage lately committed by an Indian of the St Regis tribe, was the subject of conversation. A young Georgian planter, who had visited Montreal for the benefit of his health, observed, that might he hazard an opinion, he thought the whole tribe should be transported to the West Indies as slaves; and added, that the Aborigines were scarcely entitled to the rank of human beings, at any rate.

Flora at this moment turned towards William Gordon, who was standing behind her chair. His arms were folded across his breast, his teeth gritted, and he gazed upon the speaker with an expression of intense ferocity that appalled' her very soul. His eyes gleamed like those of the rattle-snake, when about to strike. When he saw that she observed him, his features relaxed, and he resumed his wonted manner. This did not, however, prevent her from being as much pleased as ever with him. Her father remarked their growing intimacy, and rejoiced. He liked William Gordon, and judged from the style in which he lived, that he would be a very suitable partner for Flora, in a worldly point of view. The youth had now become a daily visitor at their lodgings.

An occurrence took place, that brought matters to a crisis. A sleighing party was to go to the mouth of the Utawas, on the ice, and our friends were invited to join it. The whole started in high spirits; Duncan Cameron, with his daughter, taking the lead, and Gordon following. About two miles from the city, there was a large open space, or air hole, in the ice. Cameron was driving his horse thirty yards above it, at the speed of ten miles an hour, when suddenly the sleigh and the persons in it broke through, and were swept under by the current.

The gentlemen of the party stopped their horses, and the ladies screamed. All stood aghast. But Gordon pulled off his boots, cast down his cloak, and plunged into the hole without saying a word: the whole passed in a moment. The frolickers now watched the air hole below, in breathless anxiety. They had begun to think that all three had perished, when Gordon emerged, holding Cameron up by the collar with one hand, and his daughter by the hair with the other; both too far exhausted to help themselves in the least.

As he attempted to gain a footing on the edge of the ice, it broke away under him, and it seemed that their death was inevitable. None dared approach. But luckily two Canadian *habitants* were crossing with a horse load of planks. They hastened to his aid. Laying the boards one at the end of another, the stronger of the two reached Gordon, now ready to sink: yet he insisted that Flora should be the first saved. With little difficulty, the Canadian raised her upon the ice, and drew her to a safe distance. He then returned, and extricated the old man in like manner; and last of all, Gordon was taken from the water, chilled almost to death, and unable to walk or stand. The sufferers were immediately wrapped in buffalo robes, and conveyed with all the speed the horses could make, to the city, where medical aid was instantly procured.

Cameron and his daughter had been insensible while what we have related took place, but tongues were not wanting to inform them how they had been rescued, and to magnify Gordon's gallantry. That was needless, for he had indeed ran a fearful risk. In about a week, all three had recovered from the effects of their submersion.

In a few days, Gordon made a formal proposal for the hand of Miss Cameron. Her father made inquiry of Governor Semple, who was known to be the young man's guardian, concerning his character. On this point, the Governor's testimony was in the highest degree satisfactory, but the fact which he communicated, that Gordon was a half breed, roused the family pride of the Cameron, and determined him at once to reject the suit. At the interview in which this decision was communicated to Gordon, his indignation and disappointment broke all restraint; a quarrel ensued, and the Scot forbade his daughter to hold any further intercourse with her lover.

She could not obey. Through the instrumentality of a friend of Gordon, she had an interview with him, and plighted her word never to marry another. With this he was obliged to satisfy himself, for he could not persuade her to an elopement.

Chapter 2

He is a monstrous feeder, sir. He would
Devour a bullock at one meal, and then
Pick his teeth wi' the horns. He'd eat the Devil
And sup his scalding broth; or gorge a horse
And chase the rider hard.

The Gourmand, an unpublished Comedy.

THE friend mentioned in the last chapter was a gay, light hearted young Irishman, by name Michael Cavenny. He was a clerk in the service of the Hudson's Bay Company, and was feared as an opponent by much older traders.

By the advice of Governor Semple, our hero resolved to go to Assinneboin. His guardian thought that in that wild country, where the want of all the luxuries of life must be severely felt, he would have a better prospect of overcoming Cameron's opposition than at Montreal.

The same week the bois brulé set out for Pembinaw. It is needless to relate how he accomplished the first part of his journey through the frozen wilderness on snow shoes, or what savages he encountered withal; but from Fort William, on the north shore of Lake Superior, he was attended by two Canadians who knew him not, nor were they aware that he understood French, having never heard him speak it.

One of them, by name La Verdure, was a man of gigantic stature, remarkable for an unnatural appetite, and a discontented, mutinous disposition. They carried from Fort William provisions for four days, relying on their guns and the chance of meeting with Indians for their further support. But the snow was deep, and they were too much lamed by the weight of their snow shoes [5] to pursue the few deer they saw. For four days all went well enough, but on the fifth they fasted, and La Verdure begun to talk to his comrade

91

of the good cheer they should find at Fort Douglass. The next day passed in the same manner; not a hoof nor a horn did they see, nor even a solitary prairie hen. La Verdure was sullen and silent, excepting that he occasionally muttered something about the bourgeois that had sent them so far into the desert to perish. At times he cast wolfish, hungry glances at Gordon, but quickly averted his head when he saw himself observed. The bois brulé was as brave a man perhaps, as ever lived, but he did not that night lie down before the fire without some misgivings.

Noon came on the seventh day, and as yet they had not seen an Indian, nor had an opportunity to kill anything. Then it was that La Verdure revealed his thoughts to his companion. 'Jussomme,' said he, 'I am dying with hunger. I shall not be able to walk tomorrow unless I find something to eat.'

'Why,' said Jussomme, 'this is not the first time you have fasted, I suppose? I am hungry myself, but I could travel two days more without eating.'

'I will tell you better. There is no need for either of us to fast longer than tonight. Look at that man there.'

'Well, and what then? He has nothing to give us, and we cannot eat him.'

'Why not? If we do not eat we must all three perish. Sachristie! it is better that one should die than three. He would last till we can get a supply. Let us kill him as he sleeps.'

'God forbid! God forbid! (crossing himself) that were a mortal sin. We could never get absolution. I would rather die a thousand times. Villain! I will inform the young man of your intentions instantly, unless you promise to give them up.'

'Will you so? then take care of yourself. If you offer to

tell him what I have said I will shoot you on the spot: I do not fear but I shall be able to deal with him alone. But I do not wish to hurt you: you are from my own parish. I tell you, though, that I neither can nor will live any longer without food, and if you interfere your blood be upon your own head.'

'It is a pity. It is a great pity. He is a fine lad, and he has eaten less than either of us. Do as you please, however: it is no business of mine. I wash my hands of it.'

Jussomme was physically and morally a coward, and he feared La Verdure, with whose strength and desperation he was well acquainted. Nevertheless, several times that afternoon he attempted to warn Gordon of his danger. But when about to speak he always caught the eye of La Verdure, who pointed significantly to his gun. Once he fell back and addressed the cannibal. 'La Verdure,' said he, 'when you have killed him how will you conceal it? He started with us, and we shall arrive without him: his body will be found, and it will be discovered how he came to his end. Besides, I shall be questioned.'

'If you hesitate an instant to swear to me by the passion and crucifixion of our blessed Lord, that you will never reveal what is about to happen, I will kill you too. As to the rest, trust to me: we will say that he was too weak to walk, and that we were obliged to leave him. His body will never be found. The wolves will take care of that.'

Poor Jussomme sighed bitterly. He would have given the world for an opportunity to speak to our hero: but La Verdure stuck so close to him that it was impossible. He feared, too, to hear the report of the white savage's gun at every moment. But La Verdure had formed his resolution deliberately, and had no mind to run any risk. He did not intend to kill the half breed till night. No warning was needed, for Gordon understood French more thoroughly, and spoke it better than either of them. Reluctant to shed blood, however justified by the circumstances, he prayed fervently, though silently, that a deer or some other animal might come in their way before night. But none came. At sunset they stopped, collected wood, cleared away the snow, and cut hay to sleep upon.

'How far is it to ———, La Verdure?' said Gordon.

'So far that I think you will never reach it,' replied the other.

'I am very hungry, but I think I can hold out some time yet.'

'I am hungry, too; but I shall not be tomorrow; — at least, if you have flesh enough to feed me,' he added in his own language.

'Say you so? Die, then, miscreant!' said Gordon, firing his gun at him. The ball went through La Verdure's head, and he fell and expired without a groan.[6]

Jussomme, surprised at hearing our hero speak French, and frightened at what had happened, fell on his knees and begged for mercy. Gordon quickly reassured him, telling him that he had heard and understood all that had been said; nevertheless, the Canadian slept little that night. His nerves had received too severe a shock to recover at once. Gordon's rest was little better: he had been too short a time in the Indian country to spill human blood with indifference. The next morning, having dragged their feeble steps a mile or two, they heard singing and the sound of a drum. They proceeded in the direction of the noise, and found that it came from three Algonquin lodges. They were hospitably received by the poor savages, who had hunted the deer and moose to good purpose. Here they rested two days to recruit their strength and give their swollen feet time to recover. The poor savages feasted our travellers from morning till night. One of them offered his daughter to Gordon for a wife, before he departed, herself nothing loth, but the proposal was declined.

In due time our hero and his attendant arrived at Fort Douglass, situated at the confluence of the Red and Assinneboin rivers. Gordon was received by Mr Miles M'Donald, the deputy governor of the colony, with much courtesy, and an apartment was assigned him. He had the pleasure, also, to find some of his Hohay kindred encamped on the spot. They were not slow to exact of him a considerable assortment of merchandise, on account of his connexion with them; and they asked him to go with them to their camp, an invitation which he accepted with alacrity.

The reader must not suppose that the Forts of the Indian country are constructed according to the rules of Vauban. On the contrary, they are mere stockades of pickets around the stores and dwellings of the traders and their people. These edifices are built of logs, rudely squared by the axe and plastered with clay. They contain a heterogeneous population, Indians, whites, and their squaw wives and half breed children, dogs, and in consequence, fleas innumerable. The roofs are ornamented with dog sledges, and the area inclosed by the buildings is occupied with Canadian carts. Beside this, a trading fort is the sanctuary of all evil odors.

At supper Gordon related to Mr M'Donald how he had slain La Verdure. 'You served him right,' said that dignitary, 'and deserve the thanks of the company. You have saved us from a famine. His project of devouring you was in strict keeping with his character. Why, man, his voracity was incredible. I will relate an instance of his gluttony. It is but one among many. When I' —

But here he was interrupted by the entrance of one of the

engagés with a bowl of punch. The compound was made with lime juice and high wines. Both articles being easy of transportation may be occasionally found beyond the frontier.

Gordon remained silent. But M'Donald filled the glasses and proceeded with his story.

'Two years ago,' said he, 'when I wintered at Brandon House, La Verdure was one of my people. In the spring our provisions gave out, and we had fasted a day, when an Indian brought me a fat swan. Here, said I, is enough for all five of us, for one day at least.'

'I should think it was,' said Gordon. 'A swan, if I am not mistaken, weighs something like twenty pounds.'

'Often more; but La Verdure appeared astonished at my words. "Enough!" said he, "I could eat it myself." "Very well," said I, "if you can you shall; but mind, if you do not eat the whole, I shall stop a week's wages." He took me at my word, and the fowl was skinned and boiled. Well, sir, he sat down and ate, till I feared for his life, and entreated him to stop, but he would not desist while there was a mouthful left. When he had finished he was unable to rise, and I thought he would die. However, he suffered no inconvenience: the next morning he was as well as ever.'

'I should have thought such an exploit impossible.'

'Impossible! Sir, you can have no idea of his prowess.'

'Yes I can, for I have witnessed, and had like to have fallen a victim to it.'

'Good! He was a mutinous fellow, and set a very bad example to our men in times of scarcity. I for one, am very glad of what has come to pass.'

Chapter 3

Ils tuent tous; hommes, femmes et enfans. Pour se venger
de l'époux ils mettent l'épouse à mort. Ils n'ont aucun égard
au sexe.   *Charlevoix.*

THREE mornings after, an Assinneboin brother, or cousin of
our hero, for with the Dahcotah race the words are synony-
mous, entered the fort, leading an elegant horse. The animal
was of the wild breed of Mexico, and had probably been
stolen from the Pawnees or some other tribe of the Missouri.
It was richly caparisoned in the fashion of the Hohays: the
saddle was a cushion of leather stuffed with buffalo hair,
and ornamented with porcupines' quills, as were the head
stall and crupper also. The stirrups were of wood, incased
in parchment. A rope round the under jaw supplied the
place of a bit. Indeed, the Hohays are too good cavaliers to
need such a piece of furniture.

'Come, my brother,' said Okhonkoiah (The Quick) to
Gordon. 'I give you my best horse. Get on his back and
come with me to the camp. A young man has just arrived,
and he says that the buffaloes are more plentiful than the
stars in the sky. Our people are going to pound them as
soon as we arrive. Come with me and see how your brethren live.'

The bois brulé had neither forgotten his mother tongue
nor the manner of taking the buffalo; and was therefore
more desirous to review the scenes of his childhood. He
took his gun and a blanket, and bidding Mr McDonald farewell for a while, rode off, attended by his cousin and a
dozen other Hohays. After two days' riding across a bare
prairie, in which not a tree, nor a shrub, nor a blade of grass
could be seen, they came to the end of their journey.

The camp of the Hohay nomades was pitched in a little
oasis in the midst of a boundless plain. Toward the skirts of

the wood, horses were browsing on the elm branches. A few children, at play on a slight rising ground, were the first to perceive the approaching company. The alarm was given, and mounted warriors were soon seen riding to and fro, reconnoitering the party advancing. Okhonkoiah dismounted, and made some signals with his robe that were perfectly understood by the others, for they immediately came forward to meet them, and all rode into the camp together. Dogs barked and women scolded, while the elders looked on in silence. Not a few children screamed with affright at beholding Gordon's complexion, and ran to their mothers for protection.[7]

Having given the horses in charge to the women, Okhonkoiah led the way to his lodge. It was such a tent as has been described in a previous note, and on it were painted certain hieroglyphics, which we shall not be at the pains to decypher. There were an hundred and fifty such dwellings in the camp.

A buffalo robe was spread for the visitor to sit upon, and his moccasins were taken off as he sat, by his cousin's wife. Presently a wrinkled old woman entered, and placing her hands on his head, cried aloud, and wept bitterly. The substance of her lament was the death of her daughter. Anon her tears ceased to flow, and her notes became joyful. She had now a son, she said, to take care of her in her old age; to provide meat, and steal horses for her. On inquiring who this old lady might be, Gordon was informed that she was his grandmother.

A dog was killed, and when its hair had been singed off, it was cooked and set before our hero and his friends. Before he had swallowed three mouthfuls of this savory repast, he was summoned away to feast in another lodge, and then to another, and another, and another. He who should take anything away from a table in New York or Boston, would be thought guilty of gross ill manners; but in Hohay lodges the standard of good breeding being, in this particular, exactly the reverse, Gordon was obliged to carry off all he could not eat. And so passed the time, till he was near fainting from the excess of Indian hospitality, for he could not decline eating without giving great offence. At last, being admonished to be in readiness for the hunt that was to take place the next morning, he was suffered to rest as well as the night-mare would let him.

The women had built a small enclosure of sticks and brushwood on the verge of the encampment, leaving a space open on one side, just wide enough to allow a buffalo to enter. From this opening diverged two rows of stakes, planted a few feet apart, and extending more than a mile. On the top of each was placed a large sod. By this simple contrivance are the Hohays and wandering Sioux accustomed to take the buffalo.

At day break the camp was all astir. The men mounted, some armed with guns, but more with bows and arrows. The morning was clear and frosty, just cold enough to make a little exercise comfortable. As they rode along Gordon obtained the praise of his companions. 'Eoopee!'* they cried, 'Look at him! Look at him! How he rides! He is no fool. He knows almost as much as a Hohay!'

In about an hour they came to a small herd of wild cattle, quietly turning up the snow with their noses, and cropping the grass beneath. The hunters now separated, and making a careful circuit surrounded them. As soon as the animals took to flight the Indians closed upon them, and drove them between the palisades before mentioned. Frightened by the sods on the stakes, and urged by the riders in

* An exclamation of surprise, having no particular meaning.

the rear, they plunged onward toward the pound at the end of the avenue. None of them attempted to escape laterally; such is the stupidity of the animal. As they drew near the enclosure the pursuers ceased to press them, and they entered, one by one. When they were all within, the butchery began. Men started up on all sides, and bullets and arrows were discharged in quick succession. Thus baited, and confused by the shouts of the hunters and the reports of fire arms, they ran round and round in utter amazement, till they were all killed. Upwards of an hundred were thus slain, for they did not try to break through the pound, which they might easily have done.

Then came the squaws, with horses and dog sledges,[8] and cut up the slaughtered animals. A few pounds were taken from the choicest parts of each carcass, the dogs were suffered to feast, and the remainder was abandoned to the wolves that were patiently waiting around. Such is the economy of Indians!

In a few days when all was eaten up, another hunt took place. This was a bolder and more manly sport than the first, requiring no little dexterity and horsemanship, and not unattended with danger. The buffalo, when wounded, commonly turns upon its pursuer, who must move quickly to escape from its horns. On this occasion several violent falls took place, yet none were killed or seriously injured. The worst that the discomfited cavaliers underwent, was the ridicule of their companions. Feats of archery were exhibited that excited Gordon's admiration. In more than one instance he saw an arrow driven through and through the body of a buffalo wing on its way as though it had not left a death behind.

When the chase was over the hunters divided into two parties, of which one returned to the camp and the other rode farther into the prairie, to see if any tracks of an enemy could be discerned. Our hero, fatigued with the exercise he had taken, laid himself down and slept soundly. He was awakened by a terrible uproar. An hundred voices were crying, 'A Dahcotah woman! A Dahcotah woman!' Gordon rose and ran to the spot. A woman stood in the midst of a crowd of Hohays, who eyed her with angry and threatening glances. They all spoke together, and it was with some difficulty that the bois brulé could obtain silence.

When he had at last persuaded them to speak one at a time, an old Hohay stepped forward. 'Woman,' said he, 'who is your husband.'

'I am the wife of Wawnahton,' replied the squaw.

At that hated name the clamor redoubled, for of all men, Wawnahton was the most feared by the Hohays. The women unsheathed their knives, and would have immolated the prisoner on the spot had they not been restrained by the men.

'Metah Kodah,' (my comrade) said Gordon aside, to one of those who had remained in the prairie after the hunt, 'where did you find this woman?'

'We saw three persons afar off, and gave them chace. Two were men and well mounted. They made their escape, but we caught the squaw. Do you want her for a wife, my brother?'

'No.'

'My father,' said Gordon to the ancient who was interrogating the wife of Wawnahton, 'a woman is a small gift. I am your son. All here are my brethren. Give this woman to me?'

Unable to comprehend his motive, all looked on him with surprise. 'Do you want a wife?' they cried. 'If you do, here are an hundred of the daughters of your own people, younger and handsomer, that you may take. Why do you ask for this woman, the wife of our worst enemy?'

'I do not want to make her my wife. I do not want a wife at all. But I do not wish to see her blood spilled. Have charity for her, my brethren. She is but a woman, and cannot hurt you.'

'Are you mad?' they answered. 'If she can kill none of us herself she may have children who will. Is she not the wife of him whose hand is reddest with the blood of the Hohays?'

'He slew my brother!' cried an ill favored savage, forcing his way through the crowd, tomahawk in hand. 'He slew my brother, and she shall die for it.'

And the debate promised to terminate fatally for the poor squaw, who had till now stood silent, excepting when questioned. Knives were drawn and hatchets uplifted. But Gordon snatched an axe from one of the bystanders, and thrust himself between the woman and her enemies. 'Hear me,' he cried, 'If you kill this prisoner, you shall kill your brother also. Give her to me, for I tell you she shall not be hurt. I will pay for her when I return to the fort.'

'Brother,' said Okhonkoiah, 'let there be no strife between us. Take the woman and do what you please with her. She is yours.'

And he turned round and harangued the crowd, saying that his kinsman was too young a person to be expected to know so much as a Hohay. He had moreover lived too long among 'the people with hats,' and had imbibed their foolish notions. Therefore his ignorance was to be excused.

Gordon had in the meanwhile desired that his horse might be saddled and brought to him. This done, he desired the wife of Wawnahton to mount. 'What do you mean?' said Okhonkoiah, 'Will you ruin the animal? Do you not know that a horse loses his speed as soon as a woman mounts him?'

Gordon was well aware of this superstition, but he feared a change in the popular opinion too much, to waste time in argument. He sprung on the horse before the lady, and hastened out of the camp. He asked her where she wished to go, and shaped his course according to her direction. She informed him that she was going on a visit from one Siou camp to another, in company with two of her brothers, (cousins) when they were seen and chased by the Hohays. Finding that her steed could not keep up with them; for the Sioux never suffer a woman to ride a good horse for the reason above alluded to; they left her to her fate.

When they had ridden three leagues from the camp the bois brulé dismounted. 'Make the best of your way home,' he said. 'You have no need of a guide, and you cannot be overtaken, for you sit on a horse that has no equal in the camp you have left.' He then turned, and retraced his way back.

When he arrived he was not greeted with smiles. Those who had lost friends or relations by the hands of the Sioux, reproached him with having frustrated their designs of vengeance. Little was wanted to turn their rage on him, but having a very clear comprehension of Indian character, he was silent, and the cloud soon passed away.

After passing a month with his red kindred, he returned to Fort Douglass, and when the ice broke up, he ascended the Red river to Pembinaw.

Chapter 4

'The dial spake not; but it made shrewd signs,
And pointed full upon the stroke of murder.'

IN THE mean time Mr Semple received the appointment of
Governor of Ossinneboia, and Duncan Cameron was furnished by Lord Selkirk with funds wherewith to purvey
seed and implements of agriculture for the use of the colonists. Yet the summer was far advanced before all was in
readiness for departure.

Flora had lost her gaiety, but not her hopes. Cavenny
visited her often, and through him she heard from Gordon.
The young Irishman was warmly attached to our hero and
took good care of his interests. He attended Flora to the
places where she went in compliance with her father's
wishes, and lost no opportunity to sound his friend's praises
in her ear.

Among Flora's admirers was a partner of the Northwest
Company, named M'Leod. This man was so smitten, that in
less than a week from their introduction to each other, he
made formal proposals to her father for her hand. The Cameron approved of his suit, but referred him to Flora. She
thanked him for his good opinion, but was sorry to be
obliged to reject his offer. And when pressed for her reasons, she told him with her natural frankness that her heart
was already given to another.

M'Leod was a man of black and violent passions, and he
could not forgive the slight. Never having heard of Gordon's suit, and seeing Cavenny assiduous in his attentions,
he concluded that he was indebted to the Irishman for his
failure. He had 'wintered' in opposition to Cavenny, and
had found his own skill inadequate to the contest. Perhaps
no two Indian traders ever opposed each other long with-

out being personal enemies. Cavenny had foiled M'Leod in his business, and was therefore hated by him. Injuries in trade M'Leod might have forgiven, but this imaginary wrong rankled in his breast, and he resolved that if an opportunity should offer when both would be beyond the reach of law, he would so dispose of his rival that he should never again cross his path in life.

Governor Semple becoming from the nature of his employ more intimate with Cameron, exhausted all the rhetoric of which he was master to persuade him to unite Flora with our hero. The old man listened patiently to the worthy Governor, and readily admitted that Gordon was worthy of all praise, but on the point in question he was adamant.

Cameron fell sick, and the business of the Colony and Company detained Governor Semple long. But M'Leod had already gone to his post, and the contending parties who had so far abstained from open violence now came to blows. Blood was shed, and trading forts were taken and retaken. The colonists of Ossinneboia were molested in every possible manner by the agents of the Northwest Company, who also attempted to excite the Indians to massacre the settlers. Happily, in this they failed. A large body of the erratic half breeds and gens libres was subsidised on either side, and officers were appointed under whose command these reprobates might assemble and act. The partners of the two companies wore uniforms, and assumed to be his majesty's officers; well knowing that such claims commanded the respect of the Indians. M'Leod in especial, went farther. He claimed to be a magistrate, and issued warrants under his sign manual for the apprehension of the most active partizans of the Hudson's Bay Company. Those he made prisoners in this manner were either induced to change their service by threats and bribery, or sent to Montreal;

ostensibly to be tried for alleged offences, but in reality to get them out of the way.[9]

Cavenny started for his post a short time after M'Leod. The latter was soon apprised of his proceedings, and resolved to settle all scores. He had with him a subordinate agent named Reinhard, a man who had served in the Muron regiment in the late war between the United States and Great Britain. M'Leod pitched upon this fellow as a fit instrument to execute his purposes. He gave him minute instructions, and ordered him to go and meet Cavenny before he should arrive at his post.

Reinhard met Cavenny at Lake Winnepeg, and told him, that shocked by the violence of the Northwest Company, of which he had frequently been a witness, he had resolved to leave its employ and offer his services to Lord Selkirk. Cavenny did not scruple to engage him, but he soon had good cause to repent his indiscretion.

Reinhard immediately set himself to work to corrupt Cavenny's engagés, and with two of them he succeeded perfectly. By promising that they should have higher wages, and be sent to a better post, he persuaded them not only to desert from their bourgeois, but to co-operate in measures to secure his person. The other three he sounded, but receiving unsatisfactory answers, he thought it most prudent to disclose his intentions no further.

Toward evening Angé and Le Vasseur, the two conspirators, did all in their power to irritate Cavenny; at no time a difficult task, for the Irish blood was warm in his veins. They repeatedly handled their oars so as to 'catch crabs,' as sailors term it. When rebuked by their principal, they behaved with the utmost insolence. At last, Le Vasseur let his oar fall overboard, and it became necessary for the boat to drop an hundred yards down stream to recover it. The Irishman lost patience.

'If that happens again, Le Vasseur,' said he, 'I will deduct a day's wages from your account.'

'You may do it now, if you like. My wages are small, but Heaven be praised, I can get better when I please.'

'Rogue! If you have any regard for your bones do not repeat that. If you speak so to me again, I will beat you to a mummy.'

'We are but poor engagés, Monsieur Cavenny,' said Angé, 'but we will not suffer ourselves to be beaten, for all that. Our written engagements do not stipulate that blows shall be inflicted, when we fail in our duty. Take what advantage the law allows you; you shall take no other.'

Cavenny snatched one of the boat poles, and raised it to strike the speaker. But Le Vasseur, who sat behind him, dropped his oar and seized him by the elbows, and Angé reared his oar to return the intended compliment.

'Dogs! rascals! villains!' cried the Irishman, shaking himself clear of Le Vasseur; 'wait till we get ashore, and I will make you wish yourselves at Quebec. Ho! Le Gros, put ashore instantly, — instantly.'

The steersman obeyed, and the whole party debarked. 'Now you rascals,' said Cavenny, 'I will teach you how to speak to your bourgeois. Come on!'

The other boatmen expostulated. The mutineers stood sullen and silent, and seemed afraid to begin. 'If you fear the penalties of the law provided for such cases,' said Cavenny, 'I give you my word I will take no advantage of them, whether you conquer me or not. Come, let us make an end of it.'

Reinhard now spoke. 'Monsieur Cavenny,' said he, 'you

cannot but get the worst of it. They are two to one. Any man might be afraid of such odds.'

These words had their intended effect. Cavenny furiously struck Le Vasseur a stunning blow. The battle now raged in bloody earnest. The engagés showed no lack of strength or courage, but they could not contend against the Irishman's *science*. He 'floored' them as fast as they could rise, and in ten minutes they were obliged to give in.

'There, you rascal,' said Cavenny, 'I trust I shall have no more trouble with you. It is a pity there is no law in this country to take care of such fellows. But I will have the respect and obedience that is my due, even if I am obliged to soil my hands. Return to your duty, and for this time all shall be forgiven, but beware how you provoke me again.'

The sun had now set beyond

> 'Vast savannas where the wandering eye,
> Unfix'd, is in a verdant ocean lost.'

The wolves had begun their nightly howlings, and the song of the whip-poor-will had commenced. It was too dark to proceed any farther, so Cavenny ordered his steersman to land. His tent was pitched, and a huge fire was made. The kind hearted Irishman consoled the men he had beaten with a dram, which they accepted with apparent thankfulness.

In the morning Reinhard and the two mutineers were missing. They did not take leave empty handed. The bold visage of Cavenny was somewhat blanked at this disaster, but he soon recovered his good humor. 'Well,' he said, 'at any rate I can steer the boat myself, and we have three oars left to take us to Fort Douglass. I wish however that we could see some Indians; I could then send to Mr M'Donald for a reinforcement. But never mind; 'care killed a cat;' and he sung

'O! love is the sowl of a nate Irishman,' &c.

In the mean time Reinhard and the deserters joined M'Leod. That worthy rebuked his deputy in harsh terms. 'What did I send you to Cavenny for?' said he. If he had been killed in the scuffle, it would have been done in self defence. You have let slip a fine opportunity to take him.'

'But consider, Sir, that I had but two men on my side, and the other three would have taken his part. If I had taken a share of the battle, and given him an unlucky blow, I doubt if I could have kept my neck out of a halter. I do not mean that I had any inclination to dispose of him in that manner. I would not do such a thing on any account, unless compelled. Besides, Cavenny is not so easily managed. I wish you had seen how he beat the two Canadians.'

After some further consultation, Angé and Le Vasseur were called. M'Lcod took their deposition, and issued a warrant to secure the body of Michael Cavenny for an assault and battery, by him committed on two of his majesty's liege subjects, &c. &c. This precious document was signed by M'Leod in his assumed capacity of Justice of the Peace for the Indian country. For the purpose of serving the warrant, Cuthbert Grant, a half breed well known in the Northwest, was appointed a constable. A number of Indians and bois brulés were called upon to assist, and to prevent mistakes, M'Leod resolved to attend in person. A few birch canoes were procured, and the whole posse paddled down the river.

Cavenny had stopped his boat at a convenient place, and gone after a herd of buffaloes that were grazing a short distance from the river. On his return he was seized, pinioned, and conducted before the soi disant Major.

He offered no resistance, nor did he manifest any resentment, though reviled and treated with the utmost indignity by the barbarians into whose hands he had fallen. 'Poor fellows,' said he, 'they know not what they are about.' When brought into the presence of M'Leod, who was dressed in a full suit of uniform, he did not wait for that dignitary to speak. Confronting him boldly, he drew himself up to his full height and thus addressed him. 'I demand to know on what authority I am arrested, and for what offence?'

'Show the prisoner the warrant,' said M'Leod to Reinhard, who was also dressed à la militaire, and wore a sword of portentous length.

The warrant was exhibited, fairly engrossed on a sheet of parchment. Beside the imputation of assault and battery, it charged Cavenny with having instigated divers Chippeway Indians to rob and murder certain of the lieges. It was signed —— M'Leod, J. P. for the Indian country, and Major in the Royal Canadian Corps of Voyageurs.

'M'Leod,' said Cavenny, 'what needs this farce, this vile abuse of the name of law? Since when has this Royal Voyageur Corps been organized, and from whom did you receive the appointment of major or magistrate? You well know that you are neither a soldier nor a civil officer. You must be aware that when we meet where the laws are in force we must change places. Make an end of this child's play and tell me what you intend to do, and how long I am to be kept in confinement. But why need I ask your motives? Your trade has suffered through me, and you fear that it will again, and therefore you will rid yourself of my opposition by violence. I will tell you a better way to dispose of me. Unbind my arms, tell that rascal there to lend me his sword, and draw your own.'

'Rest assured, Michael Cavenny,' replied M'Leod 'that I have sufficient authority for what I do. I will not allow it to be questioned. However, for the satisfaction of those present, I will say that my powers are derived from his Excellency the Governor General of the Canadas. The idea of fighting with a prisoner charged with high crimes and misdemeanors is too absurd to deserve a moment's consideration. You must accompany me till measures can be taken to send you to Montreal for trial. An exact inventory shall be taken of your goods and effects, at which you may be present, if you please. After the outrages committed by members of the Hudson's Bay Company, (of which some present have been witnesses) I should be inexcusable to suffer you to remain at large. In this course it is my zeal for the public good and my duty as an organ of the law that actuates me, and not the fear of your opposition as you falsely and scandalously assert. You will not dance with Miss Cameron this winter,' he added, drawing near the prisoner, and speaking so low as to be heard by him only.

Cavenny could contain his wrath no longer. 'Villain,' he cried, 'it is a burning shame that a name so pure should be profaned by the lips of such a coward and ruffian. Dog! do your worst now, for when we meet on equal terms your time will be short. Take your inventory! your scoundrelly associates will be your fittest witnesses. Do as you please with me. Henceforth I will not degrade myself by exchanging a word with you.'

In a few minutes Cavenny's boat was manned, and M'Leod gave orders to move up the river. A canoe was prepared to convey the prisoner, who, still bound, was given in custody to Angé and Le Vasseur. Before starting M'Leod took these men aside.

'You will follow us to the encampment,' he said, 'but keep out of sight, for the prisoner has a tongue that may seduce some of the men from their duty. He may try to escape from you.'

'We will take care that he does not succeed,' said Le Vasseur.

'Ay, but to be more sure, take your guns with you. If he offers any violence it is your duty to resist, whatever the consequence may be.'

'But if we should use our guns,' said Angé, 'we shall be hanged.'

'No fear of that. No one will ever hear of it. If there should be any investigation I will bear you out in what you may do in the discharge of your duty, at all events.'

'How are we to treat him if he remains quiet?'

'Why he has beaten and disgraced you, but I would not recommend any harshness. But you are not obliged to bear any abuse from him.'

'Well Monsieur, we will do the best we can.'

'Remain where you are half an hour and then follow us. If you behave properly you shall not miss a handsome reward.'

He then started with his banditti, and the Canadians remained behind with their prisoner.

Chapter 5

My conscience hath a thousand several tongues,
And every tongue brings in a several tale,
And every tale condemns me for a villain.
Richard III.

IN THINKING that the sense of shame for the chastisement
they had received, and the hope of reward, would silence
all moral feeling in Angé and Le Vasseur, M'Leod deceived
himself. They were weak, ignorant men, but not so de-
praved as to view the crime of murder without horror.

'Angé, what do you think of what Monsieur the Major
has been saying?' said Le Vasseur.

'Think? I scarcely know what to think. I believe we have
done wrong to listen to that accursed villain, Reinhard.'

'And our new bourgeois is no better.'

'It is clear that he wants us to kill Monsieur Cavenny.
But I will have nothing to do with it. He may put his own
neck into a collar if he pleases, but he shall not mine.'

'Nor mine neither. What say you, Angé? Shall we try
to make peace with our Irish bourgeois? I do not believe
that M'Leod will ever reward us as Reinhard promised.'

'Nor do I. He thinks so little of committing murder and
robbery, that I verily believe he may cheat us.'

'And he may do by us as he wishes us to do by Monsieur
Cavenny, to be safe from our evidence. Sainte Vierge! I
will go no farther in this. I will speak to the Irishman directly.'

'Monsieur Cavenny,' said he, touching his cap respectfully, 'I believe we have wronged you. If you have beaten
us, we provoked you to it. If you know how we can make
you amends, say so, and it shall be done.'

Cavenny cast on him a look of utter contempt, but did
not reply.

'Monsieur,' said Angé, 'we should not have done as we have, if Reinhard had not tempted us. But we never meant to go this length. Take us back, and stop all our wages, if you please.'

'And now,' replied Cavenny, resuming his natural gaiety, 'that you have done me all the harm you can, like two honest fellows, as you are, you resolve to do no more.'

'But your life is in danger, and we would not be guilty of your blood. Fly then to Fort Douglas with us, and there you will be safe.'

'Your master, you poor devil, dares not hurt a hair of my head. I shall get more out of him and his company, by law, than I can make in the trade. So, my fine fellows, I advise you to obey the orders of your new bourgeois.'

The men were confounded by this reply. They consulted together, and then again endeavored to persuade the Irishman to escape. But apprehending nothing more than a short detention, he thought it his duty to give his company a legal advantage over the Northwest. He returned a peremptory refusal to their proposals.

A little after sundown, they arrived at M'Leod's encampment. The ruffian hastened to the water side, and was highly enraged at seeing Cavenny. He took the boatmen apart, 'Did I not tell you,' he said, 'what to do if he attempted to escape?'

'But he has made no such attempt,' said they.

'Do you argue with me?' said M'Leod, losing temper. 'I will try to teach you your duty better.' And with his sheathed sword he beat the Canadians for their humanity.[10]

What were the feelings of this wicked man that night, we do not presume to divine. If he felt any remorse for what he had done, or compunction for what he was about to do, it never appeared in his subsequent conduct. When at last he slept, his slumbers were broken by dreams of horror. He was heard to groan heavily, and towards morning he called on Reinhard. That miscreant entered the tent, and found him sitting upright. A cold clammy sweat stood on his brow, his hands were fast clenched, and his eyes were fixed on vacancy. 'O! my friend,' he exclaimed, with the familiarity of guilt, 'stay with me. Stay with me. Not for worlds would I pass such another night. Reach me that case.' Reinhard obeyed, and his principal poured out a large glass of spirits, and drank it off undiluted.

'Are you going to get drunk, Monsieur?' said the Muron. 'Cheer up, and tell me what has frightened you.'

'Who told you that I was frightened? But I have had a frightful dream. I thought I was standing at the altar with Flora Cameron, and the priest had begun to repeat the ceremony. But when I offered her my hand, she started back, and said that there was blood upon it. I looked, and indeed it was dripping with crimson. The scene changed, and I stood at the bar with you, Reinhard. Our wrists were chained together, and Cavenny, in his shroud, bore witness against us. Then we stood upon a scaffold, and the executioner told us that we had but five minutes to live. Nature could bear no more, and I awoke.'

Reinhard laughed. 'If it should be necessary to resort to severe measures,' he said, 'I will warrant that he will never rise in evidence against us till the day of judgment, and that is so far off that I believe it will never arrive. Cheer up, Sir, this is weak and unmanly.'

We will not record the blasphemous speech of these reprobates, nor the schemes of guilt, which they concerted. The camp was roused at dawn. Notwithstanding the excess of his potations, M'Leod showed no signs of intoxication. He was indeed deadly pale, but his voice did not falter. He called before him a Chippeway Indian, a noted desperado retained by the Northwest Company. To this man he spoke in the Chippeway tongue, and the savage grunted assent to his instructions. M'Leod then turned to his prisoner.

'Mr Cavenny,' said he, 'I have been thinking that it would subject you to unnecessary hardship, to detain you in this country all winter, and have therefore concluded to send you to Montreal. There you may find bail for your appearance before a competent tribunal, as your trial cannot take place till the witnesses arrive next spring. There is your canoe, Mr Cavenny. You will go under the charge of Constable Reinhard, and Indian Joe. They have orders to treat you with all the consideration consistent with your safe custody. I wish you a pleasant journey, Sir.'

Cavenny looked daggers at him, but did not speak. He regarded the canoe, and the conviction that his death was intended flashed on his mind. It was old and shattered, and he saw that no provision, nor any of his baggage, had been put on board. But he arranged his ideas with great rapidity. He thought they would not attempt his life before night, and resolved to endeavor to escape, the first time they put ashore. If he could get possession of the Indian's gun, he would not fear them; and even if he could not succeed in this, he thought, that provided he could get out of gunshot, he could distance them both, and so was little concerned for the event. M'Leod perceived that his suspicions were awakened.

'I see that you think yourself hardly used, Mr Cavenny,' said he. 'Well, the consciousness of having done my duty must be my consolation. The Indian will mend the canoe when you encamp to-night; and he is an excellent hunter. You will not starve on the way.'

Cavenny embarked with the two savages, who exchanged

ominous glances. A rapid current soon swept them out of sight of the encampment. The canoe leaked, and was fast filling, when, coming to a sand bar, Reinhard proposed to the Indian to stop and bale it out.

The spot was about a league from the camp they had left. Seeing that he had no chance of escape, as the Indian held his gun in his hand, Cavenny sat down near Reinhard, who was busy about the canoe. The red man caught the Muron's eye, and pointed to his gun. The latter nodded to him. Placing his thumb on the dog, that the prisoner might not hear the noise of cocking, he made ready, and fired at Cavenny's back. The muzzle was so near, that the Irishman's blanket coat was blackened and scorched by the explosion. The ball passed through his body, but he did not fall. He turned and grappled his assassin, with the desperate strength of a dying man. Grasping the Indian by the throat, he hurled him to the earth with great violence, confining his arms by the pressure of his knees. Seeing his confederate thus worsted, Reinhard advanced, drew his sword, and deliberately plunged it three times into Cavenny's back. The Irishman's grasp relaxed, his eyes glared, and he rolled off his half strangled foe. Reinhard took him by the feet and dragged him to the river, his long black hair trailing in his own blood. Reader, this is no fiction. Thus died Michael Cavenny.

As soon as the Indian had recovered his breath, he set the canoe adrift, and the murderers started to join their principal by land. In a few minutes they reached the camp.[11] Not a word was spoken on either side, nor did any one ask a question relative to the fate of the prisoner. But the chief ordered the captured boat to be unloaded, and distributed the personal effects of the deceased among his followers. The Chippeway was rewarded for his share of the transaction, with Cavenny's fowling piece, and Reinhard received his linen and silver mounted pistols. M'Leod reserved nothing for himself. Ruthless as he was, he had too much pride to share in the plunder of his victim. The only redeeming trait in his character that we are able to record, was a scrupulous integrity in matters of business. Perhaps, had he passed his life where the laws are regarded, he might have passed through life with an unblemished reputation.

In the Irishman's port-folio he found many papers. One of them contained a lock of bright yellow hair, and a copy of verses, probably written by Cavenny himself, for they were in keeping with his gay but not ungenerous character. On the back of the paper were the words, 'N'OUBLIE JAMAIS,' and the text was inscribed 'To Laura.' It ran thus:

'And canst thou then so soon forget
The day, the hour, when last we met?
When first my tongue essay'd to tell
A truth already proved too well,
That every glance and every tone
Of mine already had made known?
Then heavenly bright those eyes did shine,
At each persuasive word of mine.
Then, Laura, did thy voice approve
My softly whisper'd tale of love.
Then, for thy sake, it bade me wear
This little tress of golden hair;
And said, that sooner should the sun
His wonted course forget to run,
Than Laura should unmindful prove,
Of plighted faith — of mutual love.

'But now thou say'st those sun-bright charms
Must bless a richer lover's arms;
That words like those were spoken then,
I never must repeat again.
'Tis well — I never will repine
For any love as light as thine;
The prize I have so easy lost,
Is but a woman's heart at most;
My loss I may with ease repair,
For many a maid is quite as fair.

But no – I never will again
Put faith in aught so frail and vain;
I never will again believe
A sex so practised to deceive;
For woman's smile, and woman's sigh,
I'll care not – no, indeed, not I.
One pang thy falsehood must impart,
But sparkling wine shall ease the smart.

'Yet think not that my heart is steel;
Think not that I could never feel.
How long I lov'd thee, and how well,
I cannot – may not – will not tell.
'Tis past – my dream of bliss is o'er –
I lov'd as I shall love no more;
No other e'er again shall bind,
In chains so strong, my manly mind.
Adieu! and may'st thou never know
A moment's care, a moment's wo.
The passion in my breast that burn'd,
To pity, not to hate, is turn'd.
I cast behind each fond regret,
But still, I never can forget
The hope that bound me like a spell.
Forever, false as fair, farewell!'

M'Leod read the lines, and then threw them, and the hair, into the fire. But he found other documents that interested him more nearly. These were Gordon's part of a correspondence between him and Cavenny, in which all the circumstances of his suit to Flora Cameron, and the death of La Verdure, were detailed at full length. These letters had been sent to the Irishman, by couriers bearing despatches to the Deputy Governor. M'Leod groaned with vexation, and bit his lips till the blood came, as he read and found that he had overlooked a real rival, and sacrificed an imaginary one. But it is but the 'premier pas qui coute,' and having commenced his career of crime, he began to digest a plan to get Gordon into his power. He thought that the death of La Verdure would furnish a sufficient pretext.

For this purpose he soon after rode south till he came to

a Dahcotah camp, where he had an interview with Wawnahton. He advised the Siou chief to assemble his people,
and attack the Hudson's Bay Company's fort and colony
at Pembinaw. By so doing, M'Leod told him he would
greatly injure his natural enemies the Chippeways, who
were there furnished with arms and ammunition. He held
up the plunder of the place as a farther inducement, and
above all, he promised Wawnahton a quantity of ardent
spirits in the event of his success.[12]

These arguments were irresistible. The Dahcotah promised, and what he promised he performed. He collected two
hundred men, and set forth to plunder and destroy the
devoted colony of Ossinneboia.

But the colonists were apprised of their danger by a party
of Chippeways, who had been hunting in the plains, and
had fled before the Sioux. Preparations were instantly made
to repel the attack. The women and children took refuge
in the fort. Ammunition was served out to the men and a
party of Chippeways were summoned to aid in the defence.
When, therefore, the Dahcotahs showed themselves on the
opposite bank of the river, they were greeted with a volley
that killed three of their best men, and wounded several
more. Discouraged by this, with true Indian caution, they
retired out of gun-shot.

M'Leod, who had come thither painted and disguised as
an Indian, in hopes of directing the rage of the savage warriors upon Gordon, gnashed his teeth for very spite. He
saw that the blow had failed, and advised Wawnahton to
draw his party off, and wait for a fitter opportunity. But
his counsel was not heeded.

The uncle of the chief is a man as insensible to fear as
the blade of his own knife. His name cannot be written, but
translated it means 'He who shoots his enemy in the

branches of a tree,' and he acquired it by killing a Chippeway in that manner. His silence and sullenness on ordinary occasions have procured him the title of Le Boudard, from the French of the country. He is commonly seen walking about like a chafed bear, speaking to no one, and scarcely answering, when addressed. But in times of danger, his ferocity almost amounts to insanity. He it was who answered M'Leod.

'These Khahkhahtons * shall know that the Dahcotahs are men,' he said. 'I will throw away my body to prove it. Show me where the river may be passed with least danger.'

M'Leod pointed to a bend in the river where the steepness of the banks might conceal a swimmer.

'And now; dog of an Englishman, who hast caused our people to die, shew me where is the most danger.'

'As to that, you can see it as well as I. There is the enemy in front of you.'

'Come then,' said the Boudard, throwing off all his clothing, 'come with me and let it be seen which has the strongest heart, the Dahcotah or the man with a hat.'

This proposal M'Leod very reasonably declined. But Wawnahton also stripped, declaring that his dekshee (uncle) should not surpass him in bravery. The two Indians then walked coolly to the bank, and swam over in the face of the enemy, holding their bows over their heads, that the strings might not be wetted.

When the Chippeways saw the Sioux in the water, they raised a cry of surprise and admiration. 'They honored such determined scorn of life,' and did not fire. The colonists were restrained by no such principles. They levelled their guns, and had not Gordon, who was invested with the temporary command, forbidden them, they would have shot

* People of the Rapids. The Sioux name for the Chippeways.

the desperadoes. They came ashore and boldly advanced to within a bow's length of the white men. 'Look at me,' cried the Boudard, 'you now know what a man is.'

'Brave men,' said Gordon, 'what has induced you to attack people who have never injured you? Why have you risked your lives so rashly?'

'You frighten the buffaloes out of the prairies, and you furnish our enemies with the means to destroy us,' replied Wawnahton. 'But who are you that speak our language like one of us, and are yet in arms by the side of the Chippeways?'

'I am a Hohay, and the grandson of Chuntay Paytah. Is it wonderful that I should speak the language of my mother?'

The Dahcotah uttered an exclamation of joy, and held out his hand to Gordon. Explanations ensued, and each was beginning to be better pleased with the other, when a clamor from the crowd attracted their attention.

While their dialogue was going on, the Boudard had walked through the ranks of his enemies, who gave way and opened a passage for him. As he turned the corner of one of the log huts he became aware of a Chippeway, levelling a gun at him. Drawing an arrow to the head, the Boudard rushed upon the treacherous foe and drove him into a corner. Getting so close as to make it impossible for the Chippeway to use his gun, the Dahcotah stood, with his shaft trembling on the string, and foaming with rage like a wild beast. In this posture he vaunted of his own valor and reviled his prisoner, loading him with all the opprobrious epithets in the Siou tongue. The other Chippeways had now recovered from their first surprise and begun to handle their weapons, when Wawnahton and Gordon interposed. At the command, or rather request of the former, the Boudard released his prisoner, and to prevent further collision Gordon conducted the two Dahcotahs into his own house.

The motive of the intended attack was revealed to Gordon, and he declared his intention to cross the river and punish its instigator with his own hand. To this end, after feasting his guests bountifully, he armed himself and swam over with them.

But in the mean while, M'Leod observed that the countenances of his swarthy comrades did not indicate friendly feelings toward him; and he heard them express their indignation at him whose counsels had caused the fall of their brethren. One of the braves said, moreover, that if Wawnahton and the Boudard should not return in safety, the Sagandoshee (Englishman) should pay for all. Such an event was hardly to be expected, and while the attention of the Dahcotahs was absorbed by what was passing on the opposite bank, M'Leod stealthily withdrew. He mounted his horse, and did not draw bridle till he was far out of the reach of pursuit. When, therefore, Gordon sought him among the Dahcotahs, he was not to be found, and the young man returned wet and discontented to his abode.

Chapter 6

Red is the cup they drink; but not with wine:
Awake, and watch to-night! or see no morning shine.
Gertrude of Wyoming.

GORDON had built a log dwelling for the reception of Cameron and his daughter on their arrival. It was settled between our hero and Mr M'Donald, that the old Scot should never know to whom he was indebted. The building was like all others in that country, and consisted of four apartments, three of them as rude as might be. The fourth being designed for Flora, was finished with all the taste and ingenuity Gordon could exert. The walls were squared by the axe, plastered with mud, and washed with the white clay of the prairies; the same the Indians use to cleanse their leathern garments. The floor was neatly jointed and planed, and the windows were, as we are credibly informed, the first glazed ones ever seen at Pembinaw. Those of the other houses were of oiled paper, or parchment. In short all was comfortably, if not elegantly arranged.

At this time, news came that Governor Semple, Duncan Cameron and Flora, had arrived at Fort Douglass. Mr Semple was detained there by business, and Cameron was obliged to proceed to Pembinaw; but unwilling to expose his daughter to the danger of starvation, he left her with the Governor. When the clansman arrived at Pembinaw, Gordon, under pretence of hunting, saddled his horse and rode to Fort Douglass, where he was cordially received. Flora, indeed, on the first opportunity, urged the impropriety of his visit, but as Gordon informed her that Mr Semple would ascend the river in a few days, and that his presence would add to the security of the journey, she gave up the argument.

The colonists had ploughed and planted Indian corn and such vegetables as were most likely to succeed in that climate; but when the harvest was nearly ripe for the sickle, clouds of grasshoppers swept the land like the samiel, and left not a green blade behind. The Catholic priest publicly anathematized them in vain. The inhabitants were obliged to resort to the chase for their daily subsistence, but as if all things conspired against Lord Selkirk's schemes of colonization, the buffaloes emigrated to the Missouri.[13] Provisions began to fall short at Fort Douglass, and all persons connected with the establishment were put on short allowance, to the great annoyance of the Canadians, whose digestive organs equal those of wolves in power.

In another week the new settlers for whom Mr Semple waited, arrived, and he prepared to depart. A small portion of the stores of the fort was put on board the boat, and the party moved up the river. The third day of their progress brings us to the time when our story commenced.

After leaving the boat as before related, Gordon ascended a small rising ground, and looked round for the wild cattle. His practised eye soon discovered a solitary buffalo, grazing at a great distance. The sun was fast sinking, and it was evident that to reach and kill the animal before dark, he must exert himself to the utmost. He threw his gun upon his shoulder, and was about to start, when his ear was saluted by a low whistle. He well understood it to be an Indian signal, meaning 'you are in danger; keep out of sight.' The warning came from a small ravine at the foot of the hillock; one of the thousand channels by which the snow and rain of the prairies find their way to the river. Gordon descended into the hollow and returned an answering sign. A tall Indian, mounted on a powerful charger, emerged from the ravine, and the bois brulé recognized Wawnahton. The horse appeared to have been hard ridden, and the face, hands and dress of the rider were stained with blood. His feet were placed in huge wooden stirrups, drawn up short, but he sat firm and erect, managing his steed with a cord fastened round the under jaw. Three bounds placed him at Gordon's side.

'How! metah kodah, what are you doing here?' he asked.

'I have come to kill a cow for our people. Our children are crying for food.'

'I have heard that you are as good a hunter as if you had been born in a Dahcotah lodge. But while you approach the buffalo beware that you are not yourself approached.'

'Who should approach me, if not some of your people? and they seldom come so low on the river.'

'Listen. There is a hunter who thirsts for your blood. It is the Englishman — the old woman who persuaded me to come to Pembinaw. Do you see, yonder?' he continued, pointing to a distant strip of wood, such as always fringes the border of a prairie stream. 'He is there, and nineteen half-breeds with him. There were twenty this morning.' Drawing his robe aside, he showed a scalp in his belt. 'Keep a good watch to-night, for they have been watching your boat all day.'

'You have killed one of his followers then. Why did you so? And why should he seek our lives? None of us ever opposed his trade.'

'He hates you, and if you encamp on this side of the river, not one of you will see the sun rise tomorrow. I was in quest of the Khakhatons with ten men, when we discovered the party. They were too many for us, but I was resolved not to return home without a scalp, and followed them. A man without a scalp is lying below the river bank yonder, with an arrow sticking in him. I saw that he was a Khakhaton by his features. Besides, these mongrels spoil our hunting grounds. They ride hundreds together and scare away the buffalo. I will not suffer them to hunt on my land.'

'I cannot return to the boat empty. Our women are dying with hunger. I must kill something, cost what it may.'

'That is the way with you men who wear hats. You go through fire for your women. But I have provided for that too. Do you see the wood at yonder bend of the river? I

126

killed a fat cow, and hung its flesh in those branches at noon. Your big canoe will soon be there; but mount behind me and we will be before it. Come, jump up.'

Gordon sprang on the horse behind him, and half an hour's ride brought them to the spot. Gordon had began to thank the chief, but the latter cut him short. 'When your big canoe arrives,' said he, 'make a fire and eat. Then as soon as it is dark, leave the camp and hide yourselves. Do not suffer yourselves to be surprised. I will be nigh you, and ten good bows shall not be wanting, in time of need. But stay — I have a pistol that is useless for want of ammunition; give me some of yours.' And having tied up the powder and ball he received from Gordon in the corner of his calico shirt, with a sinew, he galloped away through the wood.

When the boat rounded to at the spot where he was standing, our hero communicated the intelligence he had obtained to Mr Semple, and recommended to place the women and children in safety on the opposite shore, while the men should remain, and expect the half-breeds. 'We can make a breastwork of logs,' he said, 'to compensate for the disparity of numbers, and we shall have the Sioux on our side.'

But to these and many more good reasons for fighting, Governor Semple gave no heed. He resolved to follow Wawnahton's advice to the letter.

The engagés had toiled all day; but the sight of the meat gave them fresh spirits. They kindled a huge fire, and beguiled the time with their pipes, and a greasy pack of cards. They even heard the announcement that their labor had not ceased, without a murmur. They did not ask Mr Semple's reasons; it was enough for them that he was their bourgeois; but they said to one another, that Monsieur Gordon had probably seen signs of Indians.

It would be difficult to find a people so well fitted to endure the hardships of the Indian trade as the Canadians. They assume the manners and habits of the aborigines with perfect ease. For a stipend of from one to two hundred dollars per annum, they toil incessantly, through hot and cold, wet and dry. Carrying heavy burthens on their heads, laboring at the oar, wading for hours in rapids, and half the time subsisting on food that our dogs would reject, they are always polite and cheerful, and generally obedient.

On this occasion, when the repast was over, a number of large logs were laid on the fire, that its continued light might deceive the enemy, and the party were ordered to embark. The oars were muffled with strips of buffalo skin, and after rowing a few hours they put ashore and passed the rest of the night without molestation.

Chapter 7

With breath of foam and bloodshot eye,
    The monarch of the prairie turns:
He hurls the horseman to the sky,
    With trampling hoof the horse he spurns.
        Unpublished Poem of the Prairies.

GOVERNOR SEMPLE was prepared to find misery at Pembinaw, but the reality was beyond his expectations. On his arrival, when he asked where the town might be, his attendants pointed to thirty or forty wretched huts, scattered along the bank for a mile. Cameron's house, and the buildings in the Company's fort above, were, indeed, comfortable; for they had been erected by Canadian hands; but those built by the Scotch and Swiss, seemed about to fall with their own weight. Everything wore the garb of poverty. The colonists were ragged, and their sunken faces and hollow eyes told a tale of dearth and distress. The people angling, or drawing nets in the river, and the heaps of the offals of fishes before the doors, shewed how the inhabitants had for a long time subsisted. The very dogs seemed conscious of the general desolation. In a camp of half-breeds and gens libres, hard by, there were no such appearances. Dirt there was, and to spare, about their leathern tents; but nothing looked like starvation. They had of late found no buffaloes, but they took the beaver, otter, muskrat, and other animals, whose flesh, though not acceptable to a well educated palate, goes down very well with the rangers of the prairie. The poor emigrants, unaccustomed to such circumstances, were compelled to buy meat of these people at enormous prices, or go without. The fishery was their main dependence.

The meeting between Flora and her father was far from joyful. She flung herself on his neck and wept. He was highly displeased when he heard that Gordon had been passing his time at Fort Douglass. 'I did not think,' he said, 'when they told me he was gone to the hunting, what game he was after. And I dare to say, you were very glad to be so near him.' But when he was informed that our hero's deportment toward her had been distant; and that he had rendered the party a great service, on their journey, he was somewhat mollified.

Once installed in her new habitation, Flora discovered to whom her father was indebted for it. She found her name carved in several places on the timber, and on inquiry learned who had built the house. Yet she did not communicate her discoveries to her parent.

On his part, he found no opportunity to turn his agricultural acquirements to advantage: he was unused to the climate, and the colonists would not follow his advice with regard to their preparations for the ensuing season.

Famine soon stared the settlers in the face. The river closed, and Governor Semple promulgated an edict, directing that a part of all provisions passing through the territory should be taken for the use of the settlers. In pursuance of this law, Deputy Governor M'Donald seized a large quantity of provision, that an agent of the Northwest Company was taking down the Assinneboin River, and sent a part of it to Pembinaw. The whole country was in a blaze, in consequence, and the partners of the aggrieved company met to devise measures of retaliation.

But as the food thus obtained did not last long, though sparingly distributed, Governor Semple hired fifty half-breeds to hunt for the colonists. He advised the latter to accompany the hunters into the plains. That they might comply with his counsel, he furnished them with lodges, bought of the Indians, to encamp in; and with horses and carts to transport their families and baggage.

A herd of cattle was known to be at the river Aux Parcs, and thither the hunters were directed to go and encamp, and afterwards follow the animals in their migrations, like Indians. The procession was a curious one. There was a long line of upwards of an hundred rudely constructed carts, each conducted by a man on foot. They were laden with tents, bedding, &c. On the tops were seated the women and children. The spouses of the emigrants had found it expedient to adopt the costume of the half-breed females, as better adapted to the country than their own. It consists of a short waisted upper garment, cut and shaped like a hussar jacket, and a skirt, with a pair of leggins; all of cloth. A pair of moccasins, sometimes ornamented with porcupine's quills, a knife stuck in the girdle, and the hair hanging down the back in a queue as thick and as long as a large Bologna sausage, completed the toilet. Some of these ladies wore caps, some men's hats, and others were bare headed. At least twenty distinct languages were spoken in the cavalcade; all nations seeming to have sent their representatives, excepting the United States; for, strange to say, there was not a Yankee there. The half-breeds had indeed heard of a shrewd, *swapping*, bargaining race, called the Bostonois; but none could tell in what part of the world they resided, or who was their king. Not the least amusing of the appurtenances to our travellers, were the dog sledges, (for there was a light snow on the ground) each drawn by three or four large, wolfish dogs, tandem; their harnesses ornamented with ribbons and hawk-bells. The running horses too, the finest of the breed, were caparisoned after the Indian fashion. Some of them were decorated with collars of scarlet cloth; rewards bestowed on the animals by their owners for exertions in the chase. Altogether, a painter might go far before he would find so picturesque a subject for his pencil as the group we have attempted to describe.

Cameron accompanied the hunters; and his daughter, notwithstanding his remonstrances, resolved to go with him. When told that they might be attacked by the Sioux, she replied, that those who remained, were in still more danger from the myrmidons of the Northwest Company. When the hardships and privations of Indian life were urged on her consideration, she said, that her father's advanced age and infirmity rendered her attentions the more necessary, under such circumstances.

Gordon rode with the hunters. In two days they reached the river Aux Parcs, and encamped near a large herd of cattle. It was decided that a hunt should take place the next morning, and guns were cleaned, and knives sharpened accordingly. At sunrise, the hunters mounted and divided into parties, of which each had its allotted duties. The women ascended a rising ground to witness the sport. The animals were peacefully grazing, a league to the northward of the camp. There was a slight western breeze, and to avoid being scented [14] by the buffaloes, those whose part it was to raise them, made a circuit eastward, so that they might run toward the camp. They advanced first on horseback, and then on foot, leading their steeds by the bridles. When within two hundred yards, the animals ceased feeding, and gazed attentively. 'Mount!' cried our hero, and in an instant each was in his saddle. The buffaloes started, and the hunters followed, not however at full speed. When within a mile of the camp, other horsemen started from the hollows on the flanks, and the firing commenced. Each hunter carried his balls in his mouth, and the aperture of his horn was made large, that the powder might escape freely.

The party in the rear now closed on the herd. The buffalo, when urged to speed, has the gait of the swine, that is, the fore and hind legs are lifted alternately, and together, producing a motion something like that of a rocking-horse. The horses trained to the chase acquire a similar pace, and run beside the victim just far enough from him to get out of the way of his horns when he turns upon them, which he commonly does, when wounded. The rider, holding his piece stiffly with both hands, fires at the heart, and at the report the horse sheers off. The hunter loads again at full speed. When a buffalo is struck, it becomes the property of him who has inflicted the wound, and is left to be despatched at leisure. Though the sport is in appearance very dangerous, few accidents occur.

All these evolutions were witnessed by Flora from the stand she had taken with her father. Her cheek grew pale, for her lover was the foremost of the riders. Apart from this, the scene was terrific for a woman to look upon: the thundering tramp of the drove, the distended nostrils of the horses, as they fled from the wounded animals, the shouts of the hunters at each successful aim, the reports of the guns, and the whistling of bullets were too much for the nerves of Flora Cameron. An incident occurred that affected her yet more.

Reckless of hoofs and horns, Gordon had nine times ridden into the centre of the herd, and had each time brought down a buffalo. As the chase drew nigh the spot where Flora stood, he naturally became anxious to signalize his courage and dexterity before her eyes. There was among the rest a bull, three years old, that had turned repeatedly on the pursuers, and given them no little trouble, and Gordon resolved to attack him. Attached to the neck of his steed was a long hair rope, such as the Indians use to tether their running horses. Our cavalier dashed at the bull and fired, but the ball missed the heart, and passed through a sensitive part of the intestines. The beast rushed upon him, with a frightful roar; but the horse, true to its training, swerved, and would have carried him off clear, had not the rope above mentioned slipped from its fastening, and trailed on the ground thirty feet behind. At the end was a running noose, into which the bull put his hoof, going near to throw the horse at every bound. At this sight Flora screamed, and fell to the ground senseless.

Gordon's horse, thus entangled, plunged forward, and

the buffalo followed, the one unable to lessen, and the other to increase the distance between them. In this deadly peril, although his steed reeled and was thrice thrown upon its knees, the bois brulé did not lose his seat or his presence of mind. Shifting his gun to his left hand, he unsheathed his knife with his right, and stooping on his courser's neck, severed the rope. The bull continued his furious course, and pitched with a tremendous bellow, headlong to the ground, so near to Flora that the blood spouted from his nostrils upon her dress in a stream. The animal made a few convulsive struggles, and expired.

Gordon sprang from his horse, and ran to where Cameron was standing over his daughter, wringing his hands in utter anguish. Snatching a cup from one of the women, he ran with the speed of a frightened cabri[15] to where a hole had been cut in the ice of the river. In less than two minutes he returned, and raising Flora on his knee, he sprinkled her face with water. A faint sigh announced that she was reviving, and the first word she pronounced was his name. The women now cried that they would bring a dog sledge to convey her to the camp, but Gordon spared them the trouble. He took her in his arms and carried her to her father's lodge.

✦ ✦ ✦

The hunt had terminated, and the women, accustomed to such service, harnessed the dogs and draught horses, and proceeded to where the men were employed in cutting up the buffaloes they had killed. The carts were filled with meat. The dog sledges were laden, (at the rate of an hundred pounds to each dog,) and all returned happy to the lodges. An hundred buffaloes had that day been slain.

Now came the joys of boiling and roasting. The humps, esteemed the best part of the buffalo, were cooked for immediate use, and not to be forgotten are the tongues, still less the delicious marrow bones; to taste which is worth a journey across the Atlantic. The next business was to cure the meat, which was accomplished by a very simple process. It was cut into very thin slices and hung up in the smoke of the lodges. In this situation it soon becomes perfectly exsiccated, and as hard as wood. The worst parts were reserved for pemican. When the meat was perfectly cured, several cart loads were sent to Pembinaw. More chases took place, and consequently more remittances of provisions. The camp was repeatedly moved, in order to keep nigh the buffalo. At last, they thought they had collected food enough for the winter. But a new herd arriving in the vicinity, they could not resist the temptation, and resolved to have one more hunt before they departed.

Chapter 8

Now summon the red current to thine heart –
Old man, thy mightiest wo remains to tell:
I saw the arrow from the bow-string part;
I heard the hoarse, blood-freezing war-whoop swell –
I heard the victor's shout – the dying yell –
The bullet whizzing from the flashing gun –
Fierce was the combat where our warriors fell.
The savage fled toward the setting sun;
He bore away thy child, and thou art left alone.

Anon.

IN THE morning on which the hunt was to have taken place, Cameron walked up the bed of the river on the ice, to the place where the horses were grazing on the rushes. As he turned a short bend, he perceived a party of Indians among the animals, and turned about to retrace his steps to the camp. But he had been seen, and his retreat was cut off. Matters being in this state, he cried for help. Two Indians came up to him with threatening gestures. They seized him by the arms, and hurried him off at the utmost speed he was capable of exerting. They did not appear disposed to harm him, but they significantly put their fingers to their lips and drew their knives, to let him know that silence would be his wisest course. His first cry had, however, given the alarm, and the gens libres and half-breeds came running to save their horses. Gordon was the foremost. He came on shouting, and discharged his piece with effect at one of the hindmost of the marauders. Then seeing what had happened to Cameron, he gained upon his captors till they, aware of his pursuit, turned. A ravine twentyfive feet broad was between them. One of the savages, seeing the rescue inevitable, loosened his hold upon the old man, and drew an arrow to the head to kill him; but Gordon, exerting the physical powers of which he possessed an uncommon share, cleared the chasm at one bound, and felled the Indian to the earth with the butt end of his piece. The other uttering a wild shriek, recoiled a few paces, and let fly an arrow at Gordon. It glanced upon his powder horn, and struck Cameron in the breast, where it buried itself to the feather. Before the archer had time to draw another shaft, Gordon was upon him. Leaping up, he struck the Indian in the chest with his heels and beat him to the earth; at the same [time] receiving a deep wound in the leg from his knife. They grappled, but the struggles of the savage were unavailing. Few men could have contended with Gordon at any time, but now, he contended with tenfold energy. Seizing the wrist of his prostrate foe, he buried his dague, or broad knife, three times in his bosom. The whole passed in a moment, and the foremost of the half-breeds came up just as the Indian drew his last breath.

Gordon stood for a moment irresolute. The horse stealers had begun to recover from their confusion, and rally. At that moment one of the free men, named Le Gros, reached the spot. 'Le Gros,' cried Gordon, 'take care of the old man. Carry him to the camp, and I will fight for both of us.'

'Monsieur Gourdon,' answered the Canadian, 'he is dead. It is of no use to waste time on him. Let us rather try to save the rest of the horses.'

'No, no, he is not dead. I tell you he is not dead. Carry him to the camp, and he may recover. He cannot if he is left here. For God's sake carry him to his daughter. If you do not, I shall be obliged to do it myself.'

'I would willingly listen to your commands at any other time, Monsieur, but see, that rascal in green paint is already riding on my best horse, and there are two fellows on foot trying to catch the other.'

'You greedy rascal!' Gordon begun, but seeing that hard words would have no effect, he continued, 'I think I am more likely to regain your horses than yourself, Le Gros, and I promise you I will do it, if I can. If I do not succeed, I will pay you any price you ask for them: my word is good, I suppose.'

'O yes; your word is as good as the money. I will get my dogs, and carry the old man to his lodge; but remember, Monsieur Gourdon, I have refused an hundred and fifty dollars apiece for my horses. Do you hear, Monsieur? I say I shall expect something over an hundred and fifty dollars apiece, if you do not recover them.'

'I will pay it; I will pay it. But go, go now, for the love of God;' and Le Gros departed.

The marauders were a band of roving Yanktons, under a petty chief called Nopah Keon, or 'he who has twice flown.' M'Leod had had an interview with this dignitary, and engaged him by the promise of liquor, guns, blankets, and other articles held in high esteem by the Indians, to endeavor to get Flora Cameron and her father into his power. This effected, he had no doubt that he should be able to make his addresses acceptable. With this view, Nopah Keon had approached the half-breed camp, but the sight of the horses proved too strong a temptation to his followers. Seeing their cupidity could not be restrained, the wily savage resolved to take advantage of it to promote his designs. He detached ten men, and gained the woods in the rear of the camp, while the rest were busied catching the horses. They dismounted, and under the cover of the trees and underbrush, approached the lodges. There they waited till the alarm, which they had no doubt would be soon given, should deprive the women and children of protection. The lodge of Cameron, as well as his person and that of his daughter, had been so well described to them, that there was no danger of a mistake. But to do M'Leod justice, he had given strict orders that no violence, farther than was necessary to insure their capture, should be done to Cameron or his daughter.

But to return; Gordon, as soon as he was relieved from the care of the old man, hastened to bring the hunters into some order: courage they did not want. Nor were the Sioux unmindful of the Indian policy of war. They all dismounted, and the stolen horses were given in charge to those of the party least remarkable for skill and bravery. Each of these led five or six of the animals out of the mêlée, while a part of the warriors checked the advance of the half breeds. Other some occupied themselves in catching the horses that yet ran at large. This was not effected without difficulty. The animals were frightened, and ran about in disorder.

Shots and arrows were exchanged incessantly, but with little damage to either side. Both parties took advantage of the trees, and besides, constantly leaped about, so as to baffle any aim that might be taken with arrow or bullet. Some gallant charges were made by individuals on both sides, but the success generally amounted to driving the opponent from his cover, for none of the combatants thought of standing a conflict hand to hand. This could not last long. By dint of entreaty and exhortation, Gordon at last prevailed on the half-breeds to act together. They raised the war whoop, and drove the Sioux from their covers at once. This was not done without losing two men, and the savages suffered still more. Five of their number fell, two wounded, and three killed, all of whom were instantly divested of their scalps. By this time, the Indians appointed to catch the horses had fully succeeded. They stood in the open prairie, with the animals around them, each with a rope bridle in its mouth. The Sioux, driven from the wood by the furious charge of the half-breeds, rushed towards them, and in an instant each was mounted. The two belonging to Le Gros, more frightened than the rest, had dragged the Indian who held them to a distance from the others. Perceiving this, Gordon, calling to a man of Kinisteneau blood, named Dés Champs, ran towards them. They both came up, just as the Indian was about springing upon the back of one of the horses. Each knife was sheathed in his vitals in an instant, and while Dés Champs held the creatures by the bridle, our hero turned to the assistance of his party. It was in vain. The Dahcotahs had mounted and were already far away. At a great distance, Gordon saw ten or a dozen horsemen emerge from the bed of the river and ride in a direction crossing the course of the retreating party.

Our hero was then first sensible that he was wounded. In the heat of combat, he had paid no attention to the circumstance; but now, his leg stiffened, and he began to be exhausted by the loss of blood. Dés Champs proposed to carry him to the camp on one of the horses he had assisted to rescue, but this was found impracticable. An arrow had lodged in the body of one of them, and the other had a leg broken by a bullet. They had not a blanket with them, in which to carry him, and he was totally unable to walk or stand. He had no option but to remain where he was, until one of the men could go to the camp, and return with a dog sledge. This service Dés Champs volunteered to perform.

A fire was soon kindled, the snow was cleared away, hay was cut, and he sat down before it. His leg was washed with snow, and the bleeding staunched with the linen of his own shirt. In an incredibly short space Dés Champs returned, for he was the swiftest runner in the north-west. He said nothing to any one, nor would he answer any questions, but his brow spoke volumes. It was observed too, that he had but two dogs harnessed to the sledge. This was no objection, as two draught dogs are abundantly able to draw a man; yet it appeared singular that he had not taken three out of so many. The dogs were white, and their coats were stained with blood; yet this on another occasion would have excited no attention: they might have fought with some of their own species, or at any rate there was enough fresh meat in the camp to account for their appearance.

Some of the hunters scraped away the snow, and began to dig graves in the frozen earth, with their knives, for their fallen comrades. Others placed Gordon upon the sledge and set off with him to the camp. It presented a scene of desola-

tion. Five or six women lay on the ground in different
places, tomahawked and scalped. Before the door of Cameron's lodge, lay Le Gros, with five arrows sticking in his
body. He too had lost his scalp, but the body of a Yankton lying a few paces from him, showed that he had not
fallen alone. His teeth were close, his features still gave
token of firm resolution, and he held a pistol, with the cock
down, in his hand. Cameron was lying in his lodge, helpless.
The arrow had not been withdrawn, but he still breathed.
Flora was nowhere to be found. When Gordon was apprised
of these sad tidings, he was for a moment paralyzed. But
soon recovering he directed Dés Champs and others, to
examine the premises. Of this there was no need: the women
who had fled and concealed themselves, at the appearance
of Nopah Keon, were soon found.

They said, that while they watched the event of the
battle, an armed band of Yanktons entered the camp from
the rear. Le Gros had deposited old Cameron on his bed,
and had issued from the lodge, just as the savages broke in.
He was immediately killed, and the women and children
did not all escape, as has been already seen. The Indian
whose medal, &c,[16] declared him a chief, entered Cameron's
lodge, which he directly knew, for on it was depicted a
man in the act of shooting a deer. What passed in the lodge
they could not tell, but presently the savage came forth,
bearing Flora in his arms, insensible. He carried her into the
woods, and what became of her afterwards they knew not.
The researches of Dés Champs showed that the Yanktons
had had horses in the wood, and that they had taken a northward course. But no blood was in their tracks, and a small
comb, belonging to Flora, was picked up at some distance
from the spot where the party had taken horse; whence
they concluded that she had been carried off unharmed.

Gordon would fain have persuaded the half-breeds to pursue; but they would not listen to the proposal. Their best horses were carried off, the Indians had two hours the start, and they would not leave their wives and children without protection. He could do nothing himself, for he was so much exhausted with loss of blood, that he could not move without assistance.

The arrow was drawn from Cameron by an old half-breed, commonly called Le Docteur, from his skill in surgery and simples. It was not done without difficulty, much care being requisite to prevent the iron head from coming off in the wound.[17] The old man sighed heavily, and inquired for his daughter. When told what had befallen her, his senses failed him, and the syncope was renewed.

When he recovered, he called for Gordon. The young man was assisted into his presence, and sat down beside him. Cameron feebly stretched out his hand toward him. 'I have sinned, I have sinned,' said he, 'I have listened to the voice of pride and vain glory rather than to natural affection, and He has laid his hand heavily on me for it.' And he groaned aloud.

Gordon spoke words of comfort to the afflicted parent, and said that as soon as he was able to sit upon a horse, he would redeem his daughter from captivity, or perish in the attempt.

'Do so, do so,' said the old man. 'Rescue her from this worse than Egyptian bondage, and she is yours. I refused you before, and grievously am I punished for it.'

'I will. If it be in the power of man I will do it.'

'And I will go with you, Monsieur Gourdon,' said Dés Champs, moved to tears, by the sight of so much misery. 'You shall not want the aid that one hand can bestow.'

Indeed, Gordon was highly popular among the people of the country. His great bodily powers, his splendid courage, and his reckless generosity, were of all qualities the most likely to gain him the good will of such a race. Of his talents and acquirements they knew nothing, nor would they have cared for them if they had, but his valor they had witnessed, and they had profited by his expenditure. Flora was no less beloved. Her kindness for the aged and infirm, and the affability of her manners, had made her deservedly a favorite. They all pitied her condition, yet such is the inconsistency of poor human nature, that none but Dés Champs would risk anything for her relief.

Luckily for all concerned the Yanktons had contented themselves with taking the running horses, esteeming those destined to draught slightly. In the morning, Gordon and Cameron were placed in a cart, which was driven by Dés Champs. The women and children were disposed of in a similar manner, and they departed for Pembinaw, less joyful than they came. In three days they reached the fort. The greater number of the men had remained to take care of the camp, and the carts made several trips, before the meat and baggage were transported to the settlement.

Chapter 9

Le tumulte, les cris, la peur, l'aveugle rage,
La honte de céder, l'ardente soif du sang,
Le désespoir, la mort, passent de rang en rang.
La nature en frémit.

Henriade.

CAMERON remained in a state of utter helplessness. His lungs were injured, and bled inwardly, and he was perfectly aware that his wound was mortal. But for aught that appeared, he might survive till spring. One morning a large body of horsemen were descried in the prairie, at a considerable distance. The worthy governor had received intimations of an attack intended by the Northwest Company, and felt assured that these men were not reconnoitring the place with peaceable intent. He issued orders for a party of twenty men to assemble in arms, forthwith, and his command was promptly obeyed. He put himself at their head, and issued forth, leaving instructions for the male part of the population to be in readiness to repel any attack, and for a part of them to advance to his support with a small piece of artillery, in case help should be needed.

As he advanced, he found the number of his opponents was five times greater than that of his own escort, and he despatched a man to the rear to order up the gun, and then advanced within speaking distance of the enemy. They were under the command of Cuthbert Grant, who had caused them to dismount, and draw up in good order. Most of them had their faces painted black, after the custom of the Indians.

'Who are you, and what do you want?' cried the governor, advancing on foot and alone, to within five paces of them.

It chanced that the half breed in front of him still remained on horseback. This fellow was a noted desperado, and was known by the name of Peter Pangman, or the Bostonois. He it was, who took upon himself to answer the governor.

'You villain,' said he, 'we want our provisions, of which you have robbed us.'

'Rogue! do you dare to call me so?' said Semple, losing patience at the epithet. 'I will make you repent your insolence.'

THE BOIS BRULE

At this moment a gun was discharged at the governor, by whom, never appeared. The ball passed through his thighs. He did not fall, but stood, unable to move, on the spot where he had received the wound. The flash was followed by a general discharge of fire arms from the party of Cuthbert Grant, upon the governor's people. Those of them who were not killed on the spot, scattered and fled, and Grant's partizans broke their ranks and pursued. They fully proved their claim to Indian birth. Their savage kindred could not have behaved with more barbarity. Of twentytwo men that had come to the field, in ten minutes, but three were left alive: two, severely wounded, who had been saved from the fury of their assailants by Grant; for to do him justice, he did all in his power to mitigate the horrors of the scene. The other had fallen to the ground, in an agony of terror; three men had fallen upon him, and he owed his life to the supposition that he was dead.

When the unfortunate governor was wounded, he turned to Grant, who stood near him. 'You are a gentleman,' said he, 'and I beg you to save my life.' Grant ordered Peter Pangman to take care of him, and hastened away, saying that his presence was needed elsewhere. Pangman looked malignantly at the wounded man. 'Do you think me a rogue *now?*' asked he. 'If you were not,' answered Semple, 'you would not be here. But if anything befalls me, your own neck may pay for it.' Pangman called the Indian, Joe, the same who had assisted at the murder of Cavenny, and whose tomahawk, hands and face, were already painted bloody red. He spoke some words to the savage, in Chippeway, and left him with the prisoner. The latter saw that his last hour was come. He closed his hands upon his breast and his lips moved in prayer, though no sound came from them. The Indian stole behind him unheeded. One crashing blow,

145

and the unfortunate gentleman lay as lifeless as the corpses around him.

The party with the piece of ordnance had advanced half way from the fort, when the firing commenced. Seeing the fate of their fellows they halted, pointed the gun at the band of butchers, fired, and fled for their lives. The ball did no other harm than to kill a horse, but it had the effect to assemble the banditti round their leader. They had tasted blood, and were now clamorous to proceed to the settlement and slaughter every person in it. 'Do you see my horse lying there, Monsieur Grant?' said Pangman. 'May I die in mortal sin, if I do not have amends of these accursed planters for killing him.' And he crossed himself very devoutly. But Grant saw that too much had been done. He had received orders from his principals to take the fort, seize the provisions and merchandise, and make prisoners of all within, but his instructions were peremptory, to do no bodily injury to any one, if he could avoid it. He was himself, little disposed to commit any violence, but he was as fully possessed of the doctrine of implicit obedience to his bourgeois, as the voyageurs themselves. At present, however, he saw that reproaching his too zealous followers would have no good effect; and he contented himself with telling them that he dared not proceed without further orders from his principals. He informed them too, that their necks were in danger for what they had done, a piece of intelligence that tended not a little to damp their ardor. Pangman he assured of indemnity for his loss, and concluded by telling them, that anything more they might do, would neither be reckoned good service by the company, nor rewarded as such.

This reasoning was conclusive with a large majority of them, and the more violent, finding they were not likely to receive any support, and were themselves too weak to do anything, came to the resolution to obey Grant's orders. They all rode off the field, therefore, leaving the dead bodies of the slain to the wolves and ravens. The small cannon before mentioned, they left on the field, for they had not the means to carry it off.

As soon as they were gone, Pritchard, the man whom they had supposed to be dead, rose, and finding nothing to hinder him, walked to the fort. Stupified as he had been with terror, he had yet sense enough to perceive that the only way to save his life, was to remain quiet, and leave them in their error. But the shock had unsettled his reason. He was a man about forty years old; when he fell his hair was black, but when he arose, the snow around him was not whiter. He found his way to the fort, but to all interrogatories he responded with an idiot stare. He remained in this condition for some weeks. He would sit for hours in the same posture, his eyes covered with his hands. When at last he recovered his sanity, he was unable to give any account of what had happened. He had vivid, though indistinct recollections of a massacre, but could never connect his ideas on the subject. Afterwards when required to give evidence before a legal tribunal, his testimony was set aside by the court on this account.

The command now devolved on Gordon, who was little able to perform its duties. Yet he took measures for defence. He withdrew the settlers from their cabins into the fort, posted a regular guard, and distributed arms and ammunition. And he continued to visit his sentinels, on crutches, till Deputy Governor M'Donald relieved him.

A voyageur arrived, sent by De Reinville, (a trader at Lac au Travers) for a supply of merchandize. This man brought no tidings of Flora, but he informed our hero that the band of Wawnahton was encamped on the Wild Rice River, and thither Gordon resolved to go.

The more experienced of the Company's people advised him to wait till the requested supply should be despatched, when he might have the advantage of the carts and dog sledges. But he would brook no more delay, and departed on horseback with Dés Champs, early in a cold morning in January.

By short marches, for of long ones he was incapable, Gordon approached the camp of Wawnahton. A brother could not have tended him with more attention than did Dés Champs. He cared for the horses, prepared the food, and was ever on the look out for roving bands of Indians, from whom they might have sustained injury. But luckily, none appeared. The only danger that approached them, came in the questionable shape of a grisly bear, and was removed from their track by a bullet from Dés Champ's gun.

In nine days they came in sight of Shoankah Kahpee, (the running dog) the oasis where the tents of the Dahcotahs were pitched. Here it behoved them to use the utmost caution, for though they were sure of all kindness, when once in the lodges, the Sioux would probably have murdered them without scruple, had they found them in the open prairie. They stopped where they were, intending to enter the camp the next morning, before the light, when the savages should be asleep.

The night was cloudy, and toward morning circumstances became favorable to their enterprise. Before daybreak, snow began to fall, and the wind blew with tremendous violence. The snow was lifted from the plains, and whirled about in a thousand eddies, so obscuring the atmosphere that objects could not be distinguished at the distance of an hundred yards. In short it was one of those tremendous storms called in the language of the country *poudries*, in which neither the Indian nor the hardy Canadian dares to stir abroad, and the very wolves fly to the woods for shelter. The temperature was not much below the freezing point, but the wind pierced the garments of our travellers like a knife. The tornado was just the thing they wanted, being sure that none of the Dahcotahs would be on the watch, and that they might reach the doors of the lodges unobserved. They saddled their horses, and following the bed of the river, as a sure guide through the gloom, advanced. The banks partially sheltered them from the blast, though at times they were almost blown off their steeds. Finding that riding was the same thing as freezing, they dismounted, and led their cattle by the bridles, though the effort was exceedingly painful to Gordon. After six hours of incessant and toilsome exertion, they reached the camp. They heard singing and dancing in the lodges, but none came to question them. Turning their horses loose, they advanced directly to the tent of Wawnahton, (which had been minutely described) unmolested by any but dogs.

Chapter 10

Were I in England now, and had but these fishes painted, not a holiday fool there but would give a piece of silver; when they will not give a doit to relieve a lame beggar, they will lay out ten to see a dead Indian. *Tempest.*

GORDON and his attendant entered at once. The Dahcotah chief was sitting at the fire, carving a pipe-stem. On their entrance he looked up, and held out his hand. The women stunned the visitors with their clamor, and the cry of 'strangers arrived' brought the whole band to the lodge to gaze and ask questions. The wife of Wawnahton cast a grateful glance of recognition on Gordon, and spread a robe for him to sit on. She then took off his moccasins, and gave him others for present use. A dog was knocked in the head, singed, and consigned to the kettle with all haste. The chief took his pipe and otter-skin tobacco pouch, and gave them to the visitors, in order that they might smoke. The dog feast was scarcely over when they were asked to another in a neighboring tent, and the day passed in the exercise of over zealous hospitality.

The women set up the soldier's lodge in the middle of the camp, for the use of the strangers, and brought wood and water, without presuming to enter. Thither our adventurers repaired, with their blankets and horse furniture. One of their saddles was missing, but as soon as Wawnahton was apprised of the circumstance, a soldier, by his order, perambulated the camp, proclaiming the fact, and requiring whosoever might be in possession of the lost article, to make instant restitution, on pain of having his or her blanket and lodge cut to pieces. A general search took place, and it was discovered that a starving dog had dragged the saddle into the bushes to eat the leather.[18] The chief replaced it with one of his own.

At night the soldiers and old men assembled in the lodge, to smoke and converse. When they took leave, Wawnahton remained, and asked the occasion of Gordon's visit. It was readily communicated.

The chief pondered awhile without speaking. At last, having knocked the ashes from his pipe for the tenth time, he broke silence. 'Well, I knew that Nopah Keon had a

sick white woman in his lodge, but had I known that she
belonged to you, he should not have kept her. But if you
are in want of a woman, you need not go so far as his camp.
Choose what girl you like best in my band, and I will get
her for you. Nay, you shall have one of my wives, if you
like that better.'

To this generous offer, Gordon returned a decided negative. It was in vain to attempt to make Wawnahton comprehend the nature of his feelings toward Flora. In the
opinion of the Indian, a woman was but a kind of slave, or
beast of burthen. He might prefer one to another on account of superior beauty or industry, or because she was
the mother of his children; but he had no more conception
of such love as Gordon's than of the most abstruse problem
in Euclid. 'Why is your mind so set upon this girl?' said
he. 'Can she work moccasins better than others? Can she
carry a heavier pack or dress a buffalo robe better?' Being
answered in the negative, he added, 'Well, you people with
hats have strange notions. But I will do as you would have
me, notwithstanding.'

Gordon now proposed to the Dahcotah chief to set off
in quest of Miss Cameron on the morrow; but the latter
coolly replied that there was no occasion for haste. Nothing
is ever gained by hurrying an Indian; so our hero was
obliged to wait with what patience he might.

During the night the storm ceased and the wind fell. At
sunrise the cold was excessive. The smallest twigs were
covered with a thick rime, and the atmosphere was full of
minute glittering particles through which the sun looked,
shorn of his beams. At noon parhelia were seen in the firma-
ment, five in number, so brilliant that the true Phoebus
could not be distinguished from the false. A solitary buffalo
that approached the camp, was shot, and a little red ice

trickled from the wound. The squaws went to take a part of his flesh, but he hardened under their knives, and they were compelled to finish their task with hatchets. The nearest wood was twelve miles distant, and to attempt to reach it in such weather, was certain death. The camp could not be removed in these circumstances, and thus it remained three days longer.

The fourth morning after, was mild for the season, and the camp was raised. The horses and dogs were laden, the tents were struck, and the women made up their packs. All took the line of march. The men walked or rode indolently along, and the women followed, each bending under an immense burthen, with perhaps an infant on the top of all. The soldiers marched in front and beat the path; and at every two or three miles the whole procession stopped, to smoke and eat.

Toward night they arrived at another island, or oasis, near which a herd of buffaloes were grazing. Arrived at a suitable spot to encamp, the foremost soldier struck down a spear, surmounted with the skin of a raven, his staff of office. As the band came up, a dog passed this sacred emblem of authority. It was instantly transfixed by a shaft from one of the soldiers: a young man, who had ran to arrest the animal, had his robe cut to pieces, and was severely beaten with their bows. On any other occasion, such an indignity would have been requited with a stab, but the soldiers are an honorable kind of police, and the exercise or abuse of their authority is never resented. In this case, their rigor was intended to prevent the buffaloes from being frightened away, and they took further measures to the same purpose. The legs of the dogs were tied to their necks, the horses were picketed, and the tents were pitched, in precisely the same order in which they had stood the night before.

A few of the wild cattle were killed for immediate use. In the morning, the camp broke up, and proceeded; but not to enlarge upon the incidents of the journey, which would be a mere repetition of what has already been related, after six days' march, they arrived at the camp of Nopah Keon. It was on the side of a small lake, affording just wood enough for the kettles. A scattering discharge of fire arms gave testimony of the satisfaction of both parties at meeting; and some hours were spent in feasting and rejoicing.

Gordon found no difficulty in penetrating into the lodge where Flora lay. In an instant he was on his knees at her side. 'Flora, dear Flora,' he cried, 'nothing but death shall again sever us.'

The tears swam in her eyes; she smiled, and faintly replied, 'I had expected this of you, William; but my eyes were long, long, wearied with looking for you.'

'Do you think then, that I would have delayed an instant, if I had known where to seek you, and could have dragged one limb after the other? Take back the unjust reproach.'

'I did not mean to reproach you; I had all confidence in your affection; but I thought you were dead.'

✓ ✓ ✓

Flora informed our hero, that when she was carried off, the agitation of her mind, and the fatigue of her journey on horseback had brought on a fever, that had reduced her to the brink of the grave. She had, however, received no maltreatment, but had fared as well as the Indians themselves. Her illness had been aggravated, she said, by a proposal from Nopah Keon to become his wife, which was interpreted to her by a trader on a visit to the camp. She had been put in bodily fear too, by one of the four wives of her captor, who was jealous of a new competitor for her lord's favor. And she had also suffered from the urgency with which the old women recommended their prescriptions; for with Indians, as with white people, every one has a remedy for every disease, and presses his advice. Neither had the dancing and singing, intended to effect her cure, been of any advantage, but rather the contrary.

She now inquired for her father, and Gordon, afraid of a relapse, told her that Cameron was severely wounded, but would, he hoped, soon recover. He said too that the old man had made her redemption from captivity the price of her hand.

The crone who had been singing and shaking a rattle by Flora's side, now imagined that Gordon's visit portended no good to the interests of Nopah Keon. She left the patient and repaired to the lodge of the Grand Medicine, into which, as she belonged to the fraternity, she was instantly admitted.[19] Nopah Keon was celebrating the mysterious rites of the institution, when she informed him of what she had seen, but he was too much engrossed with his own dignity to suffer his occupation to be interrupted by anything relating to a woman.

When Nopah Keon carried Flora off, he had no other view than to deliver her into the hands of M'Leod, and get the promised reward. As soon as his party was out of danger of pursuit, he despatched a messenger to inform that wretch of the success of his machinations. The envoy did not readily find the Scotchman, and in the meanwhile the purpose of Nopah Keon changed. Nature proved too strong for him: Miss Cameron's surpassing beauty, though obscured by sickness, awakened feelings in his bosom to which he had hitherto been a stranger, and for which he could not have accounted himself. He was wont to say that he loved one of his four wives because she had a still tongue, another for having given him five boys, the third for her industry, and the fourth because she was stronger than a horse. But if any one had asked why he loved Flora better than all four, he could only have replied, that such was his pleasure. The band laughed at the lovestruck barbarian, for what they deemed his folly, and his wives loaded him with reproaches. 'See,' said one of his wives, 'your favorite cannot live in a lodge. She is sick already, and will never recover.' 'She cannot carry so large a burthen as a girl seven years old,' cried his prolific spouse. 'Who would have such an ugly, pale creature?' exclaimed the third. 'What is she good for?' shouted the fourth.

Nevertheless his resolution remained unchanged, and a trader who came to his camp with a dog sledge loaded with merchandise, served him as an interpreter to declare his love to its object. He was in no wise daunted by the indignant scorn and loathing with which she heard the proposal. On the contrary, he resolved to compel her submission, as soon as her health should be re-established, for the idea of winning her heart by gentle means never entered his head.

When M'Leod arrived, he was hospitably received, but when he demanded that the prisoner should be given up to him, Nopah Keon desired him to look round him, and take some other in her stead. For a moment he was speechless with astonishment, and then burst forth in a strain of invective. But his rage made no more impression upon the savage than rain does upon marble.

'Brother,' said He who had twice Flown, 'it is clear that you have been very ill educated, since you talk so much like an angry woman. Your heart is very weak. A man should bear so trifling a loss with patience. There are plenty of women in my camp, and I will give you any one you please, if you cannot do without a wife. You see that I am willing to deal justly with you; so be not wroth, brother.'

'I will return with a band of half breeds, and kill every one of you, if you do not give me the white woman.'

'Ha, ha! The dogs dare not come to hunt upon my grounds, unless a hundred together. I shall grow gray waiting for them.'

'You will see whether it be so or not.'

'Be pacified, brother. Give me your hand in friendship; and I will make up the loss to you. There are many girls here that I can dispose of.'

Finding remonstrance useless, M'Leod gave over. He refused to smoke with Nopah Keon, or take his hand; affronts which the Dahcotah laid up in his memory, to be remembered at a fitting opportunity.

To return from this retrospect to the course of our story; after the Great Medicine dance was over, the two chiefs held a consultation. Wawnahton urged on the unwilling attention of his countryman, that four women were enough for any man, and that by retaining Flora he would incur the ill will of all the whites, and that she was the wife of his comrade. If he must have a fifth spouse, there was no father in the tribe but would gladly bestow his daughter on such a warrior and hunter. To each and all of these reasons the chief was as deaf as the adder.

That the English girl could do no labor, he knew, he said, but his other women should work for her. He cared not for the enmity of the whites; they were a race of old women, created by the Great Spirit to make guns and blankets, and to be servants to the Indians. If they should withdraw their trade, (the worst evil they could inflict,) the Yanktons need not care, as long as there was wood enough in their country for bows, and buffaloes for food and clothing. He had buried the woman in his heart, and his wife she should be.

'You speak like a boy,' said Wawnahton, 'not like a wise man and a chief. This woman is not a fit wife for a Dahcotah: moreover, her husband is a soldier, and my comrade, and she must be restored to him. He will kill you if you refuse. Listen to me: return her, and I will give you ten swift horses: If you will not, you shall be chief no longer. I will cut your lodges; and my people shall kill all your horses and dogs. None will listen to your voice afterwards. Think well of it.'

Nopah Keon was compelled to submit. He might brave the resentment of Gordon and the whites with impunity, as he thought; but with Wawnahton he was more likely to come in contact.

If he should, by contumacy, cause the horses of his band, on which they mainly depended for support, to be killed, he well knew that his authority and influence were at an end. This was the evil he most dreaded, and he therefore yielded with the best grace he could.

'It is but a woman,' he said, 'and two chiefs should not quarrel for so small a matter. I will take the horses you offer, for my people are much in want of them. Take her, and do what you will with her.'

She was soon conveyed by Gordon and Dés Champs to the soldiers' lodge. This was contrary to Indian usages, no woman having been ever before suffered to profane that sanctuary. When informed that she was a prisoner no longer, she held out her hand to her lover. 'It is of little worth, dear William,' said she, 'but such as it is, you have won it over and over again. Take it: my heart goes with it.'

The horses were easily procured by Wawnahton, and given as the price of her ransom. In two days a dog sledge was made, with axes and knives only. This vehicle is constructed of two boards, about half an inch thick, eight

inches wide, and ten feet long. They are fastened together
with cletes, and the end is turned up like the toe of a skate,
that it may slip easily over the snow. The whole is sewed
with thongs of raw hide. Such as are intended for the con-
veyance of the traveller, have a structure upon them, in
shape like the body of a sleigh, made of parchment. Such
a one was arranged for Flora. The women of the band gave
her buffalo robes, and the grateful wife of the chief bestowed upon her and Gordon her whole stock of ornamented moccasins, the work of a year; and which had been
intended for herself and her husband. Wawnahton resolved
to escort them to Pembinaw, with thirty of his best warriors. All preparations for the journey were completed, and
even in the short time they had been in the camp, Flora's
condition was visibly improved.

In the morning all was ready for departure. The young
lady was carefully placed in her little cariole, and covered
with robes. The chief's wife laid her hands on her head,
wept and sung her regret that she should never behold her
again, her hopes that she might find her husband faithful
and kind, and that she might be the joyful mother of a boy,
before the year should elapse. This ceremony over, they
departed, and were saluted as they had been on their arrival.

Nothing material occurred on the journey. Flora's health
mended from day to day, and by the time they came in
sight of Pembinaw river she was almost well, and Gordon's
wound was nearly healed.

About two miles from the fort, they were perceived by
its inmates. Great terror and confusion was the consequence,
until one of the company's clerks ascertained, by means of
a spy glass, that two white men, and a woman, were among
the Indians. Wawnahton and his men did not care to go to
the fort, though Gordon endeavored to persuade them, and

assured them they might do so in safety. They remembered that the band of Nopah Keon had lately killed several of the colonists, and judging of the customs of the whites by their own, they dared not venture among the friends of the slain. A long colloquy was held between Wawnahton and Gordon, the former pressing upon the conviction of the latter the magnitude of his services, and the propriety of giving him a suitable reward. He wanted a few guns, blankets, kettles, axes, &c. for himself and his people, and he did not forget to mention that a quantity of silver brooches, arm-bands, wampum, beads, and above all a great keg of spirits, would be very acceptable. They might be sent, he said, by De Reinville, to Lac au Travers. Gordon would fain have had him repair to the Company's store at once, and there receive all that could be spared, but no man is equally brave at all times, and Wawnahton was not just then in a humor to throw away his body. Gordon promised, however, to comply with all his requisitions in his own way, and after shaking hands very affectionately, they parted forever.

Chapter 11

HALF an hour, and they were in the fort. Flora flew to her father's bed side, and was dreadfully shocked at his reduced and miserable appearance. At her entrance the old man turned his eyes, that shone with a feverish brilliancy, and beheld his daughter. 'And are you here, my dear child, at last?' said he. 'You are just in time to close the eyes of your old father.'

'No, no, my father, do not say so,' said Flora, speaking as fast as her sobs would let her.

'Not so, my child, my days, nay, my hours, are numbered. No man ever recovered from such a wound as mine. Perhaps you will be an orphan before sunset. But have done sobbing, and listen to the last command that I shall utter. I have promised that Gordon shall marry you. Do not turn away your head; this is no time to play the coquette. Send for My Lord, he is a magistrate; and let me see you have a protector instantly. Send for him and Gordon, and let the ceremony be performed; and then I can depart in peace.'

There was no need to send for Gordon: he had stood at the door and heard all. He advanced to the bed side. 'Father,' said he, 'if I have had evil thoughts of you, they are now removed. Believe me, your child shall never have cause to repent your goodness.'

'But father,' said Flora, 'this is no time for marrying, or giving in marriage. Consider the shortness of the notice.'

'But me no buts; what need have you of any more preparation. There is many a high born dame who would be glad to change looks with you, and give gold into the bargain, simple as you stand there. Obey me, I charge you. Come hither, young man, and take her hand. God bless you both. May your lives be happier than mine, and that your end may not be the same, leave this accursed country, where God is not feared, nor his image respected. But I feel my end draw nigh: go, William, for his lordship; or I shall not see myself obeyed.'

Gordon left the weeping bride to seek the Earl of Selkirk.

When the Earl entered, he took Flora in his arms, and imprinted a paternal kiss on her forehead. He then congratulated her on her escape from the Indians, which he attributed entirely to the gallantry and perseverance of her lover, who, he said, had fairly won her in the fashion of the days of chivalry.

The old man now said to his lordship that he felt his breath failing fast, and desired him to proceed with the ceremony. When it was completed, the parties most interested turned towards him. They spoke to him, but he did not answer. He was dead.

＊ ＊ ＊

During Gordon's absence, the myrmidons of the Northwest, under the command of M'Leod, had taken the Company's fort at Pembinaw. They had plundered the stores, and destroyed the implements of husbandry belonging to the colonists; whom they had, moreover, maltreated and menaced with expulsion. Under these circumstances many of the emigrants, driven to despair, and not knowing where to go, entered the service of the Northwest.

The Earl of Selkirk heard of these outrages at Quebec, and took measures to put a stop to them. He procured several magistrate's commissions from the Governor General; with the names left blank, in order that they might be filled at his discretion. Making all haste to Ossinneboia, he collected all the men that could be spared from the Hudson's Bay Company's posts on the route, and enlisted as many of the gens libres as he could. The tables were now turned. Pembinaw and other places were retaken; and his lordship succeeded in inspiring his colonists with new hopes, that were never to be realized. But as we have no interest in the earl, or his plans, farther than they are connected with our story, we will, for the present, take leave of them.

When Mrs Gordon recovered from the shock of her father's death, she urged her husband to leave the country. One consideration only prevented him from complying: he thirsted for vengeance on M'Leod, and information arriving that he had gone into the plains to hunt, gave him an opportunity to effect his purpose. To all the remonstrances of his wife, Gordon replied that honor bound him to see that the murderer of his friend did not escape from justice. He then requested Lord Selkirk to invest him with the proper authority, and to provide him a sufficient force. His lordship answered that the criminal had with him a band of ruffians, and that he could not, consistently with the safety of the colony, give him more than ten men. He said too, that M'Leod and his satellite Reinhard were unworthy opponents for a man of honor: but the bois brulé was unmoved by these arguments. 'If you will not give me a man, my Lord,' said he, 'I will go by myself. I will watch him till I find him alone: my friend Wawnahton taught me a lesson of that kind. He is a villain, as you say, but I do not therefore agree with you that he should be safe from my hands: he can feel a shot or a stab, my lord, as keenly as you or I. Yet I do not wish to anticipate the hangman, and I will take him alive if I can. Reinhard is a mere brute, as much at the command of his master as the horse he rides; but he is a dangerous brute, and must not be suffered to go at large. My Lord, I am resolved: will you give me the sanction of the law, or shall I take it into my own hands?'

Finding him immoveable Lord Selkirk gave him a warrant and ordered ten of the gens libres to attend him. Indians enough could have been hired, but the Earl thought it a dangerous precedent to establish. With this escort then, and his adherent Dés Champs, our hero set out.

Chapter 12

Do not repeat these things; for they are heavier
Than all thy woes can stir; therefore betake thee
To nothing but despair. A thousand knees
Ten thousand years together, naked, fasting,
Upon a barren mountain, and still winter
In storm perpetual, could not move the gods
To look that way thou art.

Winter's Tale.

OUR hero approached the camp of M'Leod cautiously, in the Indian manner, without suffering his party to be seen. He picketed his horses in a hollow three miles distant, where they might graze out of sight, and at night sent spies into his camp; but he only learned that Peter Pangman was with his enemy, sick of an intermittent fever, and that M'Leod had forty half-breeds with him. In this manner four days passed, but on the fifth night Dés Champs took upon himself the office of spy, and penetrating farther than his predecessors had done, brought back information, that on the morrow, the hunters were to chase the buffalo, and that M'Leod and Reinhard would be left alone in their lodge. On the receipt of these tidings Gordon despatched a man to raise the cattle, and drive them so far as to insure the protracted absence of the half-breeds the next day. This being effected, he moved to within a mile of the enemy with his men.

At daybreak the bois brulés saddled their horses and rode off. M'Leod came out of his lodge to witness their departure, and when they were gone re-entered it, totally unsuspicious of danger. He was first apprised of it by the entrance of Gordon with five followers, into the lodge, whom he at first mistook for some of his own people returned from the hunt. He started, and asked what had brought them back so soon.

'Rise,' said Gordon; 'rise and come with us where you must render an account of your life.'

Recognizing Gordon's voice, he started up, as did Reinhard. 'I see,' he said, 'into what hands I have fallen. But I did not kill Cavenny; no, you cannot prove it, and the law cannot condemn me. Are you come to murder me here?'

'No, miscreant; I am not. That were a deed worthy of you; not of me. Yet if I should slay you, who could blame me? There hangs a sword: if you think yourself unfairly treated; draw it, and come on. If you conquer me, I promise that you shall go free.'

'And who would trust to such a promise? If I should kill you, I should fall by the hands of your men.'

Here Reinhard broke in. 'Monsieur M'Leod,' said he, 'if you are inclined to surrender without a struggle, so am not I. Let Gordon order his men to retire, and I will trust his word. Come sir, I see you wear a sword: let us forth, and we shall see if you know how to use it.'

Gordon spoke to his men. 'If I fall,' he said, 'let them go clear. Now, base assassin, come on.'

Reinhard met him boldly. He had expected to overcome him easily, but Gordon was almost his equal in skill, and his superior in activity. Their blades crossed, and the young man attacked his opponent fiercely. Reinhard defended himself ably, but finding himself over-matched, he drew a pistol from his belt and fired at Gordon's head. He missed, and before the smoke cleared away, he received a cut across his wrist, and his sword dropped from his hand. Then he stood still and sullen, expecting a mortal blow.

His expectations were near being fulfilled: Gordon's men, who had watched the duel with intense curiosity, now levelled their weapons, and would have shot him, had not the bois brulé called to them to forbear. 'Wretch,' he cried,

THE BOIS BRULE

'I scarcely know what hinders me from staking you to the earth. Come, my men, bind up his wrist, and tie his elbows behind him. Do the same for the brave major. Dés Champs, go and bring Pangman, and their horses hither.'

M'Leod submitted, in terror, and Reinhard doggedly, without uttering a syllable. Pangman was dragged from under a heap of buffalo robes, where he had concealed himself, without respect to his feeble condition or his expostulations. Dés Champs tied his wrists so tight as to give him great pain, for it must be confessed that the half-breed, as well as others of his rank and condition, had little regard for human suffering. When the wretched invalid was brought before Gordon, the youth loosened his bonds, and rebuked his follower for his inhumanity.

'You are the master, Monsieur,' said Dés Champs. 'I hope I know my duty to my bourgeois, but please to recollect, that if we had fallen into their keeping, we should have had worse treatment. If I were master, I would not have all this trouble with them.'

'What would you do, then?' asked Gordon.

'Carry home their scalps at my horse's bridle, and help myself to whatever I liked in the camp,' answered Dés Champs.

But Gordon did not like the counsel. The prisoners were mounted on their own horses, with their ancles secured under the animals. If we were to say that the party left the camp as poor as they entered it, it would be more than would consist with strict truth. He who could exchange an old garment for a new one, did so without scruple. Sundry knives, blankets, pistols, &c, were taken. To all this Gordon offered no opposition, for he knew that the free men might, like the Indians, be led, but not driven. The spoilers left the camp in high glee. One of them had decorated his person with the gorgeous laced coat and epaulettes of M'Leod; another wore his cap and feather, a third had girt on his sword. Reinhard's apparel was disposed of in a similar manner, and the wearers of these equipments were looked upon with envy by their less fortunate companions. A great deal of the baggage of the camp, that could not be conveniently carried away was wantonly destroyed.

It is unnecessary to relate the incidents of their return to Pembinaw.

And now, gentle reader, we believe that all the incidents essential to our story have been recorded. If thy patience is not already exhausted, we bespeak thy favor in behalf of our

Conclusion

A week after Gordon's return to Pembinaw, two boats might be seen at the landing place of the Company's fort, manned, and ready to descend the river. An awning was erected on the hindmost, and under it, on a pack of beaver skins, sat Flora Gordon. Her husband and the Scottish Earl stood on the shore, in the midst of the clerks of the Company. At a little distance stood Dés Champs, leaning on his gun, and looking sorrowfully at the boats. The ceremony of leave-taking over, Gordon turned to the half-breed, and desired him to embark. He advanced, and touching his cap respectfully, held out his hand to Gordon.

'What does this mean?' said the latter, 'are you not going with me?'

'No, Monsieur. You will perhaps think me childish, or a mere Indian, to change my mind, and break my word thus. But I have slept, and considered the matter better. You have offered me a home, and a support; and if I were to follow you, I should be no more obliged to suffer cold, heat, nor hunger, and my scalp would be safe, forever. But I was once in Montreal, and I know not how it was, but I had no relish for soft beds, nor good cheer. I sighed for my native prairies; and I should again. No, Monsieur, I must keep to my horse, my gun, and my dog sledge. Adieu! you will not, I hope, forget Antoine Dés Champs. I am thankful for your kindness. May God conduct you.'

'But Dés Champs,' added Gordon, much affected, 'you can go with me to Montreal, and if you do not choose to remain, you can return in the autumn. Besides I have not yet rewarded you for your services. Indeed your determination has broken up all my plans.'

'I am sufficiently rewarded already. Nevertheless, if Monsieur Gordon pleases to bestow his gun, and his horse on me, I should not be sorry.'

'You shall have them, and everything else I leave behind. Stay, let me write a note to Mr M'Donald to that effect,' and taking out his tablets he wrote accordingly.

Dés Champs, who was a total stranger to the delicacy which would have made many white men refuse such a gift, took the paper without scruple or thanks, and thrust it under his belt. He advanced to bid Flora farewell. He paid her his awkward salutations with some appearance of feeling, and disembarked. The boatmen began to be impatient, and called to Gordon to hasten.

'Well Dés Champs,' said the young husband, 'I will no longer try to persuade you. Farewell; may God bless you. I will write to the head of the colony to provide you with stores every winter at my expense. Once more farewell.'

'Adieu, Monsieur,' said Dés Champs, shaking his hand, and raising his cap from his head. He held it in this manner until Gordon had embarked and the boat was out of sight. He then replaced it and turned away.

THE BOIS BRULE

On the arrival of the party at Montreal, M'Leod and his instruments were arraigned for the murder of Cavenny, and of Governor Semple and his people, in due course of law. The inhabitants of that city still remember how bitter was the contention of the two rival fur companies on that occasion, and what efforts were made, and what means resorted to, on the one side to produce, and on the other to suppress the evidence. The Northwest succeeded in procuring the acquittal of M'Leod and Pangman. Reinhard admitted the part he had taken in the murder of the Irishman, but informed the jury, that he had stabbed Cavenny, after he was shot by the Indian, Joe, 'to put an end to his sufferings.' Notwithstanding this humane motive, he was found guilty of manslaughter, and sentenced to be transported, for fourteen years. What has become of him, or whether he is now alive or dead, is not known.

M'Leod having refused a challenge from Gordon, found that Montreal was no place for him, and returned to the Indian country. The last we heard of him, he was trading with the Chyppewans at Great Slave Lake. Pangman returned to Pembinaw, where he is hunting the buffalo to this day.

Shortly after these occurrences, Gordon, by the command of his father, crossed the Atlantic. It is said that he now resides on the banks of the Esk with his wife, and has a large family of sons and daughters. Before he went, however, he fulfilled his promise to Dés Champs. But that person did not long live to be a tax on his bounty. In the spring of eighteen hundred and twentyone he found his death on the horns of a buffalo.

The two companies soon after discovered that strife and opposition were to the advantage of neither. They united; whereby a great number of persons were thrown out of employment, and the number of free men was greatly increased. Some of their clerks came into the United States, and formed the Columbian Fur Company, which after three years opposition amalgamated with the North American Fur Company.

Lord Selkirk returned to Scotland, and his colony died a natural death. The processions, and anathemas fulminated by the Catholic priest, availed nothing against the grasshoppers or the spring floods, and the settlers saw their crops destroyed, year after year. At last they became convinced that the country was uninhabitable, and concluded to emigrate to the United States, believing it better to risk themselves among the Bostonois than to starve at Ossinneboia. In eighteen hundred and twentyfive, not thirty of the Swiss emigrants remained at the colony. Many of them settled at Vevay, on the Ohio, where they are now cultivating the grape.

In the year eighteen hundred and twentyfour, a party of American troops arrived at Pembinaw, under the command of Major S. Long. Having ascertained that the boundary line passed through the village, the American flag was hoisted, amidst the acclamations of an hundred Canadians and half-breeds; not one of whom knew for what he shouted. The village then consisted of about twenty log huts, and a church, built of hewn timber. At present it does not exist.

WEENOKHENCHAH
WANDEETEEKAH

She bore her wrongs in deep and silent sorrow;
Endured the anguish of a broken heart
In uncomplaining sadness; saw her love
Repaid with cold neglect. But stung at last
To the bosom's inmost core, she tried the sole
Effectual remedy despair had left her.

Unpublished Play.

SHORTLY after the *coureurs des bois* began to carry packs
and drive dog sledges in the lands on the upper waters of
the Mississippi, there lived at the Kahpozhah village, three
leagues below the mouth of the river St Peters, an Indian
who was the cynosure of the eyes of all the maidens in his
band. This was because of his rare personal beauty; not of
form, for that is common to all Indians; but of countenance.
His skill as a hunter, and his bravery as a warrior, were
qualities more likely to recommend him to their parents;
but strange to say, the swarthy daughters of the forest
judged by the eye, as some authors have falsely asserted
their sex is in the habit of doing. The object of their admiration had feminine features, and a skin lighter by five
shades than the national complexion of the Dahcotahs, and
his hair, beside being light, was also fine and glossy. He
prided himself upon it, and suffered it to grow long; thereby
grievously scandalizing the male population of the village.

His toilet was usually adjusted with scrupulous accuracy; he changed the fashion of his paint five times per diem, and his activity in the chase enabled him to wear so much scarlet cloth, and so many beads and silver broaches, as made him the envy of those of his own age and sex. Those who imagine that the aborigines are all stoics and heroes, and those who think them solely addicted to rapine and bloodshed, and are therefore disposed to dispute the truth of this sketch of Indian character, are informed that there are fops in the forest as well as in Broadway; their intrinsic value pretty much the same in both places. The beau of the Northwest arranges his locks, and stains his face with mud, by a looking-glass three inches square. He of the city submits his equally empty head to the hand of a friseur, and powders his visage before a mirror in a gilt frame, in which he can behold his estimable person at full length. The former arrays his person with scarlet, and covers his feet with deer skin and porcupine quills; and the other gets a coat from Cox, whose needle, it is said, has pierced more hearts than the shaft of Cupid; and his feet prove the merits of Day and Martin. The only difference we see between the two is, that the savage kills deer and buffaloes, and helps to support his family, while the white man is often a useless member of society. Yet the elegance of the features of Toskatnay, (the Woodpecker) for so was our Dahcotah dandy called, and his taste in dress, were not his only merits. The war eagle's plume which completed his array, was an honorable evidence that he had acquired a right to call himself a man. In fact, beneath an almost feminine appearance, and much frivolity of manner, he concealed the real strength of his character. To the maidens who listened with glistening eyes to his discourse, and blushed when he addressed them, his motto seemed to be, 'let them look and die.' Exquisite as he

was, his soul was full of higher matters than love or gallantry. He aspired to sway the councils of his people, and to
lead them in battle, and if he condescended to please the
eyes, and tickle the ears of the women, it was only because
he knew that it was the surest way to exert an influence
over the men. He was not so much of a savage as not to
know so much of human nature. Yet he had no idea of marrying, but as it might further his views; and to the admiration of the young squaws he shut his eyes, while against
their complaints that 'no one cared for them,' he hardened
his heart.

With all his schemes, he had not calculated upon the
power of the blind god, as indeed, how should he, having
never heard of such a personage? The passion of which
that deity is a type, he scarcely believed to exist, certainly
never expected to feel. But his time was to come, and the
connexion he was destined to form, was to have a powerful
influence on his future fortunes. We are thus particular in
detailing his conduct and feelings, in order that our own
countrymen may take warning, and profit by his example.
There is a use to be found for everything, however mean,
and he who flirts with the brunettes and blondes that con-
gregate at Ballston or Saratoga, need not shame to take a
lesson from a Dahcotah heathen.

In the same village with our hero dwelt a damsel, whose
name, as it has not come down to us, being lost in the exploit
of which this true history treats, we cannot tell, and shall
therefore speak of her as Weenokhenchah Wandeeteekah
(the Brave Woman) the appellation which her tribe give
her, in relating the story. This girl never praised Toskatnay's attire, nor listened to his compliments, nor sought to
attract his attention. On the contrary, she avoided his notice.
Why she did thus, we do not pretend to explain. We pre-

tend not to expound the freaks of passion, any more than the profundities of philosophy, nor can we tell why love should choose to show himself in such a capricious manner. Let it suffice that she was thought to hate our hero until an event occurred that contradicted the supposition.

One hot day in July, a rabid wolf,[1] such as are sometimes seen in the prairies, came to pay the village a visit. The cornfields lay in his way, and as animals in his predicament never turn aside, he entered it. It so chanced that Weenokhenchah Wandeeteekah was at that time using her hoe therein, in company with other girls, while Toskatnay stood near them, cheering their labor and edifying their minds, pretty much in the style of Ranger in the Jealous Husband. The wolf made directly at him, and the girls seeing by the slaver of his jaws, what ailed him, shrieked and fled. Toskatnay, being no Yankee, could not guess the cause of their terror, and was looking about for it, when the animal was within five paces of him. Weenokhenchah Wandeeteekah alone stood firm, and seeing that he must inevitably be bitten, she advanced and clove the beast's skull with her hoe, contrary to the law in such cases made and provided by novel writers, which ordains that the gentleman shall rescue the lady from danger, and not the lady the gentleman. Having thus done, the color forsook her cheeks, and she swooned and fell.

Toskatnay, though an Indian fine gentleman, did not catch her in his arms, nor kneel by her. But he did what was as much to the purpose. He ran to the village, which was but a few rods distant, and sent the women to her assistance. With some difficulty they brought her to her senses.

From that hour his attentions, which had before been considered by the girls as common property, were confined to her. Love and gratitude prevailed, and for a while his dreams of ambition were forgotten. He wore leggins of different colors, and sat all day upon a log, playing on a flute with three holes, and singing songs in her praise. When she was gone to cut wood, he was not to be found in the village. He gave her beads and vermilion, and in short played the Indian lover in all points.

Indian courtships never last long, and ere the leaves began to fall, Weenokhenchah Wandeeteekah was the wedded wife of Toskatnay. For a time, he forgot his nature and his former prepossessions, and he even saw three war parties leave the village without testifying much concern. But these halcyon days did not last long. A mind like his could not be content with ignoble triumphs over the brute tenants of the woods and prairies. His excursions grew longer in duration, and more frequent in occurrence, and at last the poor bride saw herself totally neglected. Another cause concurred in this result. She belonged to a family that could boast no hero, no chief, nor any wise man among its members, and her husband saw with regret that he had formed an alliance that could never enhance his importance in his tribe. The devoted affection, and unwearied attention with which she endeavored to recall his heart, only filled him with disgust. Within the year she made him a father, but the new relation in which he stood, did not reclaim him. In the eyes of his people, he pursued a more honorable course: he joined every warlike excursion, obtained the praise of all by his valor; and once by his conduct and presence of mind, when the camp in which his lodge was pitched was surprised, he saved it, and turned the tables on the assailants. In consequence, he was thought worthy to be a leader of men, and became the head partizan in two successful inroads on the enemies' country.

WEENOKHENCHAH WANDEETEEKAH

He was envied as well as admired. Many there were, older than himself, who aspired to the objects of his ambition, and one in especial, without a tithe of his merits, outstripped him in his course by means of extended connections, and thwarted him in every particular. This was a man named Chahpah, (the Beaver) about forty years of age. He had nine wives, whom he supported in the usual style, and their relations were at his beck. Jealous of the growing influence of Toskatnay, he opposed his opinions, and turned the weak parts of his character into ridicule. The young warrior felt this deeply, and revolved in his own mind the means of making the number of his adherents equal to that of his rival. There were two ways presented themselves to his acceptance; the one to take to his lodge more wives; and the other, to continue to exert himself in the field. By the latter means, in the course of time, if he was not untimely cut off, he would attain the desired distinction. By the former his object would be effected more speedily.

An opportunity soon occurred to measure his strength with his fellow aspirant. The Beaver, not content with the limits of his harem, demanded in marriage the daughter of the Heron, a noted warrior. The father asked time to consider the proposal. While the matter was in abeyance, Toskatnay heard of it, and resolved not to lose so good a chance to further his own projects and mortify the man he hated. He went that very night to the Heron's lodge, lighted a match at his fire, and presented it to the eyes of the maiden. She blew it out, and after some conversation with her, carried on in whispers, he retired. In the morning he smoked with the Heron, and in plain terms asked his daughter to wife. The old man liked Toskatnay, and moreover, was not entirely satisfied that his offspring should be the tenth bride of any man. He accepted the offer without hesitation, and

175

the nuptials were solemnized forthwith, to the great displeasure of the Beaver.

It is unnecessary to say that he was not the only person displeased. Weenokhenchah Wandeeteeka thought this second marriage a poor requital of the service she had rendered her husband, and expostulated with him. But ambition swallows all other passions, as the rod of Moses swallowed the other rods, and Toskatnay had become intensely selfish. He desired her to mind her own affairs, and as polygamy is reckoned creditable by the Dahcotahs, she had no pretence to quarrel, and was obliged to submit. With an aching heart, she saw another woman take the place in Toskatnay's regard that she considered her own, and often did she retire to the woods to weep over her infant, and tell her sorrows to the rocks and trees. Quarrels will happen in the best of families, and so was seen of Toskatnay's. The two wives did not agree, as might have been expected, and the husband always took the part of the new comer. Moreover, when he joined the hunting camps, the Heron's daughter accompanied him, while Weenokhenchah Wandeeteeka was left at home; he alleging, that having a child to take care of, she could not so well be the partner of his wanderings. It was in vain that she protested against this reasoning. An Indian husband is, if he pleases, absolute, and she was obliged to acquiesce. It was not, in truth, that he preferred his new spouse, but he wished to conciliate her family. The poor malcontent had the mortification besides, to see that he neglected his child, and this was the unkindest cut of all.

At last, the second autumn after her marriage, it so happened that the band attached to Toskatnay was to move up the Mississippi, and hunt upon its head waters. As the journey was to be made by water, there was no objection

to Weenokhenchah Wandeeteeka being of the party, and
the two wives assisted each other in the necessary preparations. In the afternoon they came to the falls of St Anthony,
and carried their canoes and baggage round it. They encamped on the eastern shore just above the rapids. Such a
description as we are able to give of this celebrated cataract,
from recollection, is at the reader's service.

There is nothing of the grandeur or sublimity which the
eye aches to behold at Niagara, about the falls of St Anthony. But in wild and picturesque beauty it is perhaps
unequalled. Flowing over a tract of country five hundred
miles in extent, the river, here more than half a mile wide,
breaks into sheets of foam and rushes to the pitch over a
strongly inclined plane. The fall itself is not high, we believe only sixteen feet perpendicular, but its face is broken
and irregular. Huge slabs of rock lie scattered below, in
wild disorder. Some stand on their edges, leaning against the
ledge from which they have been disunited. Some lie piled
upon each other in the water, in inimitable confusion. A
long, narrow island divides the fall nearly in the middle. Its
eastern side is not perpendicular, but broken into three distinct leaps, below which the twisting and twirling eddies
threaten destruction to any living thing that enters them.
On the western side, in the boiling rapids below, a few rods
from the fall, stands a little island, of a few yards area;
rising steep from the waters, and covered with forest trees.
At the time of our story, its mightiest oak was the haunt of
a solitary bald eagle, that had built his eyrie on the topmost
branches, beyond the reach of man. It was occupied by his
posterity till the year eighteen hundred and twentythree,
when the time honored crest of the vegetable monarch
bowed and gave way before the wing of the northern tempest. The little islet was believed inaccessible, till two daring

privates of the fifth regiment, at very low water, waded out in the river above, and ascending the fall by means of the blocks of stone before mentioned, forded the intervening space, and were the first of their species that ever set foot upon it.

Large trunks of trees frequently drift over, and diving into the chasms of the rocks, never appear again. The loon, or great northern diver, is also, at moulting time, when he is unable to rise from the water, often caught in the rapids. When he finds himself drawn in, he struggles with fate for a while, but finding escape impossible, he faces downwards and goes over, screaming horribly. These birds sometimes make the descent unhurt. Below, the rapids foam and roar and tumble for half a mile, and then subside into the clear, gentle current that continues unbroken to the Rock River Rapids; and at high water to the Gulf of Mexico. Here too, the high bluffs which enclose the Mississippi commence. Such was the scene at the time of this authentic history, but now it is mended or marred, according to the taste of the spectator, by the works of the sons of Adam. It can shew its buildings, its saw mill, its grist mill, its cattle, and its cultivated fields. Nor is it unadorned with traditional honors. A Siou can tell you how the enemy in the darkness of midnight, deceived by the false beacons lighted by his ancestors, paddled his canoe into the rapids, from which he never issued alive. He can give a good guess too, what ghosts haunt the spot, and what spirits abide there.

To return to our story: Toskatnay and his band passed the falls and raised their lodges a few rods above the rapids. It so happened that evening, that a violent quarrel arose between the two wives, which the presence of some of the elders only, prevented from ending in cuffing and scratching. When the master of the lodge returned, he rebuked

them both, but the weight of his anger fell on Weenokhenchah Wandeeteekah, though in fact, the dispute had
been fastened on her by the other. She replied nothing to
his reproaches, but his words sunk deep into her bosom,
for he had spoken scornfully of her, saying that no Siou
had so pitiful a wife as himself. She sobbed herself to sleep,
and when the word was given in the morning to rise and
strike the tents, she was the first to rise and set about it.

While the business of embarkation was going on, it so
chanced that the child of the poor woman crawled in the
way of her rival, and received a severe kick from her. This
was too much for the mother. Vociferating such terms as
are current only at Billingsgate and in Indian camps, for
squaws are not remarkable for delicacy of expression, she
fastened upon the Heron's daughter tooth and nail, who
was not slow to return the compliment. Luckily their knives
were wrested from them by the by-standers, or one or both
would have been killed on the spot. This done, the men
laughed and the women screamed, but none offered to part
them, till Toskatnay, who was busy at the other end of the
camp, patching a birch canoe, heard the noise, and came
and separated them by main force. He was highly indignant
at an occurrence that must bring ridicule upon him. The
Heron's daughter he reproved, but Weenokhenchah Wandeeteekah he struck with his paddle repeatedly, and threatened to put her away. This filled the cup of her misery to
overflowing: she looked at him indignantly and said, 'You
shall never reproach me again.' She took up her child and
moved away, but he, thinking it no more than an ordinary
fit of sullenness, paid no attention to her motions.

His unkindness at this time had the effect of confirming
a project that she had long revolved in her mind, and she
hastened to put it in execution. She embarked in a canoe

with her child, and pushing from the shore, entered the rapids before she was perceived. When she was seen, both men and women, among whom her husband was the most earnest, followed her on the shore, entreating her to land ere it was too late. The river was high, so that it was impossible to intercept her, yet Toskatnay, find his entreaties of no avail, would have thrown himself into the water to reach the canoe, had he not been withheld by his followers. Had this demonstration of interest occurred the day before, it is possible that her purpose would have been forgotten. As it was, she shook her open hand at him in scorn, and held up his child for him to gaze at. She then began to sing, and her song ran thus.

'A cloud has come over me. My joys are turned to grief. Life has become a burden too heavy to bear, and it only remains to die.

'The Great Spirit calls, I hear his voice in the roaring waters. Soon, soon, shall they close over my head, and my song shall be heard no more.

'Turn thine eyes hither, proud chief. Thou art brave in battle, and all are silent when thou speakest in council. Thou hast met death, and hast not been afraid.

'Thou hast braved the knife, and the axe; and the shaft of the enemy has passed harmless by thee.

'Thou hast seen the warrior fall. Thou hast heard him speak bitter words with his last breath.

'But hast thou ever seen him dare more than a woman is about to do?

'Many speak of thy deeds. Old and young echo thy praises. Thou art the star the young men look upon, and thy name shall be long heard in the land.

'But when men tell of thy exploits, they shall say, "He slew his wife also!" Shame shall attend thy memory.

'I slew the ravenous beast that was about to destroy thee. I planted thy corn, and made thee garments and moccasins.

'When thou wast an hungred, I gave thee to eat, and when thou wast athirst, I brought thee cold water. I brought thee a son also, and I never disobeyed thy commands.

'And this is my reward! Thou hast laughed at me. Thou hast given me bitter words, and struck me heavy blows.

'Thou hast preferred another before me, and thou hast driven me to wish for the approach of death, as for the coming winter.[2]

'My child, my child! Life is a scene of sorrow. I had not the love of a mother, did I not snatch thee from the woes thou must endure.

'Adorn thy wife with ornaments of white metal, Toskatnay. Hang beads about her neck. Be kind to her, and see if she will ever be to thee as I.'

So saying, or rather singing, she went over the fall with her child, and they were seen no more.

✦ ✦ ✦

One year precisely from this time, Toskatnay followed the track of a bear which he had wounded, to the brink of the falls. He halted opposite the spot where Weenokhenchah Wandeeteekah had disappeared, and gazed on the foaming rapid. What was passing in his mind it is impossible to say. He had reached the summit of his ambition. He was acknowledged a chief, and he had triumphed over the Beaver and the Chippeways. But her for whose sake he had spurned the sweetest flowers of life, true love and fond fidelity, had proved faithless to him, and fled to the Missouri with another man. He had nothing farther to look for, no higher eminence to attain, and his reflections were like those of him who wept because he had no more worlds to conquer. A strange occurrence roused him from his reverie. A snow white doe, followed by a fawn of the same color, came suddenly within the sphere of his vision; so suddenly, that they seemed to him to come out of the water. Such a sight had never before been seen by any of his tribe. He stood rooted to the ground. He who had never feared the face of man, trembled like an aspen with superstitious terror. The animals, regardless of his presence, advanced slowly towards him, and passed so near that he might have touched them with his gun. They ascended the bank and he lost sight of them. When they were fairly out of sight, he recovered from the shock, and stretching out his arms after them, conjured them to return. Finding his adjurations vain, he rushed up the bank, but could see nothing of them, which was the more remarkable that the prairie had just been burned over, and for a mile there was no wood or inequality in the ground, that could have concealed a much smaller animal than a deer.

He returned to his lodge, made a solemn feast, at which his relatives were assembled, and sung his death song. He told his wondering auditors that he had received a warning to prepare for his final change. He had seen the spirits of his wife and child. No one presumed to contradict his opinion. Whether founded in reason or not, it proved true in point of fact. Three weeks after, the camp was attacked by the Chippeways. They were repulsed, but Toskatnay, and he only, was killed.

No stone tells where he lies, nor can any of the Dahcotahs shew the spot. His deeds are forgotten, or at best, faintly remembered; thus showing 'on what foundation stands the warrior's pride;' but his wife still lives in the memory of her people, who speak of her by the name of Weenokhenchah Wandeeteekah, or the Brave Woman.

LA BUTTE DES MORTS

The gates of mercy shall be all shut up;
And the flesh'd soldier – rough and hard of heart –
In liberty of bloody hand, shall range
With conscience wide as hell; mowing like grass
Your fresh fair virgins, and your flowering infants.
Henry V.

LA BUTTE DES MORTS * is, as its name implies, a little hill at
the confluence of the Fox and Wolf rivers, and in the angle
between them. From its summit the voyageur may have a
view of the lake of Graise d'Ours to the east, and of a long
reach of the Fox River, and many a rood of fat prairie land
to the westward. When he is tired of beholding the prospect, he may descend to the water side, and amuse himself
by shooting at the blue winged teal, the most delicious of
the feathered creation, as they fly past him in myriads. He
will do well not to fire if they fly high, for they are fattened
on the wild rice of the river, and usually burst open on
falling. Or if he is given to moralizing, he may go to the
field between the hill and the woods, and speculate on the
bones that have been whitening there for more than the
age of man.

* The Hillock of the Dead.

LA BUTTE DES MORTS

'There the slow blind worm leaves his slime
On the fleet limbs that mock'd at time.
The knot grass fetters there the hand
That once could burst an iron band.'

The last time the author was on the spot, a pit had just been dug on the top of the hillock, and in it were put, with shrieks and howling, the remains of a noted Winnebago brave, whose war cry had been heard at Tippecanoe and the battle of the Thames. At the head of the grave was planted a cedar post, on which the rude heraldry of the natives had emblazoned the rank and achievements of the deceased. Three black emblems represented three American scalps. Let us be forgiven, reader, for dwelling on the place. Silent and solitary as it now is, it is the scene of events that mayhap it will please thee to hear related. Alas, that strife and slaughter, and the extermination of a native tribe should be pleasant things for us to write, or for thee to read.

About the year seventeen hundred and twentyfive, the principal village of the Saque nation stood on the Butte des Morts. Here the Saques were accustomed to stop traders passing into the Indian country, and to exact of them a tribute; as the Winnebagoes have since done. The traders submitted with reluctance; but there was no help. At last, emboldened by impunity, the savages increased their demands; so that a total cessation of the trade was likely to ensue; and bickerings arose between the plunderers and the plundered. In the autumn of seventeen hundred and twenty-four a hot headed young Canadian trader refused to pay the customary tribute, and severely wounded a Saque who attempted to take it forcibly. He was instantly shot dead and scalped, and his boat was pillaged. Some accounts say that his men were killed too, but this part of the story, though probable, is not certain. As no notice of the affair was taken that winter by the authorities commissioned by the Grand Monarque the insolence of the Saques increased greatly, and they imagined in their ignorance that the French stood in fear of them. But in this they reckoned without their host, or rather without Jean St Denis Moran.

The Sieur Moran, a man of a decided and energetic character, held an office in the French Indian Department. He was, moreover, an old campaigner and had been at Friedlingen and Malplaquet. When tidings of what had happened were communicated to him at Quebec, his mustachios twisted upward for very anger, and he swore, sachristie! and mort de sa vie! that the Saques should repent their presumption. In order to the fulfilment of this laudable vow, he demanded of the commanding officer at Quebec that three hundred regulars should be placed at his disposal, and the request was granted. With these troops he proceeded to Michilimacinac, where he remained till the first of October, to mature his plans.

Here he caused eight or ten Macinac boats to be constructed. For fear that some of our readers may not know what a Macinac boat is, we will try to inform them. It is a large, strong built, flat bottomed boat, pointed at both ends, and peculiarly adapted to the Indian trade; in which it is often necessary to ascend and descend dangerous rapids. It is always furnished with a *parlas*, or sheet of painted canvass, large enough to protect the lading from the weather. But this equipage was never used for the purpose for which the Sieur Moran designed it before nor since.

Furthermore, he provided many kegs of French brandy, and all things being in readiness, proceeded from island to island across the head of Lake Michigan to Green Bay. Here he might have speculated on the phenomenon of a tide in fresh water, as Mr Schoolcraft and other learned philosophers have done; but different matters occupied his mind. He encamped, and sent a messenger to the Hillock of the Dead to require the instant surrender of all persons concerned in the late breach of the peace, as well as reparation for all robberies and injuries committed by the offending tribe. The Saque chief laughed the summons to scorn. 'Tell our father,' said he, 'that the Saques are men. Tell him too, that even if he should in earnest be disposed to punish his children, they have legs to take them out of the way, if he should prove too hard for them.' Having made this lofty speech, he looked around with much self-complacency, and when the concurrence of the audience had been signified, he added, 'I am a wise man.' Had he foreseen the consequences of his words, it is probable his opinion of his own wisdom would have suffered some diminution.

He smoked a pipe with the disconcerted envoy, gave him to eat, and desired him to make the best of his way back to whence he came.

On receiving this answer, M. Moran convened a band of Menomenies that had encamped in the vicinity, and whose chief, unless tradition deceives us, was called Auskinnaw-wawwitsh. To him the old soldier communicated his intention of bringing the Saques to condign punishment, and requested his assistance. 'Father,' replied Auskinnawwaw-witsh, 'what you say is good. You are a wise man. We have wished to see you a great while, because we are very poor, and we know that you are rich. We have few guns, and no ammunition or tobacco, and our women have no clothing. Above all, we want a little of your *milk*,* to make us weep for our deceased relations.[1] So kind a father will give us all these things. But wisdom requires that we should deliberate on your proposal. Father, a little of your milk will brighten

* Ardent spirits.

186

our understandings.' And to all these sayings the inferior Menomenies assented with a grunt, or groan of applause, for it might be called either.

M. Moran was obliged to acknowledge the justice of these axioms. He supplied the immediate wants of the savages, and gave them a keg of brandy. The consequence was, a frightful riot of three days duration, in which three of the intended allies were killed. Auskinnawwawwitsh required a further delay of three days, 'to cry for the slain;' and he even suggested that a little more *milk* would make the tears flow faster, and more readily. To this hint, M. Moran returned a peremptory refusal. In the mean while, the crafty Menomenie sent to the Saques a warning of their danger; but they persisted in believing that they would not be attacked, and that they should be able to defend themselves if they were.

After the mourning had terminated, Auskinnawwaw-witsh announced the result of his deliberations. 'If my father,' said he, 'will give us the land the Saques now live upon, and if he will make us a handsome present, and if he will give us more of his milk, we will assist him.' To all which postulates the Sieur Moran agreed, only stipulating that the payment should take place after the work was done.

M. Moran told the Menomenies that he should want them after two sleeps,[2] and dismissed them. Then he loaded one of his boats with merchandize, not forgetting a goodly quantity of brandy, and gave her in charge to a non-commissioned officer and four Canadian boatmen. They received his instructions to ascend the river to the Butte des Morts, and there suffer the boat to be pillaged without resistance or remonstrance. They were then to proceed a few miles further, encamp, and wait for further orders.

His orders were obeyed to the letter. The Saques plundered the boat, and drinking the brandy, were soon in no condition for attack or defence. Now was the time for Moran to act, and fearfully did he avail himself of it.

A mile below the Hillock of the Dead, and on the same side of the river, is a stream, just wide enough to allow a Macinac boat to enter, a few rods. To this the Sieur Moran succeeded in getting, at noon, the day after his advanced boat had passed. Here, out of sight of the village, he landed his Menomenies and half of his soldiers. He ordered them to gain the woods in the rear of the Saques, and there wait till the firing commenced in front. When sufficient time had elapsed for his orders to be obeyed, the remaining troops couched in the bottoms of the boats, with their arms ready, and were covered with the canvass before mentioned. This done, he put off, and the crews, disguised like boatmen, rowed up the river, singing this ditty, which is still popular in the North-west.

> Tous les printemps,
> Tant de nouvelles,
> Tous les amants
> Changent de maitresses.
> Le bon vin m'endort;
> L'amour me reveille.
>
> Tous les amants
> Changent de maitresses.
> Qu'ils changent qui voudront,
> Pour moi je garde la mienne
> Le bon vin m'endort;
> L'amour me reveille.

They were soon within ken of the village. The Saques, not expecting the entertainment prepared for them, rejoiced at the sight. They were all drunk, or at least, suffering the effects of intoxication. 'Here come the traders to supply us with fire water and blankets,' they said to each other; 'Let us make haste to the spoil.' The women screamed with delight, the children bawled in concert, and the host of dogs added to the uproar. Young and old hurried to the water side.

As the foremost boat came opposite the crowd of dark forms on shore, a dozen balls were fired athwart her course. None struck her, but the proximity was sufficiently intimate to show that her further progress would be attended with danger.[3] 'Scie, scie partout,' cried the frightened steersman, and the rowers backed water simultaneously. M. Moran rose, and commanded the interpreter to ask what they wanted. 'Skootay wawbo, skootay wawbo,' (fire water) shouted five hundred voices. 'Shore,' said Moran, and as the other boats were now alongside, they all touched the ground together.

'I let you all know, that if you touch anything in the boats, you will be sorry for it,' cried the interpreter. But an hundred hands were already dragging them farther aground, and his voice was drowned by the clamor. 'Help! help! thieves! thieves!' cried Moran, in a full deep tone. At once the coverings were thrown off, and an hundred and fifty soldiers were brought to view, as if by the spell of an enchanter. 'Fire!' cried Moran. The muskets flashed, and twenty Saques fell dead where they stood. To the poor misguided savages, the number of their enemies seemed treble the reality. They fled precipitately to their village, to prepare for defence. Two minutes sufficed for the troops to form and pursue.

The Saques found at their lodges another and more terrible enemy than the French. A Menomenie had entered the place unsuspected, and set it on fire on the windward side.[4] The wind was high, and in a few moments the frail bark dwellings were wrapped in a sheet of flame. The Saques then retreated toward the woods in the rear, one and all. Ere they were reached, Moran's reserve met them, and they were placed between two fires. Then burst forth one heart-rending, agonized shriek; and the devoted Saques prepared to defend themselves with the courage of despair. Ball and bayonet now began their bloody work. The victims were hemmed in on every side. The Menomenies precluded the possibility of escape on the flanks, and the knife and glittering tomahawk cut off what the sword had spared. The inhabitants of the village fought with unshrinking courage. Few asked quarter; none received it. They perished, man, woman, and child. The horrors of the dreadful tragedy may not be repeated, yet in less than an hour it had been enacted, and the actors were gone. A heap of smoking ruins, and a few houseless dogs, howling after the dead bodies of their masters, were the only objects the sad hillock presented. But five Saque families, that had been absent at the time, survived the slaughter; the poor remains of what had been a considerable tribe. They left their country, and emigrated to the Mississippi, where they incorporated with the Foxes, and where their descendants remain to this day.

It is due to the Sieur Moran to say, that he did all he might to mitigate the fate of his victims. But his voice was exerted in vain. Victorious troops are seldom merciful in the field, and the Menomenies would not be restrained. There was no room for rapine, for there was nothing to take; but Lust, and red handed Murder, stalked openly over the Butte des Morts on that day. From this carnage of the Saques it derived its name.

That evening, Auskinnawwawwitsh appeared before the Sieur Moran, and demanded the promised recompense. 'Let what you have seen be a warning to you,' said the leader. 'If your people, now masters of the soil, offend in the same sort, be assured, they shall drink of the same cup that the Saques have drained.'

PINCHON

Part 1

Well does he love the cork to draw,
And deep the circling wine cup quaffs;
But scorns religion and the law;
At God's own chosen priest he laughs.

His is the spirit that delights
To drag the wild wolf from his den;
To spurn the altar and its rites,
And trample on his fellow men.
New Ballad.

ANTOINE PINCHON was one of the first traders who pushed
their fortunes among the Dahcotahs. At that time the Indian
trade was profitable. Packs of beaver could then be obtained more easily than single skins now. Buffaloes and deer
abounded, and muskrats and martins were as plenty as mice.
The times have changed: the buffalo has receded hundreds
of miles; a beaver is a curiosity to a Dahcotah, and the best
hunter finds it difficult to collect a pack of rats in a season.
Yet it was not the thirst of gain that drew Pinchon into the
country; but the love of adventure and excitement, acting
upon his mind, as nettles might have operated on his flesh.

He was born near Montreal, of parents of pure Norman
descent. In his childhood, no rod, no reproof, could restrain
him from the exercise of his own free will. If he did not
learn to read and write, it was not wholly his fault, for his

PINCHON

father was a true Canadian, and held such Yankee notions
as schools in religious abhorrence. As the youth grew in
stature, he grew in iniquity also: he was a rough rider of
races on Sundays, between mass and vespers; the first at the
cabaret, and the last out of it, and by the time he was twenty he was the dreaded bully of the whole seigneurie, and
had qualified himself for the gallies, or even the gallows.
Totally ignorant; scarcely knowing right from wrong; not
a day passed in which he did not make his father's heart
ache. An intrigue with a damsel, toward whom he stood
within the prohibited degrees of affinity, finally determined
his parents to get rid of him, before worse came of it.

Among his comrades and boon companions, the voyageurs returned from the frozen north and northwest, stood
highest in his esteem. The blue capot, with the capuchon
negligently thrown back, the garnished moccasins, and the
bright sash, the usual costume of the coureurs des bois,
were certain passports to his good will. With these hardy
travellers he loved to talk, and still better to drink, while
their speech was of the wonders they had and had not seen.
He was never weary of hearing them dilate upon

—— 'Antres vast, and deserts idle,
And of the Cannibals that each other eat,
The Anthropophagi, and men whose heads
Do grow beneath their shoulders.'

For such tales would he exchange his time and coin; and
he had long resolved to become one of the class he so much
admired.

He was therefore delighted, when his father, after a long
lecture, during which he yawned most irreverently, proposed to him, as a last chance of amendment, to engage
with M. Louis Provencal, who wanted men to winter with
him on the river St Peters. He acceded to the proposal without hesitation, and accompanied his parent to the trader's

lodgings, and was straightway hired at five hundred livres per annum. *

We do not hold up this worthy as an object of admiration, nor do we ask that he should even be pitied; but as the story of his fortunes may aid our purpose to elucidate Indian manners and character, we have thought fit to communicate them to the world.

Had we the pen of Plutarch, or the greater Sir Walter, we see no reason why the exploits of the hero, or rather scoundrel of our story, should not be as much admired as the feats of Romulus, or Rob Roy, or indeed any ruffian and robber of ancient or modern times.

To return to our argument: after receiving the benediction of his father, and what he valued more, a small purse of coined silver, stamped with the effigies of the most puissant Louis, Pinchon embarked with six of his compeers on board M. Provencal's boat, and they left the quay singing the air from which Mr Moore took the hint of that elegant misnomer, 'The Canadian Boat Song.' Thus did the ditty run.

> Dans mon chemin j'ai rencontré
> Trois cavaliers bien montées
>   Lon, Lon, laridon daine,
>   Lon, Lon, laridon dai.

> Trois cavaliers bien montées,
> L'un à cheval, et l'autre à pied.
>   Lon, lon, laridon daine,
>   Lon, lon, laridon dai.

They soon reached 'Utawa's tide,' and as long as they were in the vicinity of the settlements, the bourgeois allowed his men to stop at pleasure, and fed them well with pork and beans, but once in the wilderness, there was an end to this treatment. They now only stopped at the end of the pipe or league [1] and their food was hard Indian corn and

* Six to a dollar.

tallow, a quart of one and an ounce of the other, per diem. Yet upon this fodder, they retained their health and spirits. As nothing important occurred in this stage of the journey, we shall not pretend to give an account of it. It may not be amiss, though, to state, that before the boat reached the portage at Lake Nipissing, Pinchon had fought and beaten every man in the company, M. Provencal excepted.

They coasted the northern shore of lake Huron, sometimes getting nearly out of sight of land, and crossing from one island to another, setting the sail when the wind was fair, and plying the oars when it failed. On one occasion the courage and presence of mind of our hero saved the boat, and the lives of all on board. The boat was going steadily before a fresh breeze, about four leagues from shore, when it struck upon a sunken reef of rocks. A hole, big enough to have sunk a first rate, was beaten in its bottom, yet it rubbed heavily over, and got clear. The water rushed in fearfully, yet five of the boatmen, as well as the bourgeois, instead of exerting themselves for her relief, betook themselves to their patron saints for succor. Joe Le Duc, the steersman, almost, if not altogether as great a reprobate as Pinchon, was not so absurd, yet he dared not let go the helm, as the boat might have broached to in the swell. He called to our hero to thrust his bedding into the hole, and his voice was heard, and promptly obeyed. Pinchon stuffed three blankets into the leak which was about to let in fate, and called to the rest to keep the boat free, with bowls and platters. 'Les sacrés coquins!' said he to Le Duc, 'as if God or the saints would help fools and cowards!' The water was kept under till they reached an island, under the lee of which the boat was unladen, hauled ashore, and repaired.

They crossed the head of Lake Michigan, and traversing

the opaque waters of Green Bay, arrived at the rapids of Fox river. Here Pinchon demanded of M. Provencal, that his wages should be put on an equality with those of the old hands, in consideration of his superior strength and usefulness. He had carried burthens, he said, at the several portages, of double the weight the rest could endure, and he had walked in the rapids and pushed the boat, where they had been unable to stand. If the bourgeois did not think proper to comply, he declared that he would desert, and find his way back to Macinac as he might. Rather than lose so valuable a hand, M. Provencal yielded, though the demand was mutinous, and without a precedent.

Arrived at the eastern end of Winnebago Lake, the boat was prevented from crossing by a head wind. It was now the latter part of September, and they had ample time to admire this beautiful sheet of water, as it lay embosomed between its lovely shores, and covered with ducks, geese, and countless flocks of snow white swans and pelicans. Their attention was, however, withdrawn from these things, by the arrival of three hundred savages in their war paint; the inhabitants of the neighboring Winnebago village. They swarmed about the boat, and were clamorous for the accustomed tribute, paid by traders on passing the lake, and seemed much disposed to help themselves. M. Provencal gave them something, but they were not satisfied with his liberality. The plunder of the boat seemed inevitable, and it was more than probable that the extermination of the crew would follow.

At this moment, Pinchon coolly asked M. Provencal if he wished him to save his boat, and as he stood irresolute, resolved to do that service, whether it was desired or not. Chippeway is the court language of all the northwestern tribes east of the Mississippi, and most of these unwelcome visitors understood it. So did Le Duc, who had wintered three times at Lake Superior. Our hero desired him to ask the Winnebagoes what they wanted, and the reply was, gunpowder. To work he went, and having placed all the powder kegs in the centre of the boat, in the midst of the cases of bullets, he told Le Duc to desire them to draw near. They came to him; some producing their powder horns, others their calico shirts, and in short, everything that might contain the nitre. 'Now, Le Duc,' said Pinchon, raising his voice, 'tell them to let their bravest man come forward, and take what he wants. Tell them that he who puts his hand on anything here, does it at his peril.' With these words he knocked in the head of one of the kegs, cocked his gun, and buried its muzzle in the powder.

His words were not understood by the Indians, but his motions were. In an instant all was outcry and confusion: never was such a rout seen. Those who sat on the boat plunged overboard, as did those alongside. They dived, and swam away, faster than Indians ever swam before or since. Those on shore fled on the wings of terror. Let them not, however, be branded with cowardice. Not many of these people would have shrunk from death, if duly warned. But the shock was too sudden for their nerves. Indeed, it must be allowed that to scale the skies mounted on a fiery dragon can be no very pleasing prospect to any one. The Indians gained their village with all possible expedition, and no more was seen of them.

The wind fell with the sun, and the boat proceeded. From that day a warm friendship between Le Duc and Pinchon took its date. Similarity of disposition and natural gifts cemented it. M. Provencal rued the day he had enlisted the one or the other; for they not only tyrannized over the men, but gained the ascendency over him. They leagued together for every kind of mischief, treated him with contempt, and would only obey his orders when they tallied with their own inclinations.

To return: the party proceeded onward, passed the portage, descended the Wisconsin and ascended the Mississippi to the Grand Encampment. Here they found a great body of Dahcotahs assembled. These had, though so early in the season, so large a quantity of furs, that M. Provencal thought it worth his while to stop and collect them. This could not be done without considerable delay, as the ownership of the skins was to be decided by a race, upon the result of which the greater part of them were staked, and the competitors had not all arrived.

Here, then, they remained two days, gambling, fishing, and shooting ducks and geese. The third morning the drum beat, and the racers, all active men, prepared for the trial. This was done by stripping to the skin, and rubbing their limbs with bears' oil. Never have so many manly and symmetrical forms been seen in any other part of the world. Yet here it excited no attention. Beauty of figure is so common among the Dahcotahs, that the absence of it would be the wonder.

About two miles distant, the post was set up. The racers were to touch it, turn, and return to the place from whence they started; where they were to touch another post. The wagers on the race were many. When all was nearly ready, an old man approached with a pack of beaver on his back, followed by his son, to where the whites were standing; and asked if any of them were disposed to try their speed. The challenger was a Yankton, and his boy was the swiftest runner in that sept. They had come all the way from Lac au Travers to try if any of the Munday Wawkantons (People of the Lake) might compete with those of the prairies. Le Duc brought his gun, and then untied the pack of furs. Taking out ten of the best skins, he laid them by the side of the fowling piece, and told the ancient that he was willing to run with his son on that wager. The Yankton smiled, and selecting ten more of his beaver added them to his stake, telling the Canadian that the bet should stand so. The stakes were put into the hands of M. Provencal: Le Duc stripped, and took his place beside his challenger in the line of racers.

An elder gave the signal for starting, by dropping a French flag from the end of a pole. Then were heard screams of delight from the women, as their sons, husbands, or lovers gained in the contest. The old men shouted, excited to the last degree, and the dogs howled; some of them followed their masters, and getting between the legs of the runners, entangled and threw them down, but none appeared to mind it; they rose again and strained every nerve to regain the lost ground.

At the first start, several ran abreast, and it was difficult to say which, of half a dozen, had the advantage. After the first half mile, the young Yankton was ahead, Le Duc breathing on his shoulder. The Indian exerted himself to the utmost for the honor of his band, conscious that the eyes of all were upon him. He gained the post first, seized it with his left hand, swung himself lightly round, and traced his course backward.

'So swift Camilla scours along the plain.'

But he had put forth his power too soon, and before he had run over half the ground from the distance post, it was observed that his speed slackened. Le Duc now ran abreast with him, trying to increase his confusion by asking him if a Yankton could run no faster, and the like taunts. When within three hundred yards of the goal, the white man darted ahead and came bounding to the end of the course like a race horse, leaving the Indian fifteen paces behind him.

The others arrived in quick succession, and the stakes were given up to the winners. The Yankton took the whole pack from which the beaver had been drawn, and laying it at the feet of Le Duc, said, 'I was never outrun before; and I did not think there was a man alive could do it. Take all my furs, for you have won them fairly.'

But to show that there were some things in which he could outdo all the white men that ever lived, he seized his bow and quiver. Sending the first arrow into the air, he loosened ten more from the string before the first touched the ground; and he looked at Le Duc, as who should say, 'beat that if you can.'

Pinchon demanded what the Indian had said, and being informed, cried, 'tell him, Le Duc, that there are two men living who can beat him. If he accepts the challenge, give him back his beaver, and I will put my gun against them, and run with him tomorrow morning, as soon as he gets rested.'

These words being interpreted, the young savage looked inquiringly at his father, who in his turn looked at Pinchon, and said, 'he is too big to run well.' The youth then accepted the defiance, and proposed to start instantly, declaring that he was not at all fatigued. Pinchon would not believe it, and persisted in remaining tranquil till the next day.

On the morrow, the same spectators who had witnessed the first race assembled to behold the second. Pinchon demanded four guns of M. Provencal, and having obtained them, appeared on the ground. The savages asked what he meant to do, and when he declared that he intended to run with the guns on his shoulders, a general burst of laughter proclaimed their utter scorn of his presumption. Le Duc too, entreated him to lay aside all thoughts of such a contest, but Pinchon desired him to mind his own affairs.

Without stripping, and with two guns on each shoulder,[2] he started, and beat his rival with even more ease than Le Duc had done. The laughing was now on the other side. The mortified Yankton looked around, expecting another white man to come forward to dispute the honors of the race with him. He stood sullen, with his hand on the handle of his knife, prepared to plunge it in the body of any that should offer. No one thought of the thing, and he vented his disappointment in words, which, luckily for him and all concerned, Pinchon did not comprehend.

When M. Provencal had made the most of his market, the boat moved up the river, and in due time arrived at Rocher Blanc, on the St Peters, where the voyageurs erected buildings for the winter. In the course of the season Pinchon acquired enough of the Sioux tongue for common purposes, and learned all the tricks of the Indian trade to perfection. Nothing worth recording happened at the station; but towards the spring, our hero and his friend, judging from the deportment of M. Provencal, that he intended to withhold their wages, and conscious that their behaviour had deserved it, burst into his apartment one day when all the rest were absent. Holding a cocked pistol to his breast, Pinchon compelled him to write and sign a certificate that they were the two best men he ever had under him, as also a document recommending Pinchon, as a person deserving the trust and confidence of all persons concerned in the Indian trade; and also competent to manage an outfit. Possessed of these papers, the friends stole a canoe and deserted; leaving their wives; for they had not failed to take unto themselves wives, to console themselves as they might. They soon reached old Michilimacinac, subsisting themselves on the way by their guns. On the strength of M. Provencal's recommendation, M. La Salle, the superintendent of the depot, furnished Pinchon with an assortment of Indian goods, a boat, and men to take it into the Indian country. Le Duc was also engaged as an interpreter, with a handsome salary.

Yet he could not depart from Michilimacinac without playing a prank that had nearly deprived him of the fruits of his villany. In spite of the remonstrances of his interpreter, he resolved to personate a priest who was expected from Montreal. Having procured a cassock, he caused it to be given out that the Reverend M. Badin had arrived; as indeed, he was expected before night. In his disguise our hero heard the confessions of all the voyageurs who were not in the secret. He possessed himself of their private histories, assigned them penance and received fees. Yet was he not content without playing a practical joke on the priest himself.

There was in the settlement a mangeur de lard, or pork eater, as the raw engagés are called, just arrived from Quebec. This poor fellow, as ignorant as his class in general, and being naturally none of the brightest, applied to the confessional of the supposed clergyman. The sham apostle magnified some peccadilloes that he confessed into mortal sins, and read him a sharp and severe lecture. This edifying discourse he seasoned with scraps of Latin, which he had picked up at mass, and which sunk the deeper into the penitent's mind that he did not comprehend a syllable of them. Finally addressing the simpleton by the title of 'vile sinner,' he allotted him a penance. It was to go into the fur magazine, and sit on the top of the packs till midnight. While there, Pinchon told him that the devil would appear, in the disguise of a priest, and entice him to come down. 'But mind, my son,' said Pinchon, 'that you do not consent; for if you do, you will be torn to pieces.' The fellow assured him that no consideration should induce him to descend, and having received his blessing, departed. In the evening, the real Simon Pure, the true priest, arrived. Having divested himself of his disguise, Pinchon called on him, paid his respects, and informed him that there was a man in the fur store, who appeared to be troubled in mind on account of his sins, and it was feared that he would lay violent hands on himself. Very willing to do a good action, M. Badin repaired to the spot. At the sight of him the pork eater trembled from head to foot, and his hair bristled upright. The following dialogue ensued.

M. Badin. What is the matter, my good friend? Do you not know me?

Voyageur. Ye — yes. I know y — you — we — well enough. God be merciful un — unto me a sinner! For my sins, I — I know you.

M. Bad. If you know me, come down, and tell me what ails you.

Voy. No, no. I know better than that. Good M. Badin told me what to do — blessings on him!

M. Bad. Why, my good man, my name is Badin; I am sure I never told you anything.

Voy. Ay, ay, just so. I was told how it would be. Bah! how hot it is. How he smells of brimstone.

M. Bad. Is the man mad? Do you smell brimstone already? come down; put yourself into my hands, and it may be, that I can save you from it.

Voy. Put myself into your hands! No doubt you would be glad to carry me off, but I don't choose such company. Come down — thank you, Monsieur Devil, as much as if I did. They call me a fool; but I'm not so simple as that, neither. Sancta Maria, ora pro nobis!

M. Bad. Come down you wretch; I lose all patience with you. Do you call a servant of the Holy Catholic Church a devil! Come down, I say; come down.

Voy., crossing himself. St Thomas be good to me! St Peter hear me! Pray, sir, if it is not too much trouble, let me see your foot.

M. Bad., holding out his foot. There is my foot, you foolish fellow; what do you want to see it for?

Voy. The cloven hoof may be concealed in that leather, as the tail is under the cassock, no doubt. Please to take off your boot and stocking.

M. Bad., pulling off his boots. There, wretch, are both my feet. Do you take me for the Devil still, you irreverent knave? Will you come down?

Voy. No, I will not, if you stay there till morning. The long and short of it is, Monsieur Satan, I know you, and I will not be persuaded. So you may as well be off, for here I am resolved to stay. O, for a little holy water to throw upon you.

M. Bad. Then I'll fetch you down.

Voy., seizing a fish spear. Avaunt! Mount not here, at your peril. Stand off, I say. In the name of our Saviour, stand off.

Finding his skull impenetrable, M. Badin left him to the enjoyment of his imaginery triumph. A short inquiry served to explain the matter. The other voyageurs who had been tricked, had discovered who the rogue that had tricked them of their money was. Some laughed, but more were highly indignant at the deception. M. La Salle, a strict and pious Catholic, was greatly scandalized at this treatment of all he held sacred, and he told M. Badin he would deprive

Pinchon of the outfit he had furnished, being convinced that heaven would never prosper the labors of such a sacrilegious wretch. With this sentiment the priest agreed, but it had been better, not expressed so loudly. Joe Le Duc was passing under the window, and hearing the name of his comrade, stopped to listen, and learned the intention of the superintendent, which he immediately communicated to Pinchon. The wind being fair, that gentleman assembled his men, embarked, and set sail. Six days carried him to the foot of Winnebago lake. The Indians here waited upon him with every demonstration of respect, and if they remembered the experiment he had made on their courage the season before, it was to his advantage.

As to the Mangeur de Lard, on whom he had inflicted so whimsical a penance, the fright threw him into a fever and delirium, in which he raved of Satan and Monsieur Badin. When he at last recovered, he could never be persuaded that he had not seen his infernal majesty; nor could he ever after look upon M. Badin without shuddering.

In less than a month Pinchon arrived at Lake Pepin and set up his winter quarters at Point aux Sables. He gave out the greater part of his goods, as is common in the Indian trade, to different savages on credit; for which he was to receive payment in the spring, when their hunt should be over. Le Duc kept his accounts. They sent for their wives, but did not long keep them, for they put them away and took others; according to the custom of Indian traders, before and since; caring little what might become of the children that had been born unto them in their absence. This was repeated several times in the course of the winter, for Indians are very willing to give their daughters to white men, knowing that they will not be compelled to labor.

The time did not hang heavy on their hands, for they spent it in gaming, fishing, hunting the deer, and other amusements of a wintering ground.

Part 2

No, nothing melts his stony heart,
Soft Pity never mov'd his mind;
All human ties he rends apart,
A ruthless tiger to his kind.

M. Provencal arrived at the lake a short time after Pinchon, and passing his house without stopping, proceeded to the mouth of the river St Croix, where he intended to winter. Here he stationed himself, doing Pinchon all the damage he could; visiting the camps where his debtors were hunting, and trying his best to persuade them to dishonesty, in which he was frequently successful. Pinchon retaliated in kind, and these worthies used their liquor freely to corrupt the Indians; both well knowing that they might be bribed to any act of knavery or outrage, by such means. This is the real operation of alcohol, in its various forms, upon the remote tribes; they do not get enough to do them any physical injury, but in the way it is used, it weakens or destroys the moral principle in their breasts.

As it happened, it was so used by M. Provencal, as to render Pinchon very unpopular with the Sioux. One of his debtors had been seduced to defraud him, and sell the produce of his chase to Provencal. In an evil hour for the unhappy savage, he went to the house of his injured creditor, arrayed in all his ill gotten finery. Pinchon had heard of his behavior, and when he appeared before him in a new white blanket, with scarlet leggins, and his ears stretched with the weight of their silver ornaments, the Frenchman could scarce suppress his wrath. He however curbed his temper long enough to ask the Indian what he had done with the produce of his hunt.

'I had so few furs,' he replied, 'that I was ashamed to bring them to you; I therefore sold them to the Wopayton (trader) up the river.'

'You are a dog,' said Pinchon. 'You are worse than a dog. The blanket you have on, belongs to me, and so does everything about you. You bought them with my beaver. I care not for the value, as you shall presently see; but I will not be so treated.' So speaking, he tore the blanket from his back, and cast it into the fire, holding it down with his foot, till it was utterly spoiled. The savage saw it consume with a smile of bitter contempt, and said, 'the Frenchman loved his goods too well; his heart was hurt by little things.' Had he held his peace, it had been better for him; for Pinchon, enraged at his coolness, seized him with the grasp of a giant, and wresting from him the knife he had drawn to defend himself, cut off both his ears with it, close to his head, earrings and all. Holding the silver up before his eyes, he upbraided him with his knavery, and then sent them after the blanket. When he had in some degree assuaged his choler, he thrust the man, to whom he had shown so little mercy, out of doors, with insult and violence.

Le Duc, who, ruffian as he was, was of milder mood than his principal, blamed Pinchon for this outrage in no measured terms. He told him, that he should not be surprised if he should lose all the debts due him, in consequence. He replied, that he cared not; he would never submit to insult, even if he lost his life, as well as his goods, for resenting it.

The next day, the band among whom he had trusted his goods, arrived in their canoes, and encamped beside his house. They were, most of them, related to the sufferer of the day before. He presented himself in their lodges, and related how he had been treated; declaring that he would kill Pinchon the first opportunity. The ideas of the aborigines concerning property are not very strict, and they were moved with indignation that one man should have the heart to mutilate and disgrace another, for the paltry consideration of a few beaver skins. They attributed the conduct of Pinchon to avarice, and grief at losing his merchandize. With one accord they determined not to pay him. They were resolved, furthermore, to get what they could from him, and then leave him to bite his nails. Such is Indian revenge; seldom, unless in extreme cases, visited on the person of the offender, but commonly on his property. On this occasion, had Pinchon been possessed of a horse, or a dog, it would have been shot. They would have destroyed his boat, but that they were sure from his *weak heart,* or in other words, his violent temper, it would cost whoever should attempt it his life.

It is, or it was, customary for Indian traders to give the savages a small quantity of liquor, when they came to pay their debts. The savages, on the present occasion, thronged about the house of Pinchon, and requested the performance of what they considered a duty on his part. He gave them each a dram, and promised more, when the furs should be delivered. They insisted on having it then, and he refused as positively. Finally, after much vain importunity, they went off, declaring they would pay him nothing; no, not so much as the skin of a muskrat.

'A pretty mess of pottage you have cooked for your own table!' said Le Duc. 'You will lose the whole outfit, and it will never do for us to go back to Macinac. If you had let that fellow's ears alone, you might have filled the boat with beaver. Now, all is lost.'

'Be not troubled, Joe. I will punish the villains for their insolence, and fill the boat to your satisfaction besides.'

'Despardieux! talk not of violence, or punishment. We have had enough of that already. It is doubtful if we escape with our lives. Do not make matters worse.'

'You are a fool, Joe. Let me alone, and I will set matters right.'

Confiding in the fear with which his courage and great strength had inspired the Indians, he took an axe, and going to the beach, demolished every one of their canoes, so that it was impossible for them to depart as they had threatened. Had this been attempted by another, death would have been the consequence. As it was, the women cried, 'ishtah! eenah, enah, eenomah!' and the men looked on, declaring that the Great Spirit had made him mad, but no one offered to interfere. This object effected, he returned to the house.

The morning before, he had killed a deer, and the carcass still hung entire in his store room. He pulled it down, and cut the flesh into small pieces, which he put into a large kettle and hung over the fire. When the meat was cooked, he emptied it into a great wooden bowl, and ordered all his people to quit the house. They obeyed without question, for they saw that his mood was dangerous. He then enveloped himself in a buffalo robe, and sallied forth, holding the bowl over his head.

He bent his steps toward the encampment, passed through it, and turned back, calling the dogs as he went along. Some three or four hundred of these animals, attracted by his cries, and the smell of the venison, followed him. The savages left the feast untouched, and came out of their lodges to look upon him. They spoke to him, asking what he was about, but he deigned no answer. They now believed him mad in earnest, and the looks of anger and hate which had been bent on him a few minutes before, changed to respect and admiration. He proceeded to the house, entered it, and when all the dogs had followed him in, shut the door upon himself and them. Then he scattered the meat among the animals, and sitting down, covered his whole person with the buffalo robe. The dogs, as he had expected, fell to fighting. The walls shook with the noise. Growling, snarling, and cries of pain mingled together, and the roof seemed about to escape from the hubbub.

If the Dahcotahs had been astonished at first, they were now still more so. They demanded the reasons of his conduct of Le Duc and the men, but they could give no information. One of the elders went to the door and cried with a loud voice, 'What are you doing, Tahkoo Kokeepishnay? (he who fears nothing.) Are you mad, or what is the meaning of all this?'

This was precisely the question he had wished to elicit. He replied, 'Go away, and leave me quiet. I am onsheekah, and you have made me so. You have been feasting with your comrades, and shall I not do the same with mine? I am a dog, and with dogs will I abide.'

This was touching them in the most sensitive point. Without stooping to entreaty, he had made it incumbent on them to pay him immediately. He had put himself below them in the scale of being. He had declared himself on a level with dogs; and was it for them to afflict or injure so wretched a being? No; they ran to the lodges and all; men, women, and children, joining in the work, they brought

PINCHON

their furs, and piled them up before his door. When they
had finished, he came out and liberated their dogs. He was
immediately carried to the camp and feasted, and the hand
of friendship was tendered to him.

'What do you think of it now, Joe?' said he, as he returned from the camp.

'Think? I scarcely know what to think,' replied Le Duc.
'I think that you are the devil, or that he helps you.'

'I told you I would load the boat, and punish them!'

'You have done both. Let me look at you again. Nomme
de Dieu! who would have thought of such a thing? I never
should, I am sure.'

The boat was laden, and rowed away, before the dispo-
sitions of the Indians had time to change. When it arrived
at Michilimacinac, it was acknowledged by all, that such a
cargo of furs had not been brought thither for years. He
went and confessed to M. Badin, obtained absolution, and
M. La Salle gave him another outfit.

The insults he supposed he had received from the Sioux,
rankled in his mind, which retained its impressions like
brass. He therefore resolved to be revenged on them, and to
that effect ascended the Sault de St Marie, and coasted the
south shore of Lake Superior, to Burnt Wood River, where
he set up his Ebenezer for the season, and took a wife of the
daughters of the Chippeway tribe, as did his friend and
comrade, Le Duc. He gave out his goods on credit, as usual,
and sat down to enjoy himself.

Shortly after, Wawbiskah, (The White) who had lost a
son by the hands of the Nahtooessies,[3] stung with the desire
of revenge, blacked his face, and caused a temporary lodge
to be erected in the midst of his camp. Having communicated his intentions to Pinchon, that good Catholic cheerfully gave him a yard of scarlet to hang up in the midst, and

informed the chief that he intended to consider himself a Chippeway for the time being, for which he obtained much applause. Wawbiskah then entered the lodge, and having cut some tobacco, filled his pipe and smoked.

The Frenchman, being first instructed by Le Duc how to behave, followed Wawbiskah into the lodge. He drew the scarlet through his left hand, sat down, and smoked some of the tobacco already prepared. Others, Chippeways, followed his example, and they began to tell their dreams to each other. Wawbiskah had dreamed that he had shot a deer, and when he approached the carcass, it proved to be that of a Siou. The dreams of all the party were favorable to the projected enterprise. Pinchon declared that he had dreamed of driving the whole Siou tribe into an enclosure, and destroying them like rats in a trap. As a reward for his visions, Wawbiskah said no person was so fitting as him to carry the great medicine bag.[4] This was a sack, filled with feathers, bones, skins of rattle-snakes, &c. Then the whole party, twentythree in number, repaired to Wawbiskah's lodge, where a feast of dog's flesh was provided. After the animal was demolished, a kind of kettle drum was beaten by the chief, who accompanied the music with his voice, the whole party joining in chorus. The words of the song might be something like this:

'Master of Life! look down on thy children, who have suffered wrong at the hands of the Natooessies, and are now about to avenge it.

'Master of Life! prosper our enterprise; let us not be seen by the enemy, and defend us from evil spirits.

'Master of Breath! return us safe to our wives and children, that they may eat venison and fat bear's meat, and let us take many scalps.'

The partizan then rose, and standing erect in the midst, drew his blanket around him with great dignity, and addressed his intended followers with emphasis and energy. 'They were now,' he said, 'to set their feet on the enemies' territory. The Great Spirit had approved their enterprise, and had promised to deliver their foes an easy prey into their hands, even as a salmon trout into the hands of the fisher. They were to slay the Natooessies, or lead them captive, and compel them to hew wood and draw water. If there were any present who would not believe the express words of the Almighty, now was the time for them to recede. He wished no such company. The Great Spirit had granted them an unusual favor, in giving them a white man to assist their councils with his wisdom; and to him an important trust was confided. Wherefore, he exhorted them to fear no evil, but to go on in full confidence of success.' At the conclusion of each period, a unanimous guttural sound of applause ensued, and at the conclusion, they all cried, 'That is it. That is right.' In the morning of the morrow, they set forth, in Indian file, Wawbiskah taking the lead. For the first three days, they travelled without much precaution, conversing by day, and sleeping by fires at night. Their provision for the journey was parched corn, and maple sugar, and such small game as they could strike with arrows. This was not much, for the use of these weapons had already fallen into desuetude among the Chippeways. Pinchon, painted and accoutred like an Indian, carried the great medicine bag, parting with it neither by night nor day. Not that he attached any importance to its presence or preservation, but he knew that if any accident befel it, the whole party would turn back.

On the fifth day, they entered the frontier of the Siou hunting grounds. All idle conversation was prohibited; the chief marched several furlongs ahead, observing the way before him. Towards night, they fell in with a track in the snow, and instantly stopped, smoked, and consulted. It was agreed by all to go no farther, and they slept in a small thicket, without a fire.

In the morning, two declared that they had dreamed unfavorable dreams, and were resolved to return. Their sentiments excited neither surprise nor remark. They departed on their way homeward, and the rest proceeded. Following the track seen the preceding evening, it brought them to the river St Croix, and they fell upon a broad trail, which, by indications well known to all Indians, they ascertained to have been made by the passage of two lodges of Sioux. They perceived in the snow the tracks of four men, and thirteen women and children, the usual proportion of hunters to the helpless classes of aboriginal population.

Scouts now went ahead and surveyed the route. The party moved with the utmost caution, making slow progress. Thus they went on two days. Late in the second afternoon, Wawbiskah came back at full speed, and announced to the main body, that he heard the enemy's drums at a distance. In fact, the Sioux had made a good hunt, and were now holding a feast, which was destined to be fatal to them, as it had hindered them from going abroad and discovering their enemies.

As the aborigines take no measure without smoking, the Chippeways stopped, and lit their pipes. Their measures were carefully debated. Pinchon gave his voice for moving on, and attacking immediately; but this was a degree of temerity his companions did not approve. They might lose two or three men by adopting his counsel. He was overruled by the advice of Wawbiskah, who said it was better

to remain where they were till nightfall, and then to approach, and attack just before daybreak.

When the shades fell, the moon shone forth in unclouded
brightness, and the Chippeways slowly and cautiously approached the Siou camp. Towards midnight, the sky became overclouded, and the chief proposed, in whispers, that
some one should reconnoitre the enemy, and ascertain how,
and where, the men lay, that the first volley might be conclusive. None of the Indians appearing willing to undertake
this service, Pinchon volunteered to perform it. Availing
himself of the cover of the trees, he advanced upon his
slumbering victims, and when within hearing, he threw himself on all fours, encumbered as he was with the medicine
bag, and crept onward, as the setting-dog steals upon the
partridge. He heard no voices, yet he crawled round the
lodges, till he was satisfied that all were fast in their last
sleep. He was mistaken, however. Just as he rose to depart,
he heard some one stir, and a man came out, and stood before him. While he was hastily revolving in his mind the
means to escape without giving the alarm, the Siou spoke.
'Where are you going?' said he. 'Are you on the same er-
rand as myself?'

The moment he spoke, Pinchon discovered, by the tone
of his voice, that he was the identical Dahcotah whose ears
he had cut off the preceding spring. The question was answered with a stab, which reached the heart. The Siou fell,
without a groan, into a snowdrift, which received him without betraying his fall. The white savage took off his scalp,
and rejoined his congenial comrades.

When the first approaches of daylight were seen in the
east, the Chippeways approached the lodges, with such caution that they were not discovered. Lying prostrate, they
levelled their guns parallel with the earth, and discharged a

volley, which killed and wounded half the inmates, the three men among the others. Then, rising to their feet, the valley echoed with the terrific notes of the war-whoop. The lodges were instantaneously prostrated, and their shrieking tenants discovered.

✦ ✦ ✦

By right of having taken the first scalp, our hero [5] led the van of the party on its return, and entered the camp at its head. Le Duc had so managed the trade in his absence, that his interest had not suffered, and the result of his conduct was to his temporal advantage.

Shortly after, the savages removed from the vicinity of his house, leaving but three lodges. It so chanced that the Dahcotahs soon learned the damage they had sustained, and resolved to retaliate. A party of seventeen took the war path, and after a journey we need not describe, arrived at the Burnt Wood River, where they fell upon tracks leading to Pinchon's house. While preparing for the attack, a Chippeway, who had been benighted in the chase, discovered them, as he returned. He threw down the deer he carried on his back, and gave the alarm. The Indians rose, as well as their trader and his interpreter. The Dahcotahs, burning with rage at the death of their kindred, (for they were all of the same family) and seeing that the Chippeways only counted five men, attacked instantly. The latter, posted behind the trees, and seconded by their white allies, maintained the combat resolutely, while their women loaded their canoes, in order to cross the river. The battle was, like most other Indian battles, conducted with too much circumspection to be very bloody. Yet ere morning broke, five of the assailants, and one of the Chippeways, had fallen. Two more were wounded, as were Le Duc and Pinchon. When the light increased, so that the features of the con-

215

tending parties were visible to each other, the Sioux discovered that our two friends were among their enemies. Their anger was extreme. These men had eaten their bread, married among them, and had children in their lodges. They renewed the conflict with redoubled fury, pressing on at all points. By this time, the helpless, the aged, and the five voyageurs of the establishment, were out of danger. The Indians prepared to follow, in the single canoe they had left behind, and entreated the whites to accompany them. Pinchon, now in his element, positively refused to leave his house to be plundered and burned, and for once, Le Duc agreed with him. They covered the retreat of the red men, and then darted into the building.

The Dahcotahs, thinking that their prey was now in their hands, rushed towards the house, with loud shouts, but were taught more caution by seeing two guns flash through a crevice, and two more of their number drop. They took to the trees again, and fired at the door and windows. As no second report came from within, they concluded that the ammunition of the defenders was exhausted, and they were confirmed in this view of the matter, by hearing our hero sing his death song. Nevertheless, it was but a stratagem to entice them within reach. He knew that by keeping up a distant fire he could do them little damage, and hoped to decoy them into such a position that he might destroy them all.

The Dahcotahs, encouraged at the prospect of killing the two white men, and in some degree revenging their slain, ventured from their covers and mounted the roof of the house. Here they held a short consultation. It would have been vain to apply fire, for the roof was covered with snow, and under that, with damp earth. The timbers were green, and while they were trying to ignite them, the enemy might have returned in force. No mode of access seemed so feasible as by the chimney. Down it, then, they resolved to risk themselves. The voices beneath did not seem to come from the apartment into which it afforded a passage, and they trusted to effect the entrance without being discovered: when once in, they believed that their knives and tomahawks would overcome any opposition that two men could make, whatever their strength and courage might be.

Cautiously, as if going into a panther's den, the first Indian entered the chimney. When his head was below the top, another followed, and then another. The funnel was short, and could only contain three.

'A fine condition we are in,' said Le Duc; 'before another week our scalps will be drying in the smoke of a Sioux lodge.'

'Are you afraid, Joe? I thought you a braver man,' replied Pinchon.

'I am no more afraid than yourself, but we have not another hour to live. Hark! do you hear them getting down the chimney? Let us fire our guns up at them.'

'No, no, do not be in a hurry. I tell you we shall kill them all, and winter next year on the St Peters, with their kindred. Hear them in the chimney? Yes, and I see them too.'

The legs of the lowermost savage were now on the hearth. An instant longer, and he would have been in the apartment. Rushing through the open door, Pinchon seized him by the ancles, and held him fast. 'Quick, quick, Le Duc, bring me the straw bed,' said he. The order was obeyed. Stuffing the straw into the fireplace, he applied a lighted brand. The flames ascended, and the Indians in the chimney howled in torment. Their cries soon ended. Stifled with smoke and flame, and unable to extricate themselves, their blackened bodies dropped upon the hearth, whence they were drawn one by one by Pinchon, and stabbed by Le Duc. Those above, when they saw the smoke ascend, uttered appalling cries, but did not, nevertheless, descend from the roof.

They now determined to unroof the house, and jumping down all at once, put an end to their hated enemies. Seldom do Indians persevere in this manner. On the present occasion their passions were too much excited to allow of cool reflection. Two of the slabs which composed the roof were easily torn off, and thrown to the ground. As the foremost of the Dahcotahs approached, and bent over the opening to reconnoitre the pays bas, he received the barbed points of a fish spear under his chin, and was jerked down and despatched. The thing was so quickly done, that his companions, not seeing by what means he had disappeared, supposed he had found the way clear, and sprang in. Another advancing, was likewise speared, to the further edification of the survivors. Reduced in number to five, the party lost heart, sprung from the roof, and made off, saying that the Frenchmen were *medicine men*, against whom it would be useless to contend.

When they were out of sight, Pinchon took his bullet pouch and powder horn, and throwing his gun over his shoulder, started in pursuit. Le Duc followed his example, saying that he was now convinced the devil took care of his own, and he was ready to follow his bourgeois anywhere.

They followed the backward track of the Dahcotahs at a dog trot, till night. They were both slightly wounded, and their wounds began to stiffen, but this did not abate their ardor. By good luck, the moon shone bright, so that they traced the retreating savages with ease. A little after midnight, they saw that the trail trended to a little coppice in the prairie. Here, if any of the savages were awake, it was dangerous to come: nevertheless, they reached it without being discovered.

They found the Sioux asleep, unsuspicious of pursuit, with their guns piled against a tree. Stealing upon them with noiseless pace, they took away their arms, and placed them out of reach. Then returning, they put the muzzles of their own pieces to the sides of two of the sleepers. Pinchon gave the signal, and at the word, two more were added to the number of their victims. The others jumped to their feet, and seeing their arms gone, gave one shrill yell of despair, and fled into the prairie. Two of them were speedily overtaken and slain by their inveterate pursuers. The last of the Dahcotahs was not so easily disposed of. He had not been wounded, and refreshed by the sleep he had taken, he held them a long chase, though had either of them been fresh, he would not have run far. Le Duc gave up the pursuit, but Pinchon continued to follow, as the hound follows the hurt deer. The savage held on his way untired, till day, when looking round, he saw his hunter within twenty yards of him. Finding escape impossible, he turned and faced him. The contest was brief. The white man received a deep wound, but the scalp of the Dahcotah was added to those he had already taken.

When these unrelenting ruffians reached their house, they found their men returned, with a great number of Indians. Great was the applause they received, and great was the joy of the Chippeways, that not one of the Natooessies had returned home to tell the tale. They filled the store of Pinchon with furs to the roof, before spring.

He returned to Michilimacinac, and found a welcome his deeds had not deserved. He was again trusted with an outfit, and returned to winter with the very band he had so deeply injured, having good care to take no one with him who might betray him, excepting Le Duc, who was as much implicated as himself.

One more of his exploits, for its almost incredible temerity, we shall relate, and then make an end of our story. When his boat arrived at the portage of the Wisconsin, on his return to the Sioux country, it was necessary to dry a part of the cargo, which had been wet by a shower, the night preceding. The canvass mentioned in a former sketch, as used to cover Macinac boats, was spread upon the ground to dry. While he and his men were engaged in eating, an enormous rattle-snake crept out of the grass, and stretched himself in the sun upon the canvass; thinking, it is probable, that it was placed there for his reception. It is well known that this reptile is a generous enemy, never doing any injury unless molested, nor then, without giving warning. When Pinchon and his comrade returned, they perceived the individual in question.

Le Duc seized a stick to kill it, but Pinchon held his arm, while the serpent regarded them with the utmost indifference. 'Joe Le Duc,' said Pinchon, 'we are called brave men. Should you like to try which is the best entitled to the name, of the two?'

'And how should that be tried? You do not wish to fight with me, I hope? I have no inclination of that kind myself: I would far rather drink with you.'

'Nay, it can be tried without fighting. Dare you; will you catch that snake in your bare hands?'

'Despardieux! no! I will fight the Indians with you, as long and as often as you please, but I will not fight such an enemy as that.'

'Well, then, it shall never be said that I feared man or beast. If you will not catch him, I will.'

Disregarding all remonstrance, the desperado laid himself down within a few feet of the reptile. He moved his hand towards him as slowly as the hand of a clock, while the snake raised his head, and looked him steadily in the eye, without offering to strike. When he had advanced his fingers within six inches of the serpent, he snatched it up by the neck, as quick as thought, and sprung upon his feet, holding it out at arm's length! The reptile, after a few revolutions of its tail, fixed it firmly round the man's neck, and began to contract its body. Though one of the strongest of men, he felt his arm bend, in spite of all the force of his muscles. Still his iron nerves remained firm. He grasped his right wrist with his left hand, and resisted with all his might; but the snake was too strong for him; when, at last, he saw its white fangs within six inches of his face, his courage gave way, and he cried to Le Duc to come with his knife. The snake was severed in two, and Pinchon cast the part he held from him. The animal had attained the full growth of its species, and had thirtytwo rattles.[6]

After this exploit, which was witnessed and admired by fifty Winnebagoes, he gained his wintering ground among the Sioux. His thirst of blood being insatiable, he went to war with them against his quondam friends, the Chippeways.

Such was the tenor of his life, sometimes warring upon one tribe, and sometimes upon another. Many and wonderful were his adventures, those we have related being but specimens. As a friend to morality, we should perhaps expatiate upon the misapplication of his great natural gifts, and trace his enormities to the neglect to inculcate sound principles in his mind in early youth. Yet, as no one reads such lucubrations, and more especially as such subjects have been worn thread bare by novelists and romance writers, we shall leave our readers to draw such conclusions as seem good to them.

PINCHON

The parents of this brutal desperado never had the unhappiness to behold him again. He fell by the hand of his trusty comrade, Joe Le Duc, at the age of thirtythree. He had been supplanted by this man in the affections of a squaw, and in his cups fastened a quarrel on him. Le Duc would have eschewed the contest which followed, but the ire of Pinchon was not to be appeased. Two northwest guns, and twenty yards of prairie ground decided the matter. Joseph Le Duc stood the fire of his principal without injury, for intoxication had rendered Pinchon's hand unsteady. Knowing that his opponent never forgave, he discharged his piece with better aim, and Pinchon, shot through the heart, bounded six feet into the air, and fell to the earth a corpse.

What became of Le Duc is not known. The posterity of Pinchon still flourishes among the Dahcotahs, and have lost all traces of European blood. The fifth in descent from our hero signed a treaty with the late General Pike at St Peters in the year eighteen hundred. His son is the petty chief of the Owaw Hoskah, or Long Avenue village. There he passes the summer with his band, and may be seen weekly and daily, visiting the agency to ask for 'some of his father's milk;' a harmless, worthless, drunken vagabond. Yet he has a fund of humor that frequently amuses the officers of the garrison, and procures him a bottle of whiskey. Some anecdotes of him will not, we hope, be considered out of place here.

One day, visiting Fort Snelling with his face blackened, the commanding officer asked him the reason why he had smeared himself in that manner. 'It is because my brother is dead,' was the reply.

'Why, then, do you not act as we do? When we lose a relative, we array ourselves in good black broadcloth.'

'Father, every nation has its customs. You are rich, and we are poor. Therefore, we show our grief by smearing our faces with soot, and you attire yourselves in black cloth. But as you do not approve of my following the customs of our ancestors, to please you I am willing to compromise. Give me a black dress for this occasion, and in return I will give you as much soot as shall serve for the purposes of mourning all the days of your life.'

At another time, coming to ask a present preparatory to going to Rum River with his band, the white chief asked him how that stream had acquired such an appellation. 'Is it because rum runs there, instead of water?'

'No, father,' replied the Dahcotah, 'it does not. If it did, I would live on its banks till I had drank it dry. You would never see me here again.'

Colonel Snelling once proposed to this chief and his people, in council, to give them potatoes, seed corn, a plough, &c, and to send men to their village to teach them how to use the implements of husbandry, and to raise cattle and swine. 'You see,' said the officer, 'that the chase is an uncertain support, and that you are often obliged to ask us for food, to keep you from starving. Work, then, as we do, and you will be above the necessity of begging.'

Pinchon said nothing till he had filled his pipe, and exhausted its contents. Then, deliberately knocking out the ashes, he replied:

'Father, I have been reflecting on your proposal, as its importance deserves. What you say is true. You speak with but one tongue. It is certain that we are often without anything to eat. But it strikes me, that we have no need to labor to procure corn, or squashes, or potatoes, or cattle, or pigs, while we have so good a father, who gives us all these things, without any trouble on our part.'

THE LOVER'S LEAP

Then welcome be my death song, and my death!
Gertrude of Wyoming.

THERE are some poets who esteem women slightly, assert-
ing that the sex is fickle, false, and inconstant; and others
there are, who will have it, that devotion, fidelity, and dis-
interestedness, are only to be found in the breast of woman.
Far be it from us to decide on a subject so abstruse, when
so many doctors disagree; yet we trust we shall be excused
for placing a story in our pages which would tend to make
the balance incline in favor of the fair.

Once upon a time, as story books say, there lived a woman, or, to be perfectly correct, two women, who bore to
each other the relation of mother and daughter. Tradition
has not preserved the name of either; and that of the mother
would be remembered only to be contemned, so that it is
the less matter. But it is a pity that the appellation of a being
so heroic as the daughter should be forgotten. All the Dahcotahs can say on the subject is, that she was Weenoona,
or the oldest girl of the family.[1] By this title, then, we shall
designate her. Weenoona, in the opinion of the young
hunters, was the prettiest maiden in the tribe; but the wom-
en, and more especially the girls, who ought to be the best
judges in such matters, were of a quite contrary opinion. If
we were telling this to one of those philosophers who be-

lieve with Jean Jacques, that envy and jealousy are strangers to savage life, it would probably startle him; but those who are better judges of human nature, will not be astonished when we say, that these vices, as well as all uncharitableness, are as often found in a lodge as in a palace. To return, however, to our heroine: she was tall and slender, and was accounted the best garnisher of moccasins in the village. Not less remarkable was her nicety with regard to her person, for she made it a point to wash every day, whereas her companions do not perform more than two or three ablutions per annum. Her features were the faithful index of her disposition, which was mild and yielding. She was never known to requite insult with insult, nor reproach with reproach; and when beaten by her mother, no unfrequent occurrence, she would retire to the woods and weep. Such as she was, scarcely a young man in the village took to himself a wife, without first offering himself as a candidate for her favor, and being in consequence rejected. The other maidens pointed at her, and advised the men never to take a wife like her. 'She is no hand at chopping wood,' said one. 'She cannot carry half so big a load as myself,' said another. 'She cannot hoe in the cornfield when the sun shines,' cried a third. 'What kind of creatures would the children of such a puny thing be?' demanded a fourth.

But notwithstanding all this, she was loved by many, as far as savages are capable of loving. Scarcely a night passed, that some young man did not enter her father's lodge, and hold a lighted match before her eyes. But it was invariably allowed to burn, a sign that the suitor might prefer his vows elsewhere. The advice and exhortations of her parents passed unheeded, and she bloomed in single blessedness till her eighteenth year, a circumstance not common among the Dahcotahs.

The fact was, her heart was no longer her own to bestow. She had placed her affections on a young savage, the best hunter and the most daring warrior in the band. Who danced so well as Chakhopee Dootah? * Who killed half so many deer? Who gave so many beaver skins to the trader? and who, at his age, had struck so often on the dead bodies of his enemies? But these accomplishments were lost on the parents of Weenoona. His father had accidentally killed the brother of her father. The misfortune was universally attributed to accident, and the wrath of the injured family had been appeased by gifts; the perpetrator of the mischief had long been dead, but enduring hatred still rankled in the heart of the father of Weenoona. The proposals of Chakhopee Dootah were rejected with scorn, his gifts were refused, and the poor girl was forbidden to have anything to say to him. If, therefore, she sometimes staid longer in the woods than was necessary to collect her bundle of dried sticks, and if she had in consequence to sustain the reproaches and the blows of her mother, it must by no means be inferred that she merited such treatment by disobedience.

The young man, on his part, did all that he could to extinguish the resentment of the father of Weenoona, and to gain his approbation. He was the foremost in every war party, and untiring in the chase. But it availed him nought. The old man told him in plain terms that he intended his child for the wife of a trader. If she could be married to a white man, she would be exempt from labor, and have plenty of blankets, and other worldly goods, to bestow on her aged parents. Chakhopee Dootah was a good hunter; but no hunter could command the wealth of the men with hats. To all his logic the old savage was deaf, and returned the same answer to all his proffers.

* The red war club.

THE LOVER'S LEAP

In an evil hour for the lovers, Raymond, a French trader from Montreal, erected his log house at a short distance from the village. The charms of Weenoona caught his eye, and he offered a great price for her. The proffer was very acceptable to her father, but she heard the proposition with fear and trembling. When he came into the lodge, she fled to the woods to avoid his hateful presence, or if compelled by her mother to remain, she turned his attempts at wooing in her own tongue, into ridicule, and would only accept his gifts at the express command of her parents. He was not discouraged, for he knew that very few of the Indian maidens disposed of themselves, and though force is little known in the treatment of their children among the Dahcotahs, he thought, and very justly, that perseverance might bring his wishes to pass. The life of Weenoona soon became a burthen to her. All her attempts to please were met with reproach. If she brought wood to her father's lodge, he upbraided her with her inferiority in strength to others of her sex and condition, and told her she was unfit to be the partner of a hunter and warrior. 'When he kills a deer,' said he, 'you could not go forth and bring it home on your back, and if he wanted a field of corn, or a canoe, you could not hoe and plant the one, nor cut down a great black walnut, to make the other. No, you are only fit to lead the lazy life of a white woman, and to have a white dog to do your bidding, and supply your wants. You will do very well to take the Frenchman. He is rich, and you will never need anything, and if you manage right, neither will your old father and mother.' One day, after a lecture of this kind, she had escaped from the presence of her incensed father, and repaired to the banks of a small stream in the vicinity, there to vent her grief in tears and lamentations. She had been there but few moments, when Chakhopee Dootah appeared descending the opposite bank, bearing the carcass of a deer that he had just killed. At the sight of him her cries ceased, and her countenance brightened. Coming up, he threw down his load and sat down on the trunk of a fallen tree beside her. 'What ails you?' he asked.

'My father is always angry, and scolding at me. I have a great mind to hang myself on one of these branches, or to throw myself into the water.'

'And what does he scold you for? What have you done to make him angry?'

'I have done nothing to anger him. Last night the French-man came into our lodge with a new gun, and my father wanted it. He had no furs to buy it, and the trader would not give it to him on credit; but he said he should have it, and many things beside, if I would consent to live with him. I laughed at his speech, and told him that I hated him. My father scolded, and my mother beat me, and I have had no peace since. Other mothers take the part of their children, but mine sets my father on to ill treat me. O, I wish I were dead! I wish I were dead!'

'Do not think of hanging yourself. Remember, that to reach the other world you will have to swim across a rapid river, and drag the tree after you by the neck. Live rather for me. I can maintain you as well, or better, than any white man, and your father will be reconciled to the match when he finds he cannot help it. Fly with me to-night to the Ioways, and we will remain with them till the storm blows over.'

'No, I cannot leave my parents. Though they use me harshly, they love me; and they have no child but myself. Be not afraid, they will not use force, and I will suffer everything sooner than marry the trader. I wish he would remain at home among his own nation. I hate his ugly, pale face.'

'I will watch his lodge, and the first time I catch him alone, I will send a chewed bullet through his heart.[2] He shall not stand in my way much longer.'

'Do not do so, he is not to blame. They tell me, and he tells me, that I am like a French woman; and that is probably the reason he seeks me. It is not his fault. If my father had not encouraged him, he would have given me up, long ago. If you kill him, you will bring misfortune on the whole tribe. The whites will stop the trade, and our people will not be able to get guns or ammunition till you are given up to punishment. They will slay you, for there is no buying yourself off with gifts, as there is among us. And then I shall lose you forever.'

'I care not. I am a man, and do not fear death. It will be your father, and not I, that will bring this misfortune on our people. Nay, it shall not happen at all. I will go this moment and stab him, behind his own counter, and then go strait to Prairie du Chien, and surrender myself. Do not think to dissuade me. I will do as I have said, unless you consent to elope with me.'

'Then hear me, Chakhopee Dootah; I will do as you would have me,' said she, perhaps not displeased to be thus urged. 'Sooner than such things shall happen, I will do anything you wish. But will you not hereafter reproach me with having yielded too easily? Will you not be sorry that you have taken so feeble a creature to your lodge?'

'When I do, may I die in a snowdrift, and may the wolves feast upon my carcass. Meet me then, here, to-night, when the moon rises. I will have my two horses ready, and you shall ride the best. I care not if it be spoiled. I can steal another from the Saques, but I cannot get another Weenoona.'

'You can get many better, if you will. But I will not fail you;' and with these words the simple lovers parted.

Unfortunately for the success of the assignation, it was seen and overheard. A girl who had long sighed in secret, and made advances in public, to Chakhopee Dootah, had heard the lamentations of Weenoona, as she was seeking a load of wood. She advanced towards the sound, and came in sight of the afflicted maiden, just as her lover made his appearance. She approached them under the bank, and while their attention was absorbed in each other, heard every word that passed. Forthwith she repaired to the village, and made the parents of Weenoona acquainted with the whole plan, recommending to them to watch her closely and to give her a sound castigation into the bargain. Bitter were the reproaches the poor girl was compelled to endure on her return, and hard and heavy were the blows her mother inflicted on her, with the blade of a paddle. At night she was tied to one of the poles of the lodge, and had the additional misery of reflecting that Chakhopee Dootah would look upon her as faithless to her word.

The next day she had the mortification to see him flirting with other girls, before her eyes, and looking at her with an expression that signified, 'There are as fat does yet running wild, as ever were taken.' Nor could she get an opportunity to undeceive him, for her mother was as watchful as Argus, and did not even suffer her to go for wood or water alone. Raymond, too, who had heard of her adventure, tormented her with his addresses, and upbraided her in bitter terms. But she found means, through the medium of a married woman, one of her particular friends, to explain her conduct to him. He again vowed, that he would abstain from war and the chase, till he found an opportunity to carry her off.

He was not able to keep his word. Old Tahtunker, (the Buffalo) the aged war chief, dreamed a dream. He thought that he was on the head waters of the Buffalo river, and there saw an encampment of twelve Chippeway lodges. Anon it was attacked by a band of Sioux, headed by Chakhopee Dootah. The Chippeways, at the first alarm, dug holes in the ground, within their lodges, and defended themselves desperately. But Chakhopee Dootah, throwing down his gun and tomahawk, rushed upon the camp, and in spite of a shower of balls, succeeded in setting fire to it. The enemy, thus forced from their cover, were cut off, men, women, and children. The hero of this battle appeared to be wounded in the shoulder. In the morning the old warrior assembled the young men at a solemn feast, and communicated his vision to his admiring auditors. It was unanimously admitted that the war post should be erected, and that it was the will of the Master of Life that Chakhopee Dootah should take the lead. Such a call was imperative, and he departed accordingly, with all the customary formalities.

Weenoona now obtained more liberty than before, and her father went to the chase without fear of losing his child. A misfortune full as serious in his estimation, was, however, to befall him. He encountered a she bear, fired, and wounded her. Before he had time to reload his gun, she overtook him. Defending his face with his left arm, he drew his knife, and despatched her with repeated stabs. Yet such was the animal's tenacity of life, that notwithstanding the mortal wounds she received, she scratched him sorely, and lacerated his arm, breaking it in three places before she fell. He returned to the village, and went under the hands of a juggler and physician, these two professions being commonly united in one person among the Indians.

Now it was, that he regretted that he had no son. The

meat killed by the others was indeed as free to him as to them, but he could not follow them in their hunts, and he felt the miseries of dependence, though not in the same manner and degree a white man would.

The band now moved to Lake Pepin, for the purpose of taking fish. The family of Weenoona accompanied it. They encamped with the rest, at the foot of a high precipice. The condition of our heroine was miserable indeed. She saw the suffering condition of her father, whose arm, set rudely by the Indian surgeon, kept him in continual agony, and heard his incessant and peevish complaints. Her mother told her that she was a bad child to see her parents poor and miserable, when one word from her lips would put them in possession of everything they needed. One more trial was necessary to drive her to despair, and that was not long in coming.

Raymond had not, as was the usual course, gone in the spring to Michilimacinac for a new supply of goods. He had instead, despatched three of his men with his boat, and remained himself to plant corn, with the three others. At this time he began to feel lonesome, and resolved to make a last effort to gain possession of Weenoona, and failing of success, to take another to wife. He was a gross, ignorant sensualist, and attributed the repugnance of the mistress of his affections to maiden coyness. As to her attachment to Chakhopee Dootah, he thought of it as a girlish folly, that he would soon overcome. He was not, however, of a bad disposition, and if he could have foreseen the fatal consequence of his pursuit, he would have given it over. He loaded a large canoe with merchandize, and embarking with one of his men, arrived at the encampment. The old savage and his wife came out of the lodge to gaze upon the goods as the canoe was unladen. 'All this will I give you,' said

Raymond, 'if I may have your daughter to wife.' At the same time he threw an English three point blanket over the old man's shoulders, and another of the same quality, though less in dimensions, upon his wife.

'She shall be yours,' said the old savage. 'She is my own child, and I will dispose of her as I please! Tomorrow you shall have her.'

With these words he re-entered his lodge, and summoned his daughter before him. He told here that longer delay was useless; that she must make up her mind to be the wife of Raymond; that her lover was a bad man, and was moreover gone to war, from whence he would probably never return. And that on the next night she should be carried to the Frenchman's tent, whether she liked it or not.

Weenoona laid down and spent the remainder of the day in weeping. Her heart was broken; but her grief was disregarded. The next day, the wedding feast of fish, fresh and dried, was prepared. A dance began, attended with no small uproar. The trader took his seat upon the buffalo robe spread for him, the repast was served up in wooden bowls, and Weenoona was called upon to appear. She was absent, and the girls present left the lodge to look for her. Suddenly a thrilling shriek stilled the confusion of tongues within, and all hurried out to ascertain its cause. 'Where is she?' demanded Raymond. 'There, there,' answered the women, pointing to the steep hill. All voices were hushed, in an instant, for it was evident from her tones that she was singing her death song. Raymond and some of the Indians ran to overtake her and arrest her purpose. The Frenchman was the foremost, and gained fast upon her, but in vain; she was near the top. The words of her song have been preserved, and were lately translated into English verse by a gentleman engaged in the trade. The version is furnished

with rhymes, which was not the case in the original, and has
undergone some other alterations, it being impossible to
make anything like a literal translation.

It was in the following terms:—

> Still sleeps the breeze, bright beams the sun;
> The grass grows green, the voices rise
> Of wild birds in the woodlands dun:
> The glories of the cloudless skies
> Gleam full on lake and shore.
> But on my ear the songster's strain
> And summer's breezes fall in vain:
> That light, those woods, the hill, the plain,
> I look upon no more.
> Few days are mine; my race is run,
> 'Tis ended, ere 'twas well begun.
>
> At that steep cliff ascending high,
> Dark beetling o'er the rocks below,
> The only refuge greets my eye
> That woes like mine can ever know;
> Then now be firm, my heart.
> What though a gloomy fate attends
> Who the Great Spirit's law offends,
> To other worlds, self-doom'd, who wends;
> Yet will I hence depart.
> The sorrows that I there must find,
> Are less than those I leave behind.
>
> Ay, spread the couch, and wake the song,
> The bridal feast prepare.
> Look well those joyous maids among;
> Your victim is not there.
> But turn your eyes on high;
> Your tears prepare; the song of death
> Prepare; I go to yield my breath.
> Upon the rugged rocks beneath,
> My mangled form shall lie;
> Come, cruel parents, come and see
> The victim of your cruelty.
>
> But thou wilt dearly rue my fate,
> To whom my virgin heart I gave;
> Perhaps wilt join thy martyr'd mate
> In other lands beyond the grave;
> There link thy lot with mine.
> Thou wast my love, my chosen one,

THE LOVER'S LEAP

My star, my light, my noonday sun.
No more for me its course must run,
No more its beams must shine,
Alas, on my devoted head:
To life it cannot warm the dead.

And thou, that sought an Indian maid,
Who trembled at thy nod;
Why were thy vows not rather paid
To Gain, the white man's God?
Why did'st thou sue to me?
Seek, far away, another love,
Whom honey'd words, whom gifts may move;
For now, my firm resolve must prove,
Death I prefer to thee.
Look, how the courage of despair
Can prompt the forest girl to dare.

She uttered these last words on the brink of the cliff, and as Raymond, who was now close upon her, stretched out his hand to seize her, she sprung off. He stood for a few moments, rooted to the ground, his hair bristling, and his eyes starting from their sockets with horror. Recovering, after a few moments, from his trance, he hurried down the hill to where the savages were raising the death yell over the body of Weenoona. It was literally mashed. The very form of humanity was gone.

As soon as the funeral was over, Raymond embarked, with his followers, in his canoe, leaving the goods he had brought with the afflicted parents of his bride. Fearing the vengeance of Chakhopee Dootah, as soon as he reached his trading house, he loaded his boat and pushed off. The current carried him down the river, and what became of him afterwards, we cannot say. He was never after seen in the country.

A fever, the consequence of his wound, and the violence of his grief for the loss of his child, carried off the father of Weenoona. Her mother cut her limbs so severely, to show her sorrow for her husband and daughter, that mortification took place, and the weather being hot, she only survived three weeks. There was an end of the family.

The common opinion of the Dahcotahs, was, that the poor girl would be obliged, in the other world, to carry about with her a burthen of the very stones on which she dashed herself to pieces, as a punishment. As for Chakhopee Dootah, he did not lay violent hands on himself. At first, he thrust splinters through his arms, and assumed the usual signs of mourning; but within the year he had two wives, and was as great a beau as ever. It is rather singular, that in the expedition before mentioned, of which he was the leader, he fulfilled all the circumstances of the old chief's dream. The descendants of the forgetful lover are now many.

GENTLE READER, — Our self-imposed task is completed. Having treated of some 'things unattempted yet in prose or rhyme,' we do not throw by our quill because we have no more materials on which to enlarge. No, thanks to the observations of a wandering and unquiet life, we do not lack argument whereon to employ our pen. But the labor of writing is irksome to us, and it is with heartfelt satisfaction that we approach that thrice blessed word, FINIS. Whether thou and we shall ever meet again, is more than doubtful. If not, we bid thee a sorrowful farewell.

Whether we have performed the duties we prescribed to ourselves in the preface with credit or not, is for thee, courteous reader, to say. Of the matter of which our maiden essay is constructed, it is ten to one thou knowest nothing; and if so, thou art no competent critic. But for our manner, we ask thy indulgence and favorable construction. If the crimes in prose and verse that we have perpetrated are many and great, consider that the forest has been our Alma Mater. Once more, we bid thee farewell.

Notes to the First Edition

The Captive

[1] ENGAGÉS, VOYAGEURS, and COUREURS DES BOIS, are the appellations by which the subordinates employed in the fur trade are distinguished. The experienced voyageurs are called *hivernans,* and the raw hands *mangeurs de lard,* or pork eaters.

[2] NIPPES are pieces of blankets, or other substitutes for stockings.

[3] I WILL PUT ON A BLUE LEGGIN AND RUN AFTER HER. When a young Indian of any of the branches of the Dahcotah tribe wishes to declare himself in love, he wears leggins of different colors. Thus accoutred, he sits upon a log, and plays on a flute, or sings. It may be inferred from the text, that the leggins of Washtay Wawkeeah were red.

[4] COURIR L'ALLUMETTE. The fashion of wooing among many tribes is this. The lover goes at dead of night to the lodge of his mistress, and lights a splinter of wood. This he holds to her face, and awakens her. If she leaves it burning, his addresses are not acceptable; but if she blows it out, he takes his place beside her, and communicates his intentions. The engagés call this *courir l'allumette.*

[5] DAHCOTAH. Indians are jealous and uneasy when their names are mentioned by white men in their presence. To avoid giving offence in this manner, the Canadians engaged in the trade have affixed a soubriquet to each tribe, and each prominent individual. Here follow some examples: — The Dahcotahs are called Les Sioux; the Delawares, Les Loups; the Chippeways, Les Saulteurs; the Winnebagoes, Les Puans; the Pottawottemies, Les Poux, &c, &c. By use of these nick names, traders speak of Indians in their presence, without making the subject of their conversation known. Yet they cause confusion and misapprehension in writing.

[6] CARRIED NECK AND HEELS. At Dahcotah weddings, the bride is carried forcibly to her husband's lodge, all the while resisting, and affecting the utmost reluctance.

[7] Suicide is regarded as the blackest of crimes by the aborigines. Nevertheless, it is very common for squaws to hang themselves, when

thwarted in love, or maddened by ill usage or jealousy. The men do not so often resort to self-destruction.

[8] BOURGEOIS. An engagé calls his employer, or principal, his bourgeois.

[9] DE REINVILLE is still living, and engaged in the trade.

[10] The Ioways acted in self-defence. See the public prints.

The Hohays

[1] All the labor of Indian camps devolves on the women. They have the sole care of the children, horses, and dogs; cut wood, pitch the tents, carry the baggage, and make the clothing. Hunting is the only occupation of the men.

[2] To APPROACH. Hunting the buffalo on foot is called *approaching*. The hunter first creeps on all fours, and then lies prostrate, pushing his gun before him, till near enough to fire.

[3] The Dahcotah race punish an adultress by cutting off her nose, or scarring it; or by taking away a part of her scalp.

[4] The tents or lodges of the Dahcotah race are made of half dressed buffalo skins, and may therefore be cut to pieces. It is common to destroy these dwellings, and to shoot horses or dogs, to revenge an injury. This is a matter of course. The party within always sit still while their tent is destroyed, and retaliate in kind afterwards.

[5] WINKTAH. A winktah is a man who dresses in feminine garb, and performs all female avocations. A winktah is often married like a woman, and is held in the utmost contempt. A Dahcotah may bear the terms of dog, coward, and old woman, or receive a stab, without showing resentment; but the name of Winktah he never forgives.

[6] MEDICINE DANCE. The healing art is so blended with magic in Indian minds, that one word expresses both. Their medicines are exhibited with prayers and incantations, and physic is, in their opinion, something supernatural. A medicine dance, as mentioned in the text, is simply a religious ceremony.

[7] SOLDIER'S LODGE. In large Dahcotah camps, a lodge called the soldier's lodge is set apart for councils, and the reception of strangers. The women supply it with wood and water, &c, but are not permitted to enter. The *Soldiers* are a kind of police, appointed to maintain order, and enforce the regulations.

[7] A mistake; it should be [8] Indians seldom refuse a child anything. In cases where the avenger of blood is implacable, a child is taught to plead for the guilty person.

[8] The Indians reckon it more honorable to strike on the body of an enemy than to kill him. In Indian battles, a warrior frequently falls at the flash of his opponent's gun, as if dead; and when he comes to take the scalp, rises and kills him. Therefore they say, that a coward may shoot a man at a distance, but that it requires a brave man to touch him. To strike on a fortified place, as in the text, is the same as striking on an enemy. So far is this opinion carried, that many accompany war parties

without weapons, merely to achieve this feat. The first, second, and third, who strike, share the honor among them.

The Devoted

[1] A TRIBUTE TO THE GREAT SPIRIT. Indians worship at rocks, remarkable for their size or form. They leave offerings to the supreme being upon them; usually tobacco, or worn out clothing, but seldom anything of value. The rocks themselves are addressed by the title of grandfather, and with great respect.

[2] MASTER OF LIFE, Master of Breath, and Great Spirit, are the Indian titles of the supreme being.

[3] WHEN THE DOG WAS DEVOURED. Indians believe that brutes have souls as well as men. They burn the bones of dogs, bears, and some other animals, fearing that the spirits of the deceased brutes will be angered by any disrespect or insult that might be casually offered to their remains.

[4] I WILL THROW AWAY MY BODY. Nothing is more common among the Northwestern aborigines, than to imagine themselves doomed to sorrow and dool. A run of bad luck in hunting, or two or three successive failures, are sufficient to produce this effect. On such occasions they perform voluntary penance, which frequently extends to the loss of life.

[5] The Dahcotahs sometimes bury their dead, but more frequently expose them on scaffolds, or in the branches of trees. In the latter case, it is said that the bones are afterwards interred; we believe without truth, never having witnessed it. The arms, &c, of a warrior, are buried or exposed with him: formerly, a horse was sacrificed, that the deceased might reach his future place of abode on horseback. In old times, prisoners were put to death also, that the departed might not want slaves in the next world. The Winnebagoes have observed this rite within the remembrance of many persons now living. When the corpse of a female is disposed of, her implements of labor accompany it. The men mourn for their dead relations by wounding their arms, blackening their faces, &c. The women cut their limbs with flints and knives. We have known mortification to take place in consequence of the severity of these self-imposed afflictions. In one instance we have seen death ensue. The demonstration of grief is never so energetic as when stimulated by the use of ardent spirits. The mourning is renewed at every recurrence of intoxication, and they often beg for whiskey 'to make them cry.'

Payton Skah

[1] STRUCK THE POST. Previous to the departure of a war party, a post is set up, on which the warriors strike alternately, and sing the deeds they have done, or mean to do. It is often done, too, in profound peace. The post is not indispensable, and they often perform the ceremony without taking the trouble to plant it, but it is nevertheless called 'striking the post.'

[2] HE HAD LIGHTED HIS MATCH, &C. This is explained in note 4 to The Captive.

[3] It is the duty of an Indian wife, when her husband returns from the chase, to take off his moccasins and leggins; to dry, and mend them if they require it.

[4] Usually, when an Indian kills a deer, or other animal, he leaves it on the ground, and sends the women to bring it home. He considers any labor beneath the dignity of his sex.

[5] WHICH HE HAD STOLEN, &C. Horse stealing is considered honorable by all the prairie Indians. In their lodges it is matter of pride and boast.

[6] THE EARTHEN UTENSIL. Before the aborigines became acquainted with the whites, they boiled their food in pots of earthen ware. Such are still used by the more remote Dahcotahs, and the tribes on the Upper Missouri. We have seen some, that evinced considerable taste and skill in the makers.

[7] I WEAR TEN FEATHERS, &C. For every enemy slain or struck in battle, the Dahcotahs wear a feather of the war eagle. The full dress of a Siou is a history of his life; every part expressing some action or relation.

[8] KODAH. This is a singular connection. An Indian considers the blood relatives of his Kodah his own. Thus, his father and brethren are in the same relation to his Kodah; and so on to the remotest degree of consanguinity. Kodah frequently exchange wives, temporarily or permanently, at their option; and it excites no scandal.

Charles Hess

[1] In the Indian trade, he who is entrusted with an outfit is called a clerk, whether he can write or read, or not.

[2] BRIGADE OF CANOES. In the northwest a large number of canoes is called a *brigade.*

[3] LYED CORN AND GREASE. Lyed corn is maize, boiled in strong lye to get the hulls off. A quart of lyed corn and a gill of tallow, or grease of any kind, is the daily ration of the engagés.

[4] I WAS AT MY FORT. In the Indian country every trading house is called a fort.

[5] I HAVE HOLD ON YOUR HEART. One of the few figurative expressions the Indians use, meaning 'I love you.'

[6] HIS FACE PAINTED BLACK. A black face signifies grief, or an intention of revenge.

[7] DREW HIS BLANKET OVER HIS HEAD. An Indian considers it essential to his reputation to be at all times ready to die. Endurance, in his opinion, is more honorable than resistance.

The Bois Brulé

Note. Extra. There being no accented capitals in this Printing Office, the word brulé has been printed throughout without the final acute é.

NOTES TO THE FIRST EDITION

[The accents have been supplied in this edition except in chapter captions and running headlines. J. T. F.]

[1] BOIS BRULÉS, is the name given to the half-breeds, in the Indian country.

[2] PEMICAN is thus made. The flesh of the deer or buffalo is cut into very thin slices, and hung in the smoke of a lodge till perfectly exsicated. It is then beaten to powder in a wooden mortar, and mixed in equal parts with tallow, or what is better, marrow-fat. It is a nutritious food, and when well made will keep two years.

[3] BLACKBIRDS abound all over the country west of the Mississippi and north of the Missouri. Wherever grain is sown they assemble in incredible numbers, and destroy it in the milk.

[4] ALLUME. The voyageurs stop at the end of every league to rest and smoke. A league is, in their diction, a pipe. Their admeasurement commonly exceeds the truth, by a third. We have read in the journal of a sapient English traveller, that 'a pipe' is the distance a man may walk while a pipe is being smoked.

[5] LAMED BY THE WEIGHT OF THEIR SNOW SHOES. Every one who has travelled an hundred miles on snow shoes will understand this.

[6] Such conduct as is attributed to La Verdure in the text is not unfrequently seen in the Northwest. We could bring proofs that our narrative is literally true, with the exception only of names.

[7] The children of the very remote Indians are often as much alarmed at the first sight of a white, as our infants might be at seeing an Indian.

[8] Dog sledges are the most approved and common vehicles of draught and transportation, in the region of prairie. Three dogs will draw the carcass of a buffalo.

[9] The enormities detailed in the text were actually committed. If any person doubts, let him refer to Lord Selkirk's book.

[10] This is fact.

[11] The Red River is very crooked. A man may, by intersecting the points, walk farther in one hour than a boat can go in three.

[12] Whiskey is the ultimate argument with all Indians that have once tasted it. With ardent spirits they can be bribed to commit any villany. It is thus that Indian traders use it, to their moral destruction. The remote tribes get too little to do them any physical harm.

[13] THE BUFFALOES EMIGRATED. No living can be more precarious than that which depends on hunting the buffalo. They are constantly migrating.

[14] To AVOID BEING SCENTED, &c. The scent of the buffalo is very acute. He is not much alarmed at the sight of a human being at a distance, but if a man gets to windward of him he takes to flight immediately.

[15] THE SPEED OF A CABRI. The animal called by the voyageurs the *cabri* [probably the antelope] is found only in the prairies. It is of the goat kind, smaller than a deer, and so swift that neither horse nor dog can overtake it.

NOTES TO THE FIRST EDITION

[16] THE INDIAN WHOSE MEDAL, &c. Indian agents for the British and American governments confer silver medals on the chiefs, which, as they cannot add much to their importance, are little esteemed. The British medal has on one side the arms of the United Kingdoms, and on the other the head of his Majesty. The American medal bears the effigy of the President for the time being, and a pipe and tomahawk crossed.

[17] TO PREVENT THE IRON HEAD FROM COMING OFF. Arrow heads are barbed, and are fastened to their shafts with sinews, and a kind of glue, which is apt to dissolve at a moderate temperature.

[18] Anything lost in a Yankton camp, may be recovered by hiring a soldier to cry the loss, as described in the text. Indian dogs are never fed, and therefore devour all the moccasins, saddles, &c. they can get at.

[19] THE LODGE OF THE GRAND MEDICINE. The Grand Medicine of the Dahcotahs is an institution in some respects like Free Masonry. Its rites are celebrated in secret, and it has its signs and insignia by which its members are known to each other. It differs from Free Masonry, in that women are among the initiated.

If the reader should think, that the depravity exhibited by some of the characters in the BOIS BRULÉ unnatural, we assure him that the incidents are mainly true. The outline is consistent with the history of the Northwest; the embellishments and filling up, are our own.

Weenokhenchah Wandeeteekah

[1] A RABID WOLF. In the dog days, hydrophobia sometimes occurs among the canine tenants of the prairies. In such cases, the fox and wolf forget their natural timidity, without losing their instinctive sagacity.

[2] THOU HAS DRIVEN ME TO WISH FOR THE APPROACH OF DEATH, AS FOR THE COMING WINTER. Winter is the Indian season of enjoyment. It is in winter that the aborigines hunt.

La Butte des Morts

[1] See note 5 to The Devoted.

[2] AFTER TWO SLEEPS. The Indians compute time and distance (in travelling) by the number of times they sleep.

[3] Firing across a boat (with ball) is the Indian way of bringing her to.

[4] SET IT ON FIRE. The summer, or permanent villages of the northwestern aborigines, are built of bark, and may, therefore, be easily fired.

Pinchon

[1] PIPE, OR LEAGUE. See note 4 to the Bois Brulé.

[2] TWO GUNS ON EACH SHOULDER. Tradition says, four.

[3] NATOOESSIES signifies, in the Chippeway tongue, the enemy. As the Dahcotahs and Chippeways have been at war from time immemorial, the term is natural.

NOTES TO THE FIRST EDITION

[4] THE GREAT MEDICINE BAG. Every Indian has his medicine bag, which contains articles which he considers sacred. The medicine bag in the text belonged to the institution of the *Grand Medicine.*

[5] BY RIGHT OF HAVING TAKEN THE FIRST SCALP. Among the Chippeways, he (of a war party) who has been the first to take a scalp, returns at the head of all, and has the first honor.

[6] This anecdote is well authenticated, or we should have hardly ventured to record it.

The Lover's Leap

[1] The oldest child of a Dahcotah family is called, if a boy, Cheskay, if a girl, Weenoona; the second, if a boy, Haypon, if a girl, Hahpahn, &c, as far as the fifth child. Besides these names, which only serve to mark the family relation, they have others.

[2] The Indians chew their bullets, to make them cut a bigger hole. When one of them lodges in any animal, the pain and irritation is much greater than that caused by a smooth ball.

243

Two Poems
by William Joseph Snelling

TWO POEMS

With the exception of *Truth*, the satiric and critical poem already discussed, the known verse of William Joseph Snelling consists of only two poems, "The Birth of Thunder" and "The Snow Shoe," both of which deal with the aborigines. Because they are both obscure today and because they reveal an interesting treatment in verse of the material which Snelling has handled so well in the tales, it has been thought worth while to reprint them here.

"The Birth of Thunder" narrates a Sioux legend. The scene of the poem is the country near Big Stone Lake and the sources of the Minnesota River, closely adjoining the famous red pipestone quarry of the Indians. In a cluster of small lakes or ponds lying rather below the level of the surrounding prairie and fringed with oaks was the birthplace, according to the Sioux tale, of thunder. The poem originally appeared in *The Token* for 1831 and in 1842 was reprinted by Rufus W. Griswold in his *Poets and Poetry of America*. Fragments of it also appear in Neill's *History of Minnesota*. Although poetically rather commonplace and certainly conventional in both language and meter, the work has a certain narrative vigor and is particularly interesting in its attempt to blend a rather formal technique with a native theme.

"The Snow Shoe," which also appeared in *The Token* for 1831, has been completely ignored. Yet it reveals a certain poetic competence and a lightness of spirit which give it value, and there is a pleasant simplicity in its treatment of May and December translated into savage terms and a deft use of concrete background. As one of the earliest American poems with a setting in the Northwest, it ought not to be forgotten.

The Birth of Thunder

Look, white man, well on all around,
  These hoary oaks, those boundless plains;
Tread lightly; this is holy ground —
  Here Thunder, awful spirit! reigns.
Look on those waters far below,
  So deep beneath the prairie sleeping,
The summer sun's meridian glow
  Scarce warms the sands their waves are heaping;
And scarce the bitter blast can blow
  In winter on their icy cover;
The Wind Sprite may not stoop so low,
  But bows his head and passes over.
Perched on the top of yonder pine,
  The heron's billow-searching eye
  Can scarce his finny prey descry,
Glad leaping where their colours shine.
Those lakes, whose shores but now we trod,
  Scars deeply on earth's bosom dinted,
Are the strong impress of a god,
  By Thunder's giant foot imprinted.
Nay, stranger, as I live 'tis truth!
  The lips of those who never lied

THE BIRTH OF THUNDER

Repeat it daily to our youth.
  Famed heroes, erst my nation's pride,
Beheld the wonder; and our sages
Gave down the tale to after ages.
Dost not believe? though blooming fair
  The flowrets court the breezes coy,
Though now the sweet-grass scents the air,
And sunny nature basks in joy,
  It is not ever so.
Come when the lightning flashes,
Come when the forest crashes,
  When shrieks of pain and wo,
Break on thine ear-drum thick and fast,
From ghosts that shiver in the blast; —
Then shall thou know, and bend the knee
Before the angry deity.
But now attend, while I unfold
  The lore my brave forefathers taught.
As yet the storm, the heat, the cold,
  The changing seasons had not brought.
Famine was not; each tree and grot
  Grew greener for the rain;
The wanton doe, the buffalo,
  Blithe bounded on the plain.
In mirth did man the hours employ
  Of that eternal spring;
With song and dance and shouts of joy,
  Did hill and valley ring.
No death shot pealed upon the ear,
No painted warrior poised the spear,
No stake-doomed captive shook for fear;
  No arrow left the string,
Save when the wolf to earth was borne;
From foeman's head no scalp was torn;
Nor did the pangs of hate and scorn
  The red man's bosom wring.

THE BIRTH OF THUNDER

Then waving fields of yellow corn
Did our blessed villages adorn.

Alas! that man will never learn
His good from evil to discern.
At length, by furious passions driven,
  The Indian left his babes and wife,
And every blessing God has given,
  To mingle in the deadly strife.
Fierce Wrath and haggard Envy soon
Achieved the work that War begun;
He left unsought the beast of chase,
And preyed upon his kindred race.

But He who rules the earth and skies,
Who watches every bolt that flies;
From whom all gifts, all blessings flow,
With grief beheld the scene below.
He wept; and, as the balmy shower
  Refreshing to the ground descended,
Each drop gave being to a flower,
  And all the hills in homage bended.

"Alas!" the good Great Spirit said,
  "Man merits not the climes I gave;
Where'er a hillock rears its head
  He digs his brother's timeless grave:
To every crystal rill of water
He gives the crimson stain of slaughter.
No more for him my brow shall wear
  A constant, glad, approving smile;
Ah, no! my eyes must withering glare
  On bloody hands and deeds of guile.
Henceforth shall my lost children know
The piercing wind, the blinding snow;
The storm shall drench, the sun shall burn,
The winter freeze them, each in turn.

250

THE BIRTH OF THUNDER

Henceforth their feeble frames shall feel
A climate like their hearts of steel."

The moon that night withheld her light.
  By fits, instead, a lurid glare
Illumed the skies; while mortal eyes
  Were closed, and voices rose in prayer.
    While the revolving sun
    Three times his course might run,
  The dreadful darkness lasted.
And all that time the red man's eye
A sleeping spirit might espy,
Upon a tree top cradled high,
  Whose trunk his breath had blasted.
So long he slept, he grew so fast,
  Beneath his weight the gnarled oak
Snapt, as the tempest snaps the mast.
  It fell, and Thunder woke!
The world to its foundation shook,
The grisly bear his prey forsook,
The scowling heaven an aspect bore,
That man had never seen before;
The wolf in terror fled away,
And shone at last the light of day.

'Twas here he stood; these lakes attest
Where first Waw-kee-an's footsteps prest.
About his burning brow a cloud,
  Black as the raven's wing, he wore;
Thick tempests wrapt him like a shroud,
  Red lightnings in his hand he bore;
Like two bright suns his eyeballs shone,
His voice was like the cannon's tone;
And, where he breathed, the land became,
Prairie and wood, one sheet of flame.
Not long upon this mountain height

THE SNOW SHOE

The first and worst of storms abode,
For, moving in his fearful might,
   Abroad the God-begotten strode.

Afar, on yonder faint blue mound
In the horizon's utmost bound,
At the first stride his foot he set;
   The jarring world confessed the shock.
Stranger! the track of Thunder yet
   Remains upon the living rock.
The second step, he gained the sand
On far Superior's storm-beat strand:
Then with his shout the concave rung,
As up to heaven the giant sprung.
   On high, beside his sire to dwell;
But still, of all the spots on earth,
He loves the woods that gave him birth.
   Such is the tale our fathers tell.

The Snow Shoe

Go, go away, you foolish man;
   You certainly had best
Give up all thoughts of marriage vows,
   And let a body rest.
What need to ask for whom or what
   This snow shoe I repair?
You poor old man, your tottering weight
   This shoe will never bear.

And now I think of it, I say,
   You need not come again,
To light a match at father's lodge;
   For that is toil in vain:

THE SNOW SHOE

I'll be so deaf I will not wake
    For whisper, song, or shout.
And if the match forever burns,
    I will not blow it out.

I'd rather with Keskarrah live
    In wigwams made of snow,
And eat raw fish all winter long,
    Like savage Esquimaux,
Than dwell with you in leathern tents,
    With scarlet all so fine,
And eat from copper kettles too,
    For I should weep and pine.

What if your eye like lightning flashed,
    When life was in its spring?
What if your drum and shrill war-whoop
    Made all the village ring?
Those things all happened long ago —
    No matter when or how —
Such, such, old man, as you were then
    Is my Keskarrah now.

Don't talk about your beaver packs
    With such a calf and shin,
Your legs are dwindled down to straws;
    And bearded is your chin,
Just like those ugly trader men,
    And his is smooth as mine.
His face is like the rising sun,
    His stature like the pine.

Go tell my father what you want,
    And boast your rank and birth,
Give him your horses and your guns,
    And all that you are worth.
Your powder he may shoot away,
    Your whiskey drink like water,

THE SNOW SHOE

But then, be sure, if he consents,
    That never will his daughter.

If father says I must and shall
    Make shirts and coats for you —
I'll show you both, you pumpkin heads,
    I know a thing or two.
Keskarrah's coal-black horse can beat
    A swallow on the wing;
And if the drifts should prove too deep,
    This snow shoe is the thing.

I really think another wife
    Would be one wife too many;
A man with hair as white as yours
    Can have no need of any.
Remember I am just fifteen;
    Think well of what you do.
So get away, you doting fool,
    And let me mend my shoe.